HER PERFECT MATE

PAIGE TYLER

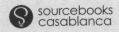

sourcebooks
casablanca

Published by Sourcebooks Casablanca, an imprint of Sourcebooks, Inc.
P.O. Box 4410, Naperville, Illinois 60567-4410
(630) 961-3900
Fax: (630) 961-2168
www.sourcebooks.com

Printed and bound in Canada.
MBP 10 9 8 7 6 5 4 3 2 1

With special thanks to my extremely patient and understanding husband. Without your help and support, I couldn't have pursued my dream job of becoming a writer. You're my sounding board, my idea man, my critique partner, and the absolute best research assistant any girl could ask for.

Love you!

Prologue

Grozny, Chechen Republic

IVY HALLIWELL STUDIED THE DILAPIDATED WARE-houses across the street, her eyes narrowing in the darkness. Casualties of a decades-long war, the buildings were mere burned-out husks of their former glory. Not to mention the perfect setting for an ambush. She scanned the broken windows and overgrown landscape. There wasn't anyone in sight, but that didn't mean someone wasn't hiding somewhere. She sniffed the air, trying to pick up a scent, but all she could smell was the sickening exhaust from the crappy rental car's idling engine.

She glanced at her partner. "I know you don't care what I think, but something's off about this."

Dave snorted. "Why? Because your Spidey senses are tingling again?"

Her feline intuition—the one that told her danger was lurking in those warehouses—wasn't one of her recognized skills, so Dave didn't put much stock in it. No, check that. Dave didn't put much stock in her, period. He didn't like working with her kind.

God, she was so sick of his attitude.

"I'm not asking you to trust my instincts because I know you won't. Going in there without checking the place out first is beyond stupid. It's dangerous."

He pulled into an alley between two abandoned

buildings, put the small car in park, and opened the door. "That's your professional opinion, based on years of field experience, right?"

She got out and followed him to the back of the car. "It's a good idea to be a little cautious on this one, okay?"

Dave checked the magazine in his .40-caliber automatic, then shoved the weapon back in its holster. "If I want an opinion on what kind of cat food to buy for my ex-wife's tabby, I'll ask a freak like you. Until then, do us both a favor and keep your mouth shut."

Ivy clenched her jaw to keep from growling. Literally. She was so close to losing her cool and ripping her partner a new one. But a rat-infested street in the middle of a dangerous crime-ridden, war-torn country wasn't the place to do it, no matter how much Dave might be asking for it. When they got stateside, though, she was done with this sham of a partnership. She was going to her boss and requesting a new partner because this one sure as hell wasn't working out. Teaming her up with a chauvinistic former jarhead like Dave Graner had been a disaster from the start.

But first, they had to make it out of Grozny alive. A couple hours ago, that didn't seem like it was going to be a problem. Now, Ivy wasn't so sure. Something was not right about this op.

Dave opened the trunk and grabbed a pair of night vision goggles—NVGs—as well as a communication headset. "Stay with the car."

"Don't be ridiculous. I'm coming with you."

He gave her a hard look as he hooked the headset over his ear and adjusted the mic. "Stay here. That's an order."

Damn him! She was his partner, not his subordinate.

She stood and watched Dave jog toward the warehouses, then grabbed the other communication headset, hooked it over her ear, and turned it on.

"Dave, the plan was to watch the guy from a distance, then pick up the bag after he makes the drop."

She heard him swear under his breath. "If the Russian can change the plan, so can I."

Typical Dave. Always trying to prove he was in charge. "Let me at least come in and cover you."

"Stay with the damn car like I told you to."

Ivy bit her tongue. The moron was going to get himself killed. She shouldn't care what happened to him, but she didn't want him getting hurt. And every instinct told her that would happen if she didn't stop him from going in those warehouses alone.

How the hell was she supposed to do that?

"Dave, please —"

"Dammit, just shut the hell up. I'm too busy right now to listen to your shit. I have eyes on our guy and the package. I'm moving toward the drop point now."

Crap.

Ivy's stomach twisted in the same gut-wrenching knot it always did when she attempted to ignore her body's internal alarm system. The hell with standing around. Let Dave report her for insubordination when they got back to DC if he wanted to. She wasn't going to be the one to let that jerk get killed. Pulling the 9mm from the holster on her hip, she ran toward the dilapidated warehouses.

The place was a pitch-black maze with twists and turns and dead ends left behind from when the building had collapsed at some point in the past. The darkness wasn't a problem for Ivy. Her eyesight automatically adjusted to the lack of light. Within seconds, the dark corners and shadows disappeared as if someone had flicked on a lamp, except without all the distortion and depth-perception problems that came with night vision goggles. Maybe part of the reason Dave disliked her so much was because she never needed NVGs. He hated the damn things.

She didn't use her heightened night vision to track Dave, though. She used his scent. It was strong on the air, too. Adrenaline mixed with fear did that.

"I'll be at your location in less than thirty seconds. Don't do anything stupid until I get there."

"Do me a favor. Go. Fuck. Yourself," he ground out. The radio clicked off.

"Dammit!" Ivy let out a growl and ran faster.

In front of her, she heard the *pop, pop, pop* of a small-caliber gun.

"Dave!" she shouted into her headset. "Dave, answer me!"

No reply.

Buildings blurred as she ran past them. She should slow down, check corners and alleys. She could be running right into an ambush.

But she didn't slow. She couldn't.

The scent of blood hit her hard as she rounded the corner of a large stone building, and she immediately froze. Less than ten feet away, Dave and another man—probably the Russian—were lying on the ground, bleeding from gunshot wounds.

She started toward them but stopped when she caught

movement out of the corner of her eye. Three men—she could tell they were men from their scent—were nonchalantly walking away from the bodies. One of them had a briefcase in his hand. Another held Dave's NVGs. She darted after them, 9mm aimed and ready to fire, but all three of them spun around at the same time and raised their weapons.

There was nowhere to take cover, and Ivy was moving too fast to even try. Instead, she opted for surprise, leaping into the air as she swiftly closed the distance between her and the men. Their eyes widened as she went airborne. Their first salvo of rounds passed harmlessly underneath her, and while she was still in the air, she took out the most dangerous target first—the guy with the MP5 submachine gun. Two shots to the chest silenced his weapon and dropped him where he stood, leaving her free to turn her gun on a second target—the man with the .45. She put two rounds in him and he flew backward.

Taking out those men left her exposed to the last shooter—the one with the small-caliber pistol. He didn't waste any time firing at her. She hit the ground and rolled, bullets zipping past her head.

The man redirected his aim to shoot her in the head. She knocked the pistol out of his grip with her free hand and leveled her gun at him. Before she could shoot, the bastard caught her weapon hand in both of his, trying to wrestle the pistol away from her.

Ivy set the animal inside free, letting out the growl that had been building low in her throat ever since she found her partner lying on the floor in a pool of blood. She didn't know for sure if this was the bastard who had shot Dave, and right now, she didn't care.

Releasing her hold on the gun, she let her fingernails extend until they became long, sharp, curved claws. The man stared at her, his eyes wide. With a hiss, she darted her right hand up and sliced open his throat.

He hit the floor, the gun falling from his useless hands.

Ivy rose from her crouch, her breathing ragged. All told, the fight had lasted less than fifteen seconds. If things had gone the way they were supposed to, she and Dave would have been in and out in that same amount of time.

Taking a deep breath, she retracted her claws, then turned and ran to Dave's side.

She carefully rolled him onto his back. He'd been shot multiple times in the chest, then another in the head. He'd never even gotten his gun out of his holster. Whatever first aid she could have offered was too late.

She sighed. "Dammit, Dave. Why didn't you just listen to me?"

She gently closed Dave's eyes, then got to her feet to check on the Russian. He was dead, too, shot once in the head.

Ivy's gaze went to Dave again and against her will, she found herself reliving the last few moments of her partner's life. Could she have done something to prevent his death?

She shook her head. Now wasn't the time—and this definitely wasn't the place—to have this conversation with herself. Even in a blown out shithole like this one, someone was bound to come snooping around to see what all the shooting had been about. In her experience, people who snooped around shootouts were not the kind of people she wanted to deal with.

She walked over to the second man she'd shot and ripped open the briefcase still clutched in his hand. Grabbing the manila folder inside, she shoved it in her coat pocket, then took out her iPhone and snapped pictures of all three gunmen as well as Dave and the Russian. She wanted to have something to back up her story if there was an investigation.

When she was done, she retrieved her 9mm, then grabbed Dave's NVGs. She didn't intend to leave anything behind that might identify them. That included Dave. Bending down, she slid her arms under his body, then lifted.

"Come on, Dave. Let's get you home."

Dave was more than twice her weight and she grunted with the effort as she hooked one of his arms over her shoulder and dragged him to the car. It was slow going, but she didn't care. Crappy partner or not, she wasn't going to leave him behind.

Chapter 1

Two Months Later
The Mountains of Afghanistan—Nuristan Province

LANDON DONOVAN CHECKED HIS WATCH. IT WAS SO dark tonight he wouldn't have been able to see his hand in front of his face if he wasn't wearing NVGs, but there was just enough glow for him to make out the time. 0200 hours.

He and five members of his 5th Special Forces A-team had moved to the final observation point in the hills above their target an hour ago. A multifamily house surrounded by a high wall in the middle of a small village perched on a mountainside—the place didn't look like much. Few places in this godforsaken country did. But it was bigger than any of its neighbors and supposedly housed the province's most infamous resident, a high-priority Taliban leader and bomb maker known only by his first name—Qari. The son of a bitch was best known for insurgent training camps that specialized in turning children into suicide bombers, but he was also a major force behind the growing number of mortar and IED attacks on local Coalition Forces. He had money and power, not to mention technical knowledge out the ass and a fair amount of religious influence. Yeah, well, none of those things were going to help him tonight. Providing everything went as planned.

Landon glanced at his teammates, checking again to make sure each of them was in position. They probably wouldn't get a peek at the compound's occupants until morning, but they'd keep at least one set of eyes glued to the scopes the entire night, just in case. He and his communications sergeant Diaz were taking the first watch.

Big Tex-Mex—otherwise known as Sergeant First Class Angelo Rios—slipped down beside Landon. "I have Marks just behind us on the back side of the ridge. Mickens is about a hundred meters downslope. We'll have warning if anyone tries to sneak up on us."

Angelo was the senior weapons sergeant on the team, and Landon used him as his second-in-command when they were running split-team ops like they were now. Part Native American, part Mexican, and all badass, Angelo was as sharp as they came.

"Good," Landon said. "Get the laser designator set up, just in case we get a chance to use it."

Angelo nodded and slipped away as silently as a ghost. For a big man, the senior noncommissioned officer could be damn quiet.

While Angelo and the other weapons sergeant, Tredeau, broke out the portable laser designator and mounted it on a small tripod, Landon went back to scanning the compound four hundred meters below, switching from his long-distance night vision scope to the thermal one.

"Holy shit," Diaz called out softly.

"What do you have?" Landon asked.

He motioned with his hand for Angelo and Tredeau to hurry up. Diaz didn't use that particular profanity lightly, so it had to be something big.

"Check out the far left window, Captain," Diaz said. "The one with the light coming through the curtains."

Landon slewed his scope from the large courtyard area he'd been scanning over to the left, focusing on the house. It took him a moment to find the window Diaz was talking about, but the second he did, he knew why the commo sergeant was so excited. Sitting there at a table, bigger than shit, was Qari. The man's beard was longer than it was in their most recent intel photo of the Taliban leader, but there was absolutely no doubt this was their guy. Landon and his teammates had studied photos of him from every angle for days on end, then quizzed each other by picking their target out of situational lineups. Every member of the team knew Qari's face better than his mother probably did.

"That's our man," Landon confirmed. "Call in air support."

Diaz turned to follow out his instructions, but then stopped and pressed his hand to his earpiece the way he always did when he listened to something on the radio. He frowned as he spoke into the mic. "Say again, all after 'abort.'"

Landon did a double take. Who the hell would be calling an abort now?

Diaz looked at Landon, a stunned expression on his face. "Captain, we've been ordered to break contact and immediately move back to the extraction point."

"Did you tell them we have Qari in our sights and were about to call in air support?"

"Yes, sir, but it was the old man himself, and he didn't give a shit. He wants us at the landing zone yesterday."

Landon swore under his breath. The original plan was

for his team to head to the landing zone once the mission was done, unless there was an emergency. There wasn't an emergency and their mission wasn't done, so why the hell would the battalion commander order them to bail? He and his team had been after Qari ever since they'd come to this country. To be pulled out now, when the big payoff was at hand, was nuts. Who knew what information they could find in that compound?

Resisting the urge to get on the radio and argue with the commander, Landon barked orders to get the gear packed.

They got to the landing zone two hours later to find a Black Hawk waiting for them, rotors turning. Landon immediately headed for it, only to stop when his executive officer, Major Bennett, stepped off the bird. Some serious shit had obviously hit the fan for the battalion's executive officer to be out here.

"Major," he said.

"Captain." Bennett surveyed Landon's teammates with a critical eye before turning back to him. "You're the only one who's going out on the Black Hawk. I'm taking over your team."

He sure as hell hadn't expected that. No formalities. No *Hey, great job finding Qari*. Just a harsh, straightforward *I'm taking over your team*.

Landon glanced over his shoulder to see his teammates looking at him in disbelief. He felt as if he'd just been hit with a ton of bricks. Well, he wasn't going anywhere without some answers. That might take time, though, and he didn't want his guys exposed out there while he got them.

"Set up a perimeter," he said to Angelo, then turned

back to Bennett. "Sir, am I being relieved of command, and if so, why?"

"No, Captain, you're not. You came down on orders. That's why you're being pulled out."

Orders? He could have handled a kick in the balls easier. "In the middle of a fucking mission? Sir, we're not due to rotate back for another month."

"Captain, I can't explain it and I'm not going to try. Battalion received the word barely three hours ago. The old man personally finalized the transfer orders himself and told me to put you on that bird ASAP." Bennett's mouth tightened. "No matter how I have to do it."

Landon looked around at his team. They'd followed his order to position themselves around the helicopter to provide security in case of an attack, but all of their attention was focused on him. They looked just as bewildered as he was.

He turned back to Bennett. "Sir, be straight with me. Did I screw up somehow?"

Bennett shrugged. "I don't know. If you did, no one in the battalion knew about it. All I can tell you is that the order to pull you out came from somewhere mighty fucking high. Above SOCOM. There isn't even a report date on your orders. They just say immediately."

He must be joking. Special Operations Command, known as SOCOM, owned all the Special Forces troops in the Department of Defense, regardless of service. Who'd be telling them where to send their own troops, especially in the middle of a deployment?

"At least tell me where I'm going," Landon said.

Bennett hesitated, and Landon thought he saw what looked like sympathy in the man's eyes. "The MDW."

The Military District of Washington? No fucking way. He must have heard wrong. He was about to ask Bennett to repeat that, but Angelo abandoned his place on the perimeter and ran up before he could.

"Landon, what the fuck's going on?"

Angelo was the only troop on his team who got away with calling him by his first name. That was because he and the NCO went way back, to a time before Landon was an officer, a time when just making it to the end of their first enlistment without getting their asses shot off was the only goal they had. Back then, Angelo had earned the right to call him anything he damn well wanted. They weren't just teammates, or even best friends. They were brothers.

Major Bennett looked like he was about to shit a brick over the delay, but Landon didn't give a crap.

"I'm getting shipped off to DC," he told Angelo.

"DC? Shit." He blew out a breath. "Is this about what happened to LT?"

Landon hoped not. He sure as hell didn't want to go there again. But some kind of shit had hit the fan somewhere for him to be yanked during a deployment. "I don't know."

"Captain," Bennett insisted.

Landon ignored him. Behind him, the Black Hawk's rotors echoed off the surrounding mountains, filling the silence. It was dangerous for the chopper to be on the ground this long. The sound of the rotors was going to attract the wrong kind of attention soon enough, and he didn't want his team here when that happened.

He swallowed hard. He'd been with his guys a long time. It felt as if he was deserting them by leaving. But he couldn't disobey a direct order.

"Tell the guys to take care of themselves," he said to Angelo. "You, too."

Landon didn't wait for a reply. Instead, he turned and climbed into the Black Hawk. Bennett slammed the door, then motioned for the pilot to take off.

As he rode back to base camp, Landon tried to convince himself he'd heard wrong, that Bennett hadn't said MDW. But Landon knew he'd heard right. He was heading to the Military District of Washington. As in Washington, DC. As in pushing pencils and making coffee for generals who didn't seem to have any work to do. There were some officers who might consider a transfer to the Pentagon—if that's where he was going—to be a peach assignment. But for a dirty-boots Special Forces warrior like him, it was the equivalent of a demotion.

What the hell had he done to earn it?

He could only think of one thing, the same thing Angelo had been referring to—the ambush that had happened eight weeks earlier. The one where his assistant commander had gotten injured badly enough for the guy to end up getting his ass shipped back to the States where he wasn't likely to ever see combat again.

Landon didn't want to believe he was getting reassigned because of that shitty episode, but it was the only thing that made sense. He snorted. It was almost ironic. He was going to be reassigned to the DC area where he'd get to come face to face with the biggest screwup of his life on a daily basis. Looked like karma was coming back to bite him in the ass.

—◆◆◆—

Landon's duffel bags were packed and waiting for him when he got back to his forward operating base. He'd figured he would at least have time to clean up before he left, but they immediately shuffled him onto another fueled-up Black Hawk and flew him directly to the main airbase in Bagram. Then he'd been the lone passenger on a C-17 cargo plane full of mail and broken equipment bound for Qatar. A Department of Defense–contracted commercial carrier had taken him from there to the Ramstein Air Base in Germany with an immediate transfer to Washington National. In all, he'd been traveling for almost twenty-four hours. Add that to the fact that he and his team had only caught an occasional catnap during the week it had taken to reach Qari's hideout, and he was flat-out exhausted. He was pretty sure he smelled, too. On top of that, he was pissed off.

He found it difficult to believe he'd been ripped away from his team, pulled out of the warzone, flown nonstop back to the States, and still didn't have a clue what the hell was going on. He didn't care what the report date on the orders in his pocket said—what kind of jackass actually wrote *immediately* on a set of reassignment orders, anyway?—he was going to find a place to stop, take a shower, and get some rest.

Great plan, but there was a man dressed in a dark suit with *Captain L. Donovan* written out on a piece of cardboard waiting for him the moment he exited the secured part of the airport concourse. He ground his jaw. Since when did the military send someone in civvies to pick up a new arrival at the airport?

Landon hiked his duffel bag higher up on his shoulder and walked over to the man.

"Captain Donovan?" he asked. "I have a car waiting outside. If you'll follow me?"

Did he have a choice?

The vehicle was a standard four-door sedan with generic-looking plates. No decals, no markings, no nothing. The guy helped Landon toss his bags in the back, then didn't say another word the entire drive except to answer the question about where they were going with a cryptic, "You'll be briefed on that soon."

Figuring he wasn't going to get anything useful out of the man, Landon stared out the window. He'd only been to DC twice to attend conferences, but he didn't remember going this way to get to the Pentagon. Landon's brows drew together as the man pulled into a parking garage underneath the offices of the Environmental Protection Agency. What the hell?

"I'm being assigned to the frigging EPA?" Landon asked as he got out of the car and shut the door.

The man gave him a smile. "Not exactly. They'll brief you on everything inside."

Yeah, well someone damn well better brief him. And they'd better do it soon.

Landon followed the man through a set of unmarked, glass double doors and into a huge lobby. He hoped there'd be some official looking emblem on the wall to clue him in on what the place was, but no such luck. There wasn't anything but some framed black-and-white photos of the various monuments in the DC area, and they weren't very helpful.

The man led him to the U-shaped reception desk. "This is Captain Donovan, Vivian."

The blonde looked up from her computer to give him a warm smile. "Captain, we've been expecting you. Let me show you to the conference room."

Vivian was pretty, with a curvy body that looked damn good in the sleeveless blouse and tight skirt she was wearing. Something he would have appreciated if he wasn't so irritated.

He did a quick recon of the place as she escorted him to the conference room. The people working there wore nothing that indicated they were in the army, or even with the Department of Defense. There were a few people in black uniforms similar to the Army Combat Uniform he had on, but they didn't have any rank on them, which meant they probably weren't military. At least no military he was familiar with.

"Can I get you some coffee?" Vivian asked when they got to the conference room.

He shook his head. "I'm good, thanks."

"Are you sure?" She smiled. "I make a mean pot."

"I'm sure."

"Okay." She seemed so bummed, he almost changed his mind and said he'd take a cup, but she hurried on. "Well, someone will be with you shortly. Go ahead and make yourself comfortable," she said, then closed the door behind her.

Landon almost laughed. Make himself comfortable. Right. He scanned the room, once again looking for something that would tell him where he was, but except for the immense television screen at the front of the room, the walls were bare. He didn't like the feeling he was getting. Special Forces qualified as black ops, sure, but an organization hidden in the garage of the EPA? That was another thing altogether. This had CIA written all over it and that wasn't going to work for him. He was a warrior, not a spook. And he was going to tell that to whoever was in charge when he or she walked in. Which could be a while, so he might as well try to make himself comfortable while he waited.

Pulling out one of the chairs, he sat down and prepared to settle in, but the door opened as soon as he did. He immediately got up, wanting to be on equal footing with whoever walked in.

Landon did a quick assessment of the man who entered. Average height, salt-and-pepper hair, expensive suit, wire-rimmed glasses. He looked like he should be teaching at an Ivy-League school somewhere.

He held out his hand. "Captain Donovan, I'm John Loughlin. Have a seat."

Landon did, then immediately went on the attack. "You in charge here?"

If Loughlin was taken aback by the direct approach, he didn't let it show. "I'm the director, yes."

Director. Well, that just screamed CIA, didn't it?

"What the hell is this place?"

Loughlin leaned back in his chair. "First, let me tell what it isn't. It's not the army or any other branch of the military. Nor is it the NSA, the FBI, or the CIA Special Activities Division. It's called the Department of Covert Operations. DCO for short."

"Never heard of it."

Landon's frustration made him speak harsher than he normally would, but he didn't care. Loughlin didn't seem to mind.

"Very few people have heard of it, and we like to keep it that way. We were created after 9/11. Technically, we're a special organization within Homeland Security."

"That's great," Landon said. "But what if I don't want to work for the DCO?"

The man smiled. "We can discuss that later."

Which was code for saying it wasn't the kind of assignment he could turn down. Landon swore silently. This sucked. It was hard enough to get a good-looking evaluation report in the Special Forces since almost everything he did was classified and redacted. He couldn't imagine what they'd look like now. If he even got an evaluation report. It would be damn hard to get the Army Promotion Board to recognize a performance review when he wasn't assigned to a branch of the Department of Defense.

When he mentioned it to Loughlin, the man waved a hand dismissively. "Don't worry about that. Your records will indicate you've been transferred to the Department of Homeland Security. All performance areas on your evaluations will still be redacted, of course, but your service will be properly recognized."

Yeah, he was screwed big time.

"How long is the assignment?" Landon asked.

"There's no formal length of duty with the DCO. It really depends on your performance. Let's just call it indefinite right now."

Bend over, here it comes again, Landon thought. So much for ever making major. Anybody reviewing his records for promotion would figure he'd screwed up and been transferred into some rear echelon job to keep him out of the field.

"So, how did I get selected for this assignment? If I may ask." Then, because this guy was his new boss, he added, "Sir."

"We're not as formal here as they are in the army,

Landon. Call me John. And to answer your question, the DCO keeps an eye out for people with your unique skill set. You were handpicked from a long list of candidates to serve in one of the toughest and most important assignments in the world. The DCO takes only the best and brightest."

He was really in trouble if the guy had to lay it on that thick.

"Unlike standard agents with the Department of Homeland Security, you'll have worldwide responsibilities," John continued. "You'll be paired with another agent who is just as highly trained as you are, only with a different set of talents."

Landon frowned. "I'll be on a two-person team? Doesn't that drastically limit the types of missions we can perform?"

"Not at all. We've learned from experience that a two-person team can perform more efficiently when it comes to the type of work you'll be doing."

"Exactly what kind of work is that? You still haven't said."

"We'll get into more detail later," John said. "But your primary job will be to cover your partner's back while they apply their special talents."

That was vague. What kind of special talents did this partner of his have? "That's it? You yanked me out of a warzone to pull babysitting duty?"

"That's not all you'll be doing, no. You'll be involved in direct action as well, but many times oversight will be a large part of your job, yes."

Landon sensed a "but" coming.

"However," John said, right on cue, "you do have one additional task. In fact, it's one of the most critical

functions you can be asked to perform. Consider it the
first general order for the DCO. It's something of a for-
mality, but I have to discuss it with you. In the event
your team is compromised and it appears likely your
partner is about to be captured, it will be your task to
eliminate them."

What the hell? John did not just say what Landon
thought he did. "I think I must have misunderstood. By
them, I assume you mean the enemy we're up against?"

"No, Landon, you didn't misunderstand me. One of
the most valuable services the DCO provides to the lead-
ership of the United States is plausible deniability. Your
partner possesses certain attributes that could prove embarrassing for our county if they were exposed. Therefore,
it's critical that your partner never be captured. Part of
your selection involved an assessment of your ability to
follow out this particular job requirement."

Landon didn't think much of any assessment process
that could determine he'd be okay with executing his
teammate. What the hell had these assholes seen to
make them think that? One of the founding principles of
the Special Forces—the army in general—was that no
one got left behind. There wasn't an army unit out there
that wouldn't risk every single member in it to go back
into enemy territory and rescue one of their people. It
was the cog that made everything else work.

The idea that he'd be asked to kill his own partner
was beyond distasteful. It was flat-out repugnant. Just
what kind of attributes did his partner have that would
make this person an embarrassment to the United
States anyway?

He didn't care if he could turn down the assignment

or not. Let them court-martial his ass. He was walking out of here right now. Landon started to get to his feet, but John held up his hand.

"I see this particular issue is difficult for you," he said. "Let me assure you we don't take this lightly, Landon. The requirement has been evaluated at the very highest levels of authority, and it's been determined to be reasonable and required. That said, it isn't a common occurrence at the DCO. In fact, it's never happened, and we hope it never does. If it helps, you can look at it another way. It's your responsibility to make sure your partner is never put into a position where you have to kill them."

That wasn't much better, but Landon could live with it, especially since he sure as hell wasn't going to let any teammate of his get compromised.

"Is my partner aware of this order?" he asked.

John nodded. "Yes. All EVAs are fully aware of this stipulation and have signed the necessary documents to acknowledge and accept the consequence of their capture."

Landon had no idea what the hell an EVA was, but they must be seriously committed if they could work for an organization that would execute them.

John picked up the phone on the table and pressed one of the buttons. "Olivia, please have Todd and Kendra come in."

Since there were two of them, neither one was probably his new partner. Another team, maybe? He was about to ask John when the door opened.

The man and woman who walked in weren't dressed in the black uniforms Landon had seen earlier, so they probably weren't operatives. The business casual look they were rocking didn't give much of a hint as to what jobs they did. Neither did the clipboards in their hands.

John stood, so Landon did the same.

"Landon, this is Todd Newman and Kendra Carlsen," John said. "They'll be your training officers as well as be your handlers after you and your partner are certified for fieldwork."

Landon studied the man and woman closer as he shook their hands. Todd looked like he could have played linebacker when he was in college, but he was a little too soft in the middle to be lighting up guys on the field anymore. Kendra was cute, blond hair pulled back in a messy bun, reading glasses perched on her head, a spray of freckles across her cheeks.

He glanced at John. "What if my partner and I don't successfully complete the certification course?"

"You'll be debriefed and sent back to your unit." John smiled. "But something tells me you won't have to worry about that."

Landon hoped it wasn't the same something that told John he'd be okay with killing his partner. He'd never failed at anything and he wasn't about to start now, even if he didn't want to be here.

Kendra smiled. "Come on. Todd and I will introduce you to your partner."

It was about time. Landon gestured toward the door. "Lead the way."

Landon expected Todd and Kendra to take him to another conference room, so he was surprised when they led him into what looked like a workout room. Mats covered the floor and a heavy bag hung from a hook in one corner. Weights and workout equipment filled a good portion of the room. A woman was seated cross-legged in the center of it, her eyes closed, her hands loosely resting on her knees. At their entrance, she gracefully uncurled herself from the floor and got to her feet.

She was wearing a pair of black workout pants like his ex-girlfriend used to wear when she went to yoga class, and a form-fitting tank top. He couldn't help but notice her curvy, athletic body, expressive dark eyes, and full lips. With little makeup and her long, dark hair pulled up in a ponytail, she looked like the girl next door. Only more exotic than any girl he'd ever lived next door to, that was for sure.

He didn't care how tired and irritated he was, this was a woman he definitely wouldn't mind stopping to appreciate. Hopefully, one of his new training officers would introduce them before she left to give them the room.

"Landon, meet Ivy Halliwell, your new partner," Kendra said. "Ivy, Captain Landon Donovan, Special Forces."

They were going to have to pick his jaw up off the floor because Landon was damn sure that's where it was after hearing that announcement. No way this walking wet dream was his partner. She looked like she couldn't hurt a fly, much less do any kind of covert ops. They had to be messing with him.

"Your first mission is to put her on her ass," Todd said.

He'd had some big what-the-hell moments in his life—most of them within the past twenty-four hours—but this had to be the biggest.

Landon narrowed his eyes at the man. "Excuse me?"

"Take her down."

Was this guy serious? This was his new partner and they

wanted him to kick her ass? Ivy was about half his size and looked like she should be walking down a fashion runway somewhere, not trading blows with a trained combat killer.

Landon shook his head. "Forget it. I'm not going to take a swing at her, much less put her on her ass." He folded his arms across his chest. "You want entertainment? Maybe I should put you on your ass."

Kendra must have thought that was funny because she hid a smile behind her clipboard.

Ivy wasn't so subtle. She laughed outright. And damn if it didn't have a sexy sound to it.

"That's chivalrous of you, Donovan," she said. "You putting Todd on his ass is something I'd like to see, but he isn't going to let us leave this room until you learn the lesson you're here to learn. So, let's get this over with."

She didn't wait for a reply, but instead slowly circled around Landon on her bare feet. He instinctively turned to follow her. She moved with the sure-footed grace of a cat, making him think she was probably well-trained in one or more martial arts.

"Well?" she demanded.

He assessed her stance. "You're not ready."

Ivy rolled her eyes. "Tell you what. I'll make it easier on you. I'll hit you first. How's that sound?"

"That implies I'd let you hit me."

She shrugged her slim shoulders. "Oh, I'll hit you all right."

He laughed, but the sound was cut short as she twisted in a blur and her leg came around in a spinning heel kick that would have taken off his head if he hadn't backed away just in time.

"Shit," he muttered. He was way too tired for this

crap. "Stop screwing around, okay? That kick would have done some damage if you landed it."

Ivy didn't heed his warning, though. Instead, she immediately followed up with the same kind of a kick, this time in the other direction. Landon quickly backpedaled to avoid her foot, only to smack against the wall. He dropped to one knee, instinctively thrusting out with his hands to both knock her away from him and put some space between them. But instead of falling back, she moved out of the way, avoiding his hands. For a moment he didn't realize what she'd done. Then it struck him.

She'd darted sideways while she was in mid-kick. That shouldn't even be physically possible.

Ivy landed lightly on her feet, a smile curving her lips. "I knew I could get you to take a shot at me, even if it was lame. Then again, I didn't expect much from another oversized grunt like you. I don't know why they keep pairing me up with guys like you all the time. Can't they find anyone with a brain?"

Landon rose from his crouch and moved to the center of the room. When she came at him again, he didn't want a wall getting in his way. "Guys like me? You're trying to insult me now? Think that's going to get me to take a punch at you? What are you, a masochist?"

Her smile broadened. "I already got you to do that. And I'd only be a masochist if you ever got your hands on me."

He snorted. "Lady, that wasn't a punch. You'd know it if I wanted to hit you."

"All talk and no action," she scoffed. "Isn't that the Special Forces motto or something?"

Landon knew what she was trying to do and it wasn't going to work. She must have figured it out, too. She gave up on the verbal jabs and resorted to real ones, coupled with those damn spinning roundhouse kicks again.

He stripped off his camo overshirt and threw it across the room, so he could get down to serious business.

He blocked most of her strikes with his hands and the others with his shoulders, biceps, and thighs. He sure as hell felt them, but he got the feeling she wasn't hitting him nearly as hard as she could.

His plan was to lure her in close enough to get his hands on her. That way, he could put her down without being forced to throw a serious punch. She might be agile as hell, but if he connected with anything real, he'd break something. His best bet was to get his hands on her and pin her to the floor so he could end this stupid game.

That was easier than it sounded. Ivy was faster than lightning and could twist her body into a pretzel to get out of his grasp. He had her in a perfect jujitsu take-down position several times only to have her spoil it by not going down like she should have. He even planted his knee in her stomach and yanked her backward with him in a throw that should have landed her hard on her back, groaning in pain. Instead, she turned the move into some kind of gymnastic flip and came down as softly on her feet as if she stepped off a street curb.

Out of the corner of his eye, he saw the two training officers taking notes as they watched. Kendra was actually smiling. Landon clenched his jaw. What a couple of asses.

On the other side of the room, Ivy spun around to face him. Eyes narrowing, she ran directly toward him. He automatically braced himself for another blow, but at the last second she darted to her right, jumping at the wall and rebounding off it like she was an extra in some Jackie Chan movie, then ricocheting back at him, her right leg coming around in a roundhouse kick.

Instead of getting out of the way like any sane person would have, he moved closer, getting underneath her swinging leg and grabbing her shoulders. He avoided her foot, but ended up taking a knee to the left side of his rib cage. It hurt, but it got him inside her defenses. He was going to get a grip on her, and this time she wasn't going to get away.

That's when he realized her kick had only been a distraction. He'd been so busy watching her feet he hadn't even noticed her open hand coming toward him. He did a double take. She was going to *slap* him? His mind registered surprise for half a millisecond before her hand angled down to sweep across the front of his T-shirt.

Landon felt the fabric tug and swore he heard a ripping sound. He even felt a sting. But he ignored it. Tightening his grip on her shoulders, he spun them both around, letting the momentum from her rebound take them down to the floor.

He twisted at the last second, taking the impact of the floor on his right shoulder before yanking her to his chest in a bear hug. If he'd been trying to kill her, he would have crushed a hell of a lot harder. Instead he squeezed just enough to let her know he could hurt her if he wanted to.

They came to a stop with him on his back, Ivy pinned to his chest. She didn't fight him, simply laid there with her face close to his neck, breathing deeply. Landon couldn't help but notice how soft her body was against his, and how nice it felt to have her on top of him.

His cock noticed, too.

Shit. This was going to be embarrassing.

"Okay, you two," Todd said. "I think we've gotten everything out of this demonstration I intended."

It took a moment for the words to register—probably because all the blood had left his head to rush to another part of his anatomy. Landon reluctantly loosened his hold on Ivy. He waited for her to get up, but she stayed firmly planted on top of him, which alarmed him. He thought she would have jumped up the moment he released her. God, he hoped he hadn't hurt her with that take down.

He gently tilted her chin up with his fingers. "Hey. You okay?"

Ivy blinked at him, her beautiful eyes filled with something that looked almost like wonder. Then she gave herself a little shake. "I-I'm good. You?"

"Yeah. Fine."

"Good."

She gazed at him for a moment longer, then quickly pushed to her feet. She crossed the room to slip on a pair of flip-flops she had left there. When she turned back to him, her face was the perfect mask of composure he'd seen when he first walked in.

"No hard feelings, I hope?" she said as he stood. "That's just the way the DCO likes to introduce me to my new partners. I don't know why."

He knew why. The DCO realized the fastest way to get a man to appreciate the talents of his female partner was to have her kick his ass. At least she hadn't done it to him.

"Not at all," he said. "I suppose we can call this match a tie."

Her lips curved. "You think so?"

Reaching out, she flicked his shirt with her fingers, then turned and walked away.

Remembering the bizarre open-handed swipe she'd given him across the chest, he looked down to see four diagonal tears in his T-shirt. He pushed the material aside, frowning when he found four identical scratches on his chest. If he didn't know better, he'd think he got scratched by a cat—a big cat. They weren't deep or bleeding, but there was no mistaking what had made them—fingernails. Ivy's fingernails.

Not exactly standard-issue hand-to-hand combat technique. He got the feeling nothing about this place was standard issue. Especially his new partner.

Landon scooped up his camo overshirt and walked over to where Ivy was talking to the two training officers. Her face was still flushed from their wrestling match, but if it wasn't for that, he'd never know they'd been rolling around on the floor a few minutes ago. She was back to being the girl next door again. And when she looked like that, there wasn't a man alive who wouldn't underestimate her. Given that, it was okay to cut himself some slack for doing the same thing.

"There's some administrative paperwork we need to take care of before you leave, Landon, but then you can take off early," Todd said.

Landon would have preferred to have a long conversation with his new partner about her fighting technique than do mounds of paperwork, but he silently followed the two training officers back to the conference room. One thing was for sure. He'd be smart not to take anything, including Ivy, for granted until he learned more about the DCO and what his part in it was going to be.

Chapter 2

IVY HATED THAT THEY'D PAIRED HER UP WITH ANOTHER combat killer. She thought they would have learned from that mistake after the debacles with her two previous partners—both of whom had been military. But the DCO seemed so enamored with the training military guys brought to the table that they simply didn't understand why these guys couldn't work with a woman like her.

It was true Landon hadn't tried to humiliate her like some of the others had, but she wasn't holding her breath that the chivalrous treatment would last long.

Ivy adjusted her crossbody shoulder bag as she stepped off the Metro at Pentagon City and fell in with the rest of the people making a mad dash for the escalators. Outside the station, she turned right and headed toward the grocery store where she regularly stopped on her way home.

She grabbed a cart and wandered through the aisles, letting her mind do some wandering of its own—right to Jeff Peters, Navy officer and her first partner at the DCO. For about the first year, she and Jeff had gotten along great. Or at least she'd thought so. They'd worked well together, hung out after work, become good friends. Then Jeff wanted to take the partnership somewhere she wasn't comfortable going—the bedroom. Everything had gone downhill from there. The final straw came when he decided to take what he wanted. She'd fought back, practically ripping off his face in the process, something that earned her a reputation as a tease, a slut, and a ball breaker. Along with a brand new nickname— Poison Ivy.

After that, it was almost guaranteed her second partnership would start off on bad footing. And it had. Dave might not have wanted to get into her panties, but his open dislike for her had made working with him just as hard.

Ivy had begged John to give her someone from the FBI or CIA, someone who wasn't another type A asshole. She'd even tried to talk him into pairing her up with another EVA. But the DCO didn't pair up EVAs with other EVAs. That was department policy.

So, she was saddled with Landon, for better or worse. Hopefully for the better, given the way he'd handled himself during their sparring match.

That twisting takedown he'd used to end the match? She'd never seen anything like that. Clawing his chest hadn't even distracted him from overpowering her. She smiled as she remembered the confusion on his face when she pointed out his shredded T-shirt.

She picked up her grocery bags and walked out of the store. The biggest surprise hadn't been Landon's reluctance to fight her because she was a woman, but her reaction to him as a man.

He looked better in uniform than any man had a right to. A military uniform, particularly the camouflage Army Combat Uniform, was cut to make all men look good, but on Landon it was downright criminal. The man was six-foot-four and built. When he'd pinned her against him, it had taken every bit of her self-control to stop from leaning over to lick him. She was completely comfortable with her animal side, but sometimes she felt as if someone else was in charge of her baser desires. Like back in that room when she'd been locked in Landon's arms.

Regardless of her physical attraction to him, though, she was sure going to keep Landon at arm's length. Even if department policy didn't prohibit partners from getting romantically involved, there was no way she'd ever get friendly with a military grunt. He might seem nice now, but it wouldn't last. Sooner or later, something would set him off and he'd go right back to being the asshole he probably was.

That unpleasant thought accompanied her home. A corner unit in a high-rise building with a view of downtown DC, the apartment was her sanctuary from the rest of the world. It was big and comfortable, and with the addition of various things she'd collected on her travels, she'd slowly made it feel more like home.

Her cell phone rang as she walked in. Rather than try to extricate herself from the grocery bags to answer it, she let it go to voice mail, then checked her messages after she set the bags on the granite counter in the kitchen. There were four other messages in addition to the one she'd missed. She scrolled through them and groaned when she saw that three of them were from Clayne Buchanan, one of the other shifters at the DCO. He'd always been a good friend, but lately he'd made it obvious he wanted to be more than that. He was a great guy, and she wished she felt the same way about him, but she didn't and was sure she never would. That didn't stop him from trying to change her mind. She should call him back, but knew if she did, he'd read too much into it. She'd see him at the DCO tomorrow before she and Landon went to the training complex.

The fourth call was from Kendra.

"Hey, girl! You took off so fast after the admin briefing with Landon that I didn't get a chance to talk to you, and I'm dying to know what you think about your new partner. God, what a hottie. Gotta love a man in uniform, huh? Anyway, call me."

Ivy shook her head. As if she hadn't noticed how gorgeous Landon was. Friend or not, she wasn't going to call Kendra back, at least not right away. She was still mad at Kendra for not telling her ahead of time that her new partner was Special Forces.

The message she'd missed while juggling grocery bags was from her mom. She dialed her parents' number, then turned on the speaker so she could talk while she put the groceries away. Her mother answered on the second ring.

"Ivy, dear! I'm so glad you called back."

"Don't I always?"

"Except when you're on one of those trips you keep going on. I never know where you are."

Ivy didn't say anything. Her father had always shielded her mother from the dangers of his job as a police officer, and Ivy had found herself doing the same thing when she joined the DCO. Her mom didn't know she risked her life for her country every day, or that Jeff had gotten the boot because he'd tried to rape her, or that Dave had been killed on a mission. And while her mother might suspect, Ivy knew her mom preferred to be blissfully ignorant.

"You're coming to Layla's graduation party next weekend, aren't you?" her mom asked. "Everyone's going to be here and they all want to see you. Including your father and me."

That was her mother's way of saying she hadn't visited in a while. Ivy chewed on her lower lip as she put a box of cereal in the cabinet. Her parents lived in Virginia, so it was close enough for her to stop by and see them on a regular basis, but things had been crazy since Dave died. She couldn't tell her mom she'd been busy with endless psych evaluations for the past couple of months.

"I'll try to make it, Mom, but I'm breaking in a new partner again, so I'm going to be insanely busy at work."

Which was a pain. She really wanted to be there for her sister's party, especially since she hadn't been able to go to Layla's college graduation. But she had no idea how long training with Landon would take, or if Todd and Kendra would make them work through the weekend.

"Again?" Her mother's voice took on a note of disapproval. "I don't understand why they keep changing your partners. It doesn't seem very efficient. How are you supposed to get to know any of them?"

Mom had always been big on Dad bonding with his partners, too. Ivy opened the freezer and put a stack of frozen dinners inside. "I know, Mom. Hopefully, this will be the last one for a while."

"Well, will we at least get a chance to meet him? Or is this new partner a woman?"

"It's a guy. I don't know about you meeting him, though. We'll see."

It was a lie, but it placated her mother, who launched into a funny story about how hard it had been finding the perfect graduation gift for Layla. Ivy laughed, relieved to talk about something besides her new partner. She wanted to keep work—and Landon—as separate from her personal life as she could.

The same guy who'd picked Landon up at the airport drove him and his bags to a furnished apartment in Alexandria. In addition to finding his Ford F150 parked in a space out front, he discovered half a dozen pairs of black Army Combat Uniforms, four duffel bags, and a stack of boxes in the center of the living room, along with the keys to his truck. It was his stuff from Fort Campbell. Well, the DCO was nothing if not efficient.

He looked at the small pile of possessions. It was pitiful. But he'd never been big on material stuff. If he had a bed, a couch, and a television, he was good. Based on what Todd and Kendra had said during the briefing, it didn't sound like he was going to have any more free time working for the DCO than he'd had with his unit.

According to the two training officers, he and Ivy were going to be doing a lot of training over the next few months. That wasn't a big deal. Special Forces had pretty much cornered the market when it came to training. Between Basic, AIT, Airborne School, Special Forces Assessment, SFQC, SERE, and LET, it took two years to become a Green Beret, so he didn't have a problem with that part. He was surprised when Todd said there was no way of telling how long the training would take. If he and Ivy did well, it would be weeks. If they did poorly, it was going to be a hell of a lot longer than that. All Landon knew for certain was that he and Ivy would be staying at the DCO training complex in Virginia for the duration of it. He was more interested in what kind of work he and Ivy would be doing anyway, and found out they'd specialize in infiltration, recon and surveillance, intel acquisition, and "elimination" work.

Landon sighed and looked at the boxes. Unpack or not to unpack. Not. Definitely not. He was way too tired. All he wanted to do was shower, crash, and make up for two weeks' worth of sleep deprivation. But there was something he had to do first.

He took a quick shower, then pulled on jeans and a T-shirt. Grabbing the keys to his truck, he picked up his cell phone and googled directions to Walter Reed Military Medical Center in Bethesda as he walked out the door. It was going to be hard, but he needed to face the demons that had been haunting him and go see Jayson.

It was always rough when a brother went down in combat, but he and Jayson Harmon had bonded the moment the lieutenant had become his assistant detachment commander two years ago. Next to Angelo, the other officer was his closest friend. Which was why the idea of Jayson lying in a bed broken hurt Landon so much. That and the fact Landon was responsible for him being there.

Landon kept thinking of the ambush that left Jayson injured. The brutality of it gave many soldiers flashbacks and left them in a cold sweat, even now. He swore under his breath, quickly squashing the images. He couldn't go there right now. He needed to walk in that room and be strong for Jayson, not tearing up like a teenage girl.

He only wished he knew what he was walking into. Unfortunately, he and his teammates hadn't been able to get many details about Jayson's condition after he'd been medevaced out. But they knew it had been bad. Then again, people with hangnails and paper cuts didn't get sent to Walter Reed Military Medical Center. The only soldiers who went there were the ones with severe injuries.

The facility was bigger than he thought it would be. It took Landon a while to find Jayson's room. When he got there, he didn't go in right away. He stood outside the door, psyching himself up and rehearsing what he wanted to say.

Hey, Jayson. Just stopped by to see how you're doing. Since the doctors dug all that shrapnel out of your back, I mean.

Yeah, that was what Jayson needed. A reminder of what happened to him. As if he wasn't reminded every time he looked down at his useless legs.

Landon took a deep breath. *Stop being such a coward and get your ass in there.*

Not wanting to disturb Jayson if he was sleeping, Landon didn't knock, but instead slowly pushed the door open. He hadn't been sure what to expect—that Jayson would be lying flat on his back in bed, he guessed—but his friend was sitting in a chair by the window overlooking the common area. He looked thinner than the last time Landon had seen him and had a serious case of bedhead, but otherwise, he was the same as Landon remembered.

Landon knocked softly on the open door.

Jayson turned at the sound, doing a double take when he saw Landon.

"Captain! Damn. What are you doing here? Come in."

Landon hoped he was wrong about Jayson's legs, and that his friend would get up and meet him halfway, but then he saw the walker by the chair. Jayson probably couldn't stand on his own much less walk. It could be worse. He could be in a wheelchair.

Jayson's handshake was just as firm as it had always been. That was something.

"I'd get up, but..." He nodded to the other chair by the window. "Sit down."

Landon took him up on the offer. The place didn't look like the usual hospital room. There was no obvious disinfectant smell lingering in the air or dingy curtain hanging from the ceiling ready to shield the bed. No medical equipment, either. Instead, there was a twin-size bed, a writing desk, a corkboard on one wall, and a TV mounted on the other. If Landon didn't know better, he'd think he was in the barracks on an army post.

He and Jayson sat in silence, like they were two strangers instead of friends who'd gone to battle together. It was uncomfortable, but Landon couldn't think of anything to say. Even if he could come up with something, he was so choked up he probably couldn't have gotten the words out.

"So, what are you doing here?" Jayson finally asked. "Did the unit rotate back early?"

He shook his head. "No, the guys are still on deployment. I came down on orders to DC."

Jayson frowned. "In the middle of a rotation?"

"I know. It surprised the hell out of me, too."

Jayson was silent, as if he was trying to come up with something else to say.

"You're at the Pentagon, then?"

Landon hesitated. His training officers said he couldn't tell anyone he was working for the DCO. They hadn't said he couldn't say he was working for the Department of Homeland Security.

Jayson's eyes went wide at that. "The Department of Homeland Security, huh? Wow. You're moving up in the world, I guess."

Landon cringed. Jayson was sitting here wondering if he was ever going to be able to get around without using a walker, and he was boasting about a new job. Would it make it better if he said it was a crap assignment and that he'd rather be back in the unit? Probably not.

"How're the guys?" Jayson asked, filling the god-awful silence again.

Landon grinned. "Diaz met a girl on Facebook and thinks he's in love. Mickens still thinks the meatloaf in the MREs is made of dog food. And Angelo...well...is still Angelo."

A ghost of a smile appeared on Jayson's face, only to fade just as fast.

Silence filled the room again. Landon cleared his throat. "How's the rehab going?"

Jayson shrugged. "Okay, I guess. I had to do the wheelchair thing for a while, but they've got me up and walking around using this thing now." He jerked his head at the walker, then looked out the window, his gaze suddenly distant.

Landon felt his throat clog up. Why did Jayson have to be so nice about it? He'd gotten the guy blown up for Pete's sake. He swallowed hard. Dammit, it should be him sitting in that chair, not Jayson.

He wanted to say something reassuring, but "I'm sorry," wasn't going to cut it. What do you tell a guy whose life has just derailed? If not for the accident, Jayson could have risen through the ranks all the way to general, like his father.

Luckily, a knock on the door saved Langdon from having to come up with some kind of meaningless platitude.

"Sorry to interrupt," said a redheaded nurse from the doorway. "I didn't know you had a visitor, Jayson. I'll come back later."

Landon got to his feet a little faster than he intended. "No. Stay." He practically shouted the words. "I should be going anyway." He looked at Jayson. "I've got training tomorrow, but I'll come back to see you when I can."

Out in the hallway, Landon leaned against the wall, closed his eyes, and pinched the bridge of his nose. Inside the room, Jayson and the nurse were talking, but their voices were too soft for him to make out what they were saying. Something about a sleeping pill, he thought.

Whatever it was, it didn't keep the nurse in there long, and Landon intercepted her when she walked out.

"Got a minute?"

She smiled up at him. "Sure. What can I do for you?"

"How is Jayson?" he asked her. "Really."

"Are you family?"

"No, but I'm the closest thing he's got to one. His parents are both dead," Landon said. "I was his commanding officer."

"Oh." She sighed, her smile disappearing. "Physically, he's doing exceptionally well considering the amount of nerve damage he has. Mentally and emotionally? Not so much. A good portion of physical therapy is mental and emotional, so he's not doing as well as he should be. As you're probably aware, there isn't a lot motivating him right now. Hopefully, with you coming by to see him, that will change. Something has to get him up and moving or he may never walk on his own again."

Damn. Now Landon felt even guiltier.

———

When he got back home, Landon undressed and fell into bed, too exhausted to do anything. But instead of falling asleep, he stared up at the ceiling.

He'd been deployed for so long, he'd forgotten what it was like to sleep in a real bed. It felt strange, especially not being around his teammates. Had they gone back to Qari's compound after he'd left? If so, had they all made it out okay? Bennett had taken over command to finish up the mission they'd been on, but who was going to lead the team for the rest of the deployment? With Jayson sitting in a hospital, that left only Master Sergeant Johnson and Angelo. Both of them were born leaders, but the battalion would probably assign another officer to take charge. He ground his jaw. He'd spent the past four years training the team to be the best damn Special Forces unit in the Army. He didn't want some staff weenie going in there and fucking around with his well-oiled machine.

Landon gave himself a mental shake. He had to stop thinking about them as *his* A-team. He was part of a new team now.

His mouth edged up as he thought of Ivy. He'd never seen a woman so sexy in his life. It wasn't only her exotic good looks, sultry dark eyes, and athletic body that got his pulse racing. She exuded sensuality in everything she did—from circling around him before they'd sparred to walking away from him after they were done. When they'd been fighting and he dragged her down on top of him, it had felt amazing. Her body was curved in all the right places, and those curves molded to his body as if she'd been made for it. Just thinking about it made his cock stiffen.

He swore under his breath.

Get a grip, jackass. You're not some horny teenager!

Tell that to his dick.

Landon groaned. If he wasn't so tired, he'd jerk off and be done with it. He could control his physical attraction to Ivy, especially since he had good reason not to act on it. What he couldn't control was his curiosity about these special talents of hers. His gut told him it was more than her martial arts skills.

He ran his fingers over the scratches on his chest. The raised welts were still there, but they didn't sting anymore. He couldn't believe her fingernails had done that. He'd snuck a glance at her delicate hands during the briefing to see if her nails were sharpened to points or something. But no. She had nice, normal, feminine fingernails, not overly long, but not short, either. And they certainly weren't sharp enough to rip open his shirt and claw his chest.

The proof was there, though, in the form of four diagonal marks. And when he saw Ivy tomorrow, he was going to ask how she'd done it.

Chapter 3

LANDON FELT LIKE A SOLDIER OF FORTUNE AS HE drove to work in the DCO-issued black uniform the next morning. It had no name, no rank, no nothing. He was more uncomfortable than if he was driving his truck naked.

Ivy was waiting for him in the lobby when he walked in, looking as cool and standoffish as she had yesterday. But damn if she wasn't Lara Croft sexy in that black uniform with her hair in a ponytail.

"Ready to head to the training complex and get settled in? Kendra thought it would be easier if you just followed me there." She glanced over her shoulder as she started for the door and looked him up and down. "See if you can keep up."

Landon refused to let her get to him. She wanted to play the bitch, fine. "Not much you can do without me, I'd imagine," he drawled.

At that, she turned and strode down the hall, while he took great pleasure in watching her ass every step of the way.

The training complex was south of DC, near Quantico. Once they got through the guarded checkpoint, he followed her to a two-story building and pulled into the empty space beside her.

"These are the dorms," she explained. "We'll be staying here during the main phase of our training. It's easier to park here and jog over to the training areas. We don't have to meet Kendra and Todd for another thirty minutes yet, so I'm going to bring my bags up. You might want to do the same."

Landon grabbed his duffel bag from the seat and followed her inside the building and up to the second floor. The stairwell opened onto a landing with two doors. Ivy headed for the one on the right. He wasn't sure what he expected to find when he walked inside, but the small living room/kitchen combo complete with a microwave oven, full-size fridge, comfy looking couches, and sweet LED television were a nice surprise.

When she'd said dorms, he envisioned the open barracks room he'd called home for the nine weeks he'd been in Basic Training. It had been a huge room with ten to twelve beds separated only by wall lockers. Perhaps this training wouldn't be so bad after all.

Ivy gestured to a door on the other side of the living room. "Bathroom's in there. I'll take the room on the left. The other's yours." And with that, she hustled away to unpack her gear.

Landon put his bag down on his designated bed, then went back into the common area. Ivy was in the kitchen checking out the contents of what was a surprisingly well-stocked fridge. He'd sure never been in a dorm that came with food.

"Don't even have to go to the grocery store. Looks like the DCO thinks of everything," he remarked.

She shut the fridge door. "They usually do."

Which was either a good thing or a bad thing. He leaned back against the counter.

"I get the feeling you've been through yesterday's

briefings before," he said. "How many partners have you had?"

From the look on her face, he might as well have asked how many guys she'd had sex with.

"Two."

"Things didn't work out?"

"No."

He waited for her to give him a few more details, but she didn't. He thought that was her way of saying she didn't want to talk about it. He wouldn't push, but he was curious.

"John mentioned you have some special skills," Landon said. "I'm guessing martial arts is one of them. What are the others?"

She didn't answer, her dark eyes unreadable. He was about to prompt her again when her cell phone rang. She glanced at the call display, then held it to her ear.

"Hey, Kendra," she said, then listened for a moment. "We'll be right there."

Ivy looked at him as she slipped the phone back in her pocket. "Kendra and Todd are waiting for us."

Landon caught her arm when she started for the door. "You didn't answer my question. About the special skills you have."

Her lips curved into a smile. "You look like a smart guy. You'll figure it out soon enough."

He frowned. "What's your problem, Ivy? Is it me, or are you this nice to everyone you work with?"

She looked ashamed he'd called her out, and for a moment he thought she might actually apologize, but then she turned and walked out the door.

Landon snorted as he watched her go. Hell of a nice partnership they had brewing.

———◆———

Ivy swore. She should have gone easier on Landon, especially since he was obviously trying to be friendly. But it wasn't like she could come out and tell him she was a shifter. She'd tried that approach with Dave and it had backfired. It hadn't helped that her enemies had fed him a load of crap about her, all of which had been lies. Unfortunately, those same jerks were still at the DCO, so there was nothing to stop them from turning Landon against her, too.

Ivy glanced at Landon as he fell into step beside her. Some damage control might not be a bad idea. She might have to depend on him for her life someday, and she didn't need to get on his bad side—more than she already was.

"What kind of training are we doing?" He gave her a sidelong glance. "Unless that's a big secret, too."

She deserved that. "Something the DCO likes to call team building. Hope you're not afraid of heights."

"Can't be afraid of heights and be in Special Forces. What are we doing? Rappelling? Air assault ops?"

"Nothing nearly that fun. You remember the last time you played on a confidence course?"

Ivy smiled at the tortured expression on his face. Landon was clearly one of those people who thought the term *confidence course* was an oxymoron. Maybe this was going to be fun after all.

Kendra and Todd were waiting for them along with a medic named Tim. Kendra smiled at Ivy while Todd immediately started briefing them on what they'd be doing.

"You're going to have to work as a team to make it

through the confidence course, and how well you work together is as important as getting through it," Todd told them.

"Time is a factor, too, so no dilly-dallying," Kendra added.

Easy for Kendra to say. She wasn't climbing up to the top of a forty-foot tower with a partner she just met and wasn't sure she could trust to not slip up and drop her ass.

Landon looked at Ivy. "After you."

Ivy turned to survey the confidence course. A series of balance beams, ladders, and towers, it was higher than anything Landon would have seen in the military, but he didn't so much as blink at the prospect of climbing it. Self-assurance like that was attractive in a man, but it could also be dangerous. If he got too cocky, he could end up getting both of them hurt.

Her heart was beating faster than normal as she led the way over the balance beam and up the ladder to the first real obstacle—an inverted tower. She hesitated at the bottom of it. Fifty feet high, it was a series of square platforms. It looked like the floors of a building, only with no walls. The problem was that each floor was wider than the one below it, meaning a person had to lean out over empty space to climb onto it. The only way to get up an inverted tower like this was for one person to boost the other up to the next platform. Then whoever was on top had to lean over the edge and help drag the other one up. It was simple enough—if the two people trusted each other.

She poised to jump up and grab the edge of the first platform when Landon dropped down to one knee and laced his fingers together.

"Here," he said. "I'll give you a boost."

She opened her mouth to tell him she didn't need it, but quickly closed it. Another problem with this obstacle was that the floors got farther apart the higher they got. Higher up, she'd definitely need his help, and if she refused now, he probably wouldn't help her later and they'd fail their first training exercise. Besides, she'd promised herself she would be nicer to him.

Mumbling her thanks, she put her booted foot in his hands and allowed him to lift her up. Landon was tall enough to climb up to the first platform without help, but not the next. Though she didn't think he'd take it—either because he didn't think she'd be strong enough to pull him up or didn't want to tarnish his manhood—Ivy reached down to offer him a hand. He hesitated a second and then jumped up to grab her hand.

When he got up on the platform, he gave her an appraising look. "You're a lot stronger than you look."

"I thought you figured that out yesterday." She grinned. "Gonna give me a boost up or what?"

Landon chuckled and laced his hands together.

Ivy couldn't believe how fast they were moving, probably because they were working as a team. That was a different experience for her. She had to admit having a guy as athletic—and hot—as Landon helping her get through the confidence course made it more fun than it should have been. When Landon planted his big, strong hands firmly on her ass to boost her up onto the topmost platform, she found herself breathing a little harder. And when it was her turn to help him, she couldn't resist grabbing his butt to drag him up. His ass was muscular. He must do nothing in his off time but work out, which made her wonder what the rest of his body looked like underneath that uniform. She had to force herself to really focus as they completed the rest of the course.

When they reached the ground, Ivy had to catch herself from high-fiving her new partner. "You were good up there," she told him.

He seemed surprised at the compliment. "Thanks."

Kendra glanced at something over's Ivy's shoulder. "Yikes. Clayne's here. I'll go intercept him."

Ivy stiffened. Dammit.

"Problem?" Landon asked.

"No," she said. "He's just a friend of mine."

"Friend, huh?" Landon glanced at Clayne, sizing up the tall, muscular shifter the way a man would an opponent he was about to fight. "The way he's looking at you makes me wonder if he knows that."

Clayne was assessing Landon like he wanted that fight.

"Okay. Break's over," Todd called. "Time to move to the next tower."

Ivy sighed with relief. Putting the cap back on her water bottle, she set it down and fell into step beside Landon as he headed for the tower. She needed to focus on their next challenge, not Clayne, especially since the obstacles on this part of the course were tougher and higher.

Again, Landon let her go first, and Ivy quickly climbed the rope to the first level, then ascended the ladder to the top of a tower and waited for him there. He made it up almost as fast as she had.

Landon frowned at the next obstacle—a thirty-foot solid wood wall. On a normal military confidence course, the same wall might be ten feet high. Tough to get over by yourself but doable for a two-person team. Nobody could get over this one, even with teamwork. No average human anyway.

Landon glanced at her. "I don't suppose you can fly, can you?"

"Not quite." She hesitated, then added, "But I can climb it."

He raised a brow. "Climb it? You've gotta be kidding me." When she didn't answer, he folded his arms across his chest. "This I've gotta see."

Ivy's pulse quickened. Part of the reason the DCO made them do the confidence course was to expose Landon to her true nature so he could recognize its value. Or cringe in revulsion.

Time to see if he could handle it or would go running off for a psych evaluation.

Turning to face the wall, she let her fingernails extend until they were as long as those of the great cat with which she shared her DNA. Then she took a deep breath and ran toward the wall. Jumping onto it, she dug her claws into the wood and climbed hand over hand all the way to the top. Heart pounding, she peeked down at Landon, praying she wouldn't find the disgust she'd seen so many times before. But he just stood there with an amused expression on his face.

"If you expect me to climb the wall like that, we're going to be here awhile," he called. "Hope you brought lunch."

Huh? No shock, no freaking out, no fear in his eyes. She couldn't believe it.

"Well?" he prompted.

She gave herself a shake. "There's a rope up here. I'll toss it down."

Just because he hadn't freaked out didn't mean he wouldn't demand answers when he got to the top, and Ivy braced herself for a barrage of questions. But he only reminded her that Kendra and Todd were timing them so they'd better hurry.

Since Landon hadn't freaked out after seeing her sprout claws and scale a thirty-foot wall, Ivy didn't see the need to hold back anymore, particularly when they got to a rope bridge stretched between two towers fifty feet high. She could get across the bridge in the dark with one arm tied behind her back, so she didn't need to use the safety rope above her head, like Landon did.

She didn't know what happened. Maybe she wasn't paying as much attention as she should have. Or maybe she was showing off for Landon. The next thing she knew, her foot slipped off the rope and she fell. She instinctively tried to grab the rope bridge, but missed it.

Crap. The fall wouldn't kill her, but it would hurt like hell—her pride most of all.

Suddenly, her hand hit something. She grabbed whatever it was, hoping it was strong enough to stop her descent, when she felt a hand wrap around her wrist. Amazed, she jerked her head up to see Landon holding on to her.

"I've got you," he said, his voice calm and reassuring.

Ivy didn't know how he managed to get to her so fast. Or how he was keeping himself from falling. Dragging her gaze away from his soulful brown eyes, she saw that he was hanging from the rope bridge by his legs like a circus performer. That probably wasn't a standard Special Forces move. Maybe he had some monkey DNA and didn't know it.

"Um, Ivy. Not to rush you or anything, but this isn't really comfortable. Think you can find a way to climb up me without ripping me to shreds or knocking us both down?"

That's when she realized her claws were out and dug into his wrist like spikes. That had to hurt.

"Oh God, I'm sorry!"

She retracted her claws and carefully climbed up Landon's back onto the rope bridge. Grabbing the top rope, she quickly moved forward so he could get back up on the bridge. But Landon didn't bother. Instead, he swung hand over hand on the bottom rope until he got to the tower, then dragged himself up onto it. Careful to hold on to the safety rope this time, Ivy hurried across the rope bridge to join him.

She grabbed his wrist to see how much damage she'd done. There were five bloody puncture marks around it that were already starting to swell. She winced. They looked painful. She might not be crazy about the guy, but she hadn't meant to hurt him.

"I really am so sorry," she murmured.

"I'm fine," he said. "I'll get it checked out when we're done. You okay?"

Ivy blinked up at him. He'd almost gotten killed saving her butt from her own stupidity, and he was asking if she was okay?

"Yeah. I'm fine. Thanks. For catching me, I mean."

"No problem. What's a partner for?" He flashed her a devastating grin. "Come on, let's get moving. We're eating up the clock."

———— ∽∿∽ ————

As he and Ivy jogged to the cafeteria, Landon tried to comprehend what had happened up on the tower. Not the whole saving-Ivy-from-falling thing. He'd saved plenty of guys' asses on training exercises before, and he'd had someone save his ass from a screw-up once or twice. What had him confused was the whole claws-and-wall-climbing thing. And that wasn't even the most bizarre part, which had come when she'd looked up at him after he'd caught her mid-fall. Her eyes had gone from their usual dark, beautiful brown to an iridescent, light green, and her pupils narrowed to slits, like a cat's.

But that was impossible, right? Yeah, well so were claws.

He glanced at Ivy. He wanted to ask her about it, but that wasn't something they could talk about while they were jogging. So he shelved his questions for later.

In the cafeteria, he and Ivy grabbed some food, then found a table. Although the chili he'd chosen would never be considered gourmet by any stretch of the imagination, it was better than the stuff he was used to in Afghanistan.

"Thanks again for saving my ass back there," Ivy said as they ate. "How'd you do that thing you did with the rope?"

"You mean hang upside down from it?" He gave her a lopsided smile. "I don't know. I saw you fall and instinctively leaped to catch you. I think hooking the rope with my legs was more luck than skill."

Landon studied her over the rim of his Gatorade bottle. Since she'd brought it up, he figured it was a good time to ask about her feline tendencies. Before he could say anything, however, Ivy mumbled something about talking to Kendra, then grabbed her tray and got up.

A lot of people watched Ivy cross the room. That wasn't a surprise. She was an attractive woman who made the DCO uniform look good. But not everyone eyed her with appreciation. Some of them were looking at her with hatred. What the hell had she done to earn that kind of animosity? Besides having claws that allowed her to scale a thirty-foot wall and puncture flesh? Not to mention eyes that seemed to glow. He could see how that would make some people look at her differently.

Claws. Eyes that glowed. What the hell was he thinking? That Ivy was what…part cat? He took another gulp of Gatorade, trying to get the thoughts out of his head, but he had the puncture wounds on his wrist to prove it.

"Mind if we sit?"

Landon looked up to see two men standing in front of him. One was short and stocky, with curly hair. The other was a tall African American. "Go ahead."

"I'm Foley," the stocky guy said. "This is Hightower."

"Donovan."

"We thought we should come over and offer our condolences on being partnered up with Poison Ivy," Foley said.

Poison Ivy? He had to be kidding. What, were they in fifth grade again? Landon took another swig of Gatorade. "That so?"

"Yeah." Foley leaned back in his chair. "Got her first partner deep-sixed from the DCO. Got her second partner killed while they were on a mission. If she weren't an EVA, she'd be out on her ass for the shit she's pulled. Freaking bitch."

Landon had to tighten his grip on the plastic bottle to keep from balling his hand into a fist and punching

Foley in the face. It was obvious Foley was a dumbass who liked to spread rumors about crap he didn't know anything about. The man's opinion of Ivy didn't mean shit to him. When he wanted to know about her previous partners, he'd ask her.

"Thanks for sharing," he replied.

Foley looked like he had more to say, but he backed off when four men casually sauntered up to the table. Three of the men looked nondescript, but the fourth guy was quite memorable. Easily six-foot-seven, he was blond and built like a pro wrestler. Or the guy from that *Thor* movie he'd seen over in Afghanistan. He was also the one Foley must have disliked the most. The curly haired man threw a scowl his way, then nudged Hightower.

"Let's go." Foley gave Landon a pointed look as he stood. "Watch your back."

Landon didn't say anything. The four newcomers sat down, the pro-wrestler lookalike sitting across from Landon.

"Was Foley filling your head with lies about Ivy?" asked the dark-haired one with blue eyes and a neatly trimmed beard and mustache.

"He tried to," Landon said. "I didn't buy what he was selling."

The bearded man nodded. "Good. Because he's full of shit. Ivy's one of the best operatives at the DCO, and if Foley wasn't such an asshole, he'd realize that. I'm Tate Evers, by the way." He nodded at the two men sitting next to Landon on each side. "That's Brent Wilkins and Gavin Barlow. And this big guy"—he jerked his thumb at the pro wrestler—"is Declan MacBride. He's the EVA part of our team."

Landon looked at the big blond man. He couldn't imagine him growing claws and scaling a wall. "EVA?"

"No one told you what that stands for yet? I'm not surprised." Tate snorted. "The DCO always does a lousy job of explaining stuff. EVA is short for extremely valuable asset."

Asset. As if the DCO didn't think of Ivy and Declan as people. Landon swung his gaze back to Declan. "You can do what Ivy does?"

Declan laughed. "Not on a good day."

Tate grinned. "Declan's skills are different than Ivy's. You two didn't have the talk yet, huh?"

The talk? That sounded ominous. "Apparently not."

"Then I won't be the one to steal her thunder. After this morning's training, I'm sure you've already figured out she's special, right?"

"Very."

All four men regarded him thoughtfully, but once again, it was Tate who spoke.

"Look, you're going to run into people like Foley who'll tell you people like Declan and Ivy are freaks. That's bullshit. She and Declan and people like them aren't any different than you, me, Brent, and Gavin. They just have special skills that make them unique. Regardless of what Foley told you, you can trust Ivy to have your back. And she needs to know she can trust you in return."

"She can," Landon said without hesitation. That was a given, regardless of what happened with her previous partners.

"Good," Tate said. "Because in this job, both your lives depend on it."

—∿∿—

It was cowardly to use Kendra as a buffer between her and Landon, but Ivy couldn't help it. Her new partner might not have freaked out at the sight of her claws—or that she'd dug them into his arm—but she wasn't quite ready to have the talk with him yet.

"What do you think of Landon?" Kendra asked Ivy.

Ivy's gaze strayed to her partner to find him looking at her. She quickly turned her attention back to Kendra. "He seems okay. You could have warned me he's military."

"Why? So you could obsess about how awful he'd be every waking minute until you met him?" Kendra bit into one of the two chocolate chip cookies on the tray in front of her. "So what if he's Special Forces? You two obviously work well as a team. And he's definitely nice to look at."

"That's not the point. I thought you were going to have some say in picking my next partner."

Kendra scowled. "You guys were great together on the course. Stop being so closed-minded."

Ivy finished off the cookie she'd been nibbling on. "I'd better do some damage control before our next round. I might have to depend on Landon to save my ass again."

She grabbed her Gatorade and got to her feet, almost smacking into Declan as she turned around. She really must be preoccupied if she hadn't heard him come up behind her. The bear shifter wasn't exactly stealthy. He was, however, one of the sweetest guys she'd ever met.

Ivy smiled up at him. "Hey."

"Hey. I just met your new partner. He seems like a

good guy." Declan turned his baby blue eyes on Kendra.
"Um…Hi, Kendra."

Ivy hid her smile behind her Gatorade bottle as she
took a sip. Poor Declan. She couldn't believe a guy who
was this big and tough could get so tongue-tied when it
came to talking to a woman. But he had a serious crush
on Kendra.

"I was…um…wondering if you…might want to…
you know, grab something to eat."

Kendra frowned in confusion. She looked down at
her empty tray, then up at Declan. "Thanks, but I already ate."

He flushed beneath his tan. "Right. I knew that. I
just…you know, thought you might want to go out to
dinner this weekend."

"Dinner? Oh."

Kendra glanced at Ivy, looking helpless and in desperate need of a life preserver, but Ivy wasn't tossing
one to her. If Kendra was going to give him the brush-
off—yet again—she was going to do it without Ivy's
help. Something Kendra must have quickly figured out
because she turned back to Declan.

"Thanks for the offer, Declan, but I'm kind of
swamped right now with training and everything."
Kendra gave him a small smile. "Maybe after Ivy and
Landon are certified."

As brush-offs went, it wasn't rude, but from the way
Declan's shoulders sagged, Kendra might as well have
told him he didn't have a snowball's chance in hell of
ever going out with her. Ivy couldn't blame him. What
she couldn't understand was why he kept asking Kendra
out after she'd shot him down so many times. Wasn't

doing the same thing and expecting different results the definition of insanity?

To his credit, Declan didn't let the hurt show. He even managed a grin. "Sure. Sounds good." He gave Ivy a nod. "See you around."

He hesitated, as if he wanted to say something else to Kendra, but after giving her one more puppy-dog look, he turned and headed for the cafeteria's big double doors. Ivy frowned as she watched him go. He looked even more upset this time than he usually did when Kendra turned him down. She'd have to tell Tate to keep an eye on Declan. She didn't want the shifter getting himself or someone else hurt because he was in a depression-induced fog.

Ivy looked at Kendra. "Why don't you just give the poor guy a break and go out with him?"

Her friend's brow rose. "Declan? You're not serious?"

"Why not? He's obviously crazy about you."

"I know. Which is why I feel awful turning him down every time he asks me out. But he's just not my type."

Of course he wasn't. Kendra's type was Clayne, a guy who didn't have the time of day for her. As a result, Kendra missed out on what could be a good thing with Declan. And Clayne was missing out on a good thing with Kendra because he only had eyes for Ivy. And she wasn't interested. In him or anyone else.

Sometimes she wondered if the DCO was a high-speed government covert-ops organization or a dysfunctional soap opera.

Chapter 4

IVY BRACED FOR A CONFRONTATION WITH LANDON, BUT he was as nice to her after lunch as he'd been before. Either Foley hadn't said anything nasty about her, or Landon hadn't believed him. She hoped it was the latter. Although she was dying to know what the two men had talked about, she didn't ask. The curiosity, however, was enough to distract her.

Luckily, that afternoon's training didn't require a lot of concentration. It was physically demanding, though, and by the end of the day they were both dirty, sweaty, and exhausted.

"Man, I reek," Landon said when they got to their dorm.

Actually, he didn't reek at all. He was half covered in mud and soaked in sweat, but he was far from stinky. To her, he smelled of musk and masculinity. The combination was so delicious, she had to keep from burying her nose in his neck so she could take a closer whiff.

Sometimes, she really hated having an enhanced sense of smell.

Cheeks coloring, she reached up to tuck a stray strand of hair behind her ear. "Do you want to flip a quarter to see who gets to use the shower first?"

Unless you want to share. Like she'd trust herself enough to be in such a confined space with all that potent masculinity.

"Nah. You can go first." His mouth edged up. "I might stink like a pig, but I'm still a gentleman."

And underneath all the mud and sweat covering her, she was enough of a lady to appreciate the gesture. "Okay. Thanks."

Grateful to put some space between her and his sexy scent, she grabbed her robe and toiletry bag from her suitcase, then ducked into the bathroom. Unfortunately, the door didn't do a thing to shut out the pheromones he was emitting. She should have jumped in the shower and turned on the water full blast, but instead she stood there with her mouth partially open, breathing in his scent and getting more aroused by the second.

Ivy closed her eyes and inhaled deeply, moaning as warmth pooled between her thighs. She'd never had such a strong reaction to a man before. Not even the ones she'd slept with.

She pushed away from the door. Stripping off her uniform, she climbed into the shower and turned it on full force. It was cold, but she didn't care. Hoping the coconut-scented body wash would help mask Landon's scent, she squeezed some into her palm and lathered up. As she ran her hands over her breasts and down her stomach, she imagined it was her new partner washing the sweat and dirt away. The fire between her legs engulfed her whole body and she slid her hand down to touch herself.

A few circular motions on her clit with her fingers and she'd orgasm. But she couldn't. Not here. Not with Landon just outside.

She caught her bottom lip between her teeth to stifle a moan and reluctantly pulled her hand away. Why the heck hadn't she thought to pack her vibrator? On second thought, maybe it was better she hadn't. Masturbating while thinking of her partner was not a good idea.

Regardless of how scrumptious he smelled, she was not going to fantasize about having sex with Landon. And she was most definitely not going to give in to her animal side and actually have sex with him. No matter how intoxicating he smelled or how hot he looked in his uniform.

Landon had to stifle a groan when Ivy came walking out of the bathroom. Seeing her in nothing but a short robe with her long, wet hair hanging down her back and her slender legs bare was enough to make him go hard in his pants. Now he understood why the army didn't allow women on the A-teams. To say they'd be a distraction was an understatement.

Disappearing into the bathroom before Ivy could see the tent he was pitching, he took off his boots and uniform, and jumped in the tub. He showered quickly, turning the water all the way to cold in the hope it would get rid of his raging hard-on. Thankfully, it worked. Though he wasn't sure how long the effect would last if Ivy was still wearing that robe when he went back into the living room.

Fortunately, she wasn't. Unfortunately, she was wearing something just as sexy—shorts and a tank top. The kind that showed lots of skin and hugged every one of her curves. His cock immediately stiffened in his jeans.

Ivy turned as he walked into the kitchen. Landon's gaze locked on her perfect breasts. He swore under his breath and forced himself to focus on her face instead. Or more precisely, her beautiful, brown eyes. A guy could get seriously lost in those eyes.

"I was just going to make a sandwich," she said. "You want one?"

His stomach growled at the mention of food. He hadn't even realized he was hungry. How could he? He'd been too busy thinking about what his partner looked like naked under her robe. "Sure. Thanks."

"Peanut butter and jelly okay?"

"That's fine."

Actually, it was better than fine. He hadn't had a peanut butter and jelly sandwich since his forward operating base got a big shipment of care packages in from the States. That had been months ago. Most people didn't think much of peanut butter and jelly, but it was something you sure missed when you couldn't get it.

He leaned against the counter, watching as she spread peanut butter on a slice of bread. "Can I ask you something?"

She dug more peanut butter out of the jar for the second sandwich. "That depends on what it is."

Fair enough. "Well, I guess we won't know unless I ask, so at the risk of offending you, I'm just going to come out and say it. Are you some kind of government experiment, like on *X-Files* or something?"

Ivy stopped spreading peanut butter on the third sandwich to look at him, surprised. Then she burst out laughing. "No. I'm definitely not a government experiment."

He waited for her to continue, but she only finished up with the peanut butter and started on the jelly.

"If you're not a government experiment, what are

you then? Other than an extremely valuable asset to the DCO, I mean?"

She shook her head, the hint of a smile curving her lips. "The DCO loves their labels, don't they? You're a norm. I'm a paranorm. You're valuable. I'm extremely valuable."

Paranorm. That sounded like something from the SyFy channel. "What do you prefer to be called?"

She gave him a smile. She had a gorgeous smile. "Ivy works for me."

He grinned back. "Ivy it is then."

She set the plate with the sandwiches on the small breakfast bar. "There's bottled water in the fridge. Can you grab a couple?"

"Wouldn't you rather have milk? It goes better with peanut butter."

She made a face. "I don't like milk."

Who didn't like milk? He grabbed water for her and milk for himself, then sat down on the stool beside her. "You didn't answer my question. About what you are."

She chewed on her bottom lip as if debating whether to answer or not. "I'm a feline shifter."

A feline shifter. As in cat. Okay. He'd been right about her eyes then. Shouldn't she like milk then? "Were you attacked by a werecat?"

She coughed up the water she'd been sipping. "A werecat? You watch way too many movies."

Now that he thought about it, the idea was pretty ludicrous. But she'd just told him she was a feline shifter. What the hell was he supposed to think? He picked up his sandwich and took a bite. "I'll take that as a no."

"I was born a shifter," she explained. "And no, before you ask, my mom didn't have sex with a lion."

"The idea never crossed my mind."

Like hell it hadn't. In addition to watching too many movies, he sometimes had a very twisted imagination.

Ivy bit into her sandwich, chewed, then washed it down with water. "The scientists at the DCO said that somewhere in the past, feline DNA got mixed in with one of my ancestors' DNA."

Landon felt his mouth twitch. "Ah. So, your great-great-great-grandmother slept with a saber-toothed tiger?"

She made a face at him. "No one slept with any saber-toothed tigers. According to the geneticists, there's a little bit of this mixed-up DNA in everyone. Even you."

He downed the rest of the first sandwich and started on the second. "Yeah? Then how come I can't do what you can do?"

"Because the genetic coding didn't become active and cause changes in your physiology when you were a teenager like mine did."

"Changes in your physiology. Like claws and cat's eyes?"

Her eyes, soft and brown now, went wide. "You saw my eyes change? When?"

"When you latched on to my arm with your nails on the confidence course. They changed for a second, but then went back to your natural color so quickly, I wasn't sure I'd seen right."

"I usually only do that at night so I can see better. But they can change whenever I'm stressed. Or emotional." She looked at him sheepishly. "I feel awful about clawing you. It was an instinctive reaction. I really am sorry."

"Don't worry about it. They don't even hurt now," he said. "Any other feline superpowers I should know about?"

"Well, I'm a lot stronger and faster than a woman should be," she admitted.

He grinned. "Yeah, I kind of figured that when we were sparring yesterday. Anything else?"

"I can heal twice as fast as a normal human. So, while that fall from the rope bridge would have hurt, it wouldn't have killed me."

"Damn." That would be one hell of nice superpower to have in Special Forces. "What else?"

"I'm more athletic and agile than a regular person."

"Right." He chuckled. "Like that graceful demonstration on the rope bridge this morning."

"Not quite." She blushed. "That was me showing off. When you didn't freak out after seeing me climb a wall, I got a little carried away. I'm not normally that careless. Especially out in the field. So, no worries."

Was that her way of telling him she wasn't going to let what happened to her previous partner happen to him? Whatever that was. He should have asked, but right now he was more interested in learning about her animal side.

"Can you turn into a bobcat or lion, or whatever breed your DNA is from?"

She laughed. "You really do watch too many movies. No, I can't turn into a bobcat. Or a lion. Or a cheetah."

He'd been hoping she could. That would have been really cool.

Ivy pushed her plate away so she could rest her forearms on the counter. "Okay. How come you're not freaking out about all this? About me and what I am."

Good question. He shrugged. "I don't know. Would you believe me if I said I've always been a cat person?"

Ivy smiled, giving him a glimpse of perfect white teeth. "Maybe. If I didn't know you were lying."

She was right. He was more of a dog person. But it was either lie or come clean and tell her he'd always had a thing for Catwoman. An image popped into his head of Ivy dressed in a shiny leather catsuit complete with ears and a long tail. Now he was hard again.

"You can't read minds, can you?"

She laughed. "No."

"What about the other shifters at the DCO?" he asked, partly because he was curious and partly because he had to do something to get the sexy image of a leather-clad Ivy out of his head or he was going to really embarrass himself. "Do they have feline DNA, too?"

"Some of them. But others have wolf, bear, whatever."

"How many of you are there?"

"Working for the DCO? About a dozen or so."

"Have you ever been partners with any of them?"

She shook her head. "The DCO doesn't pair shifters with other shifters. They say it's because their studies show pairing a human with a shifter creates the strongest teams, but I'm not sure I buy that. I think it's because they don't trust two shifters to work together without adult supervision."

Or the people in charge were worried one shifter wouldn't carry out orders to kill the other if he or she became compromised. Landon wanted to ask Ivy how she could work for an organization that would rather see her dead than have someone know they had people like her on their payroll, but he changed his mind. He didn't want her thinking he was focusing on it. That situation was never going to happen because he wasn't going to let it happen. So there was no reason to talk about it.

Landon glanced at his watch. As much as he hated to cut the conversation short, he needed to get moving if he wanted to see Jayson before visiting hours were over. He slid off the stool.

"I'm going to take off for a while," he told Ivy.

"Oh." Was it him or did she almost look disappointed? "Okay."

He picked up their empty plates and carried them over to the sink so he could wash them. Ivy'd made the sandwiches, so he figured it was only fair for him to do the dishes. She followed, leaning casually against the counter as she watched him work.

"Thanks," she said. "For not freaking out about me being different."

The way she said it made him think she didn't get that kind of reaction from people very often. That wasn't surprising. It wasn't every day you ran into someone who was part cat. "Thanks for trusting me enough to tell me."

She gave him a small smile. "It's not like I had a choice. You'd find out anyway, and it was better you found out from me. I'm just glad you're okay with it."

Was he okay with it? He didn't know. Maybe he just hadn't wrapped his head around it yet. Or maybe he was still too sleep-deprived to care.

Setting the plates in the rack beside the sink, he grabbed his keys and headed for the door. He opened it to find himself face to face with Clayne, the guy who'd showed up at the confidence course that morning and gotten under Ivy's skin. While the man wasn't quite as big as Declan, he was still taller than Landon. Did that make him a shifter?

Clayne looked past Landon as if he weren't even there, his gaze going to Ivy. "Hey."

"Hey." She walked over. "Landon, this is Clayne Buchanan. Clayne, my new partner Landon Donovan."

Landon held out his hand, but instead of taking it, Buchanan brushed past him and walked into the living room. Landon snorted. Ignoring Buchanan, he turned to tell Ivy he'd see her later, but the words died in his throat when he saw how stiff she was. She looked as tense as when she'd seen him earlier in the day.

"Do you want me to stay?" he asked her, leaning close and lowering his voice so Buchanan wouldn't hear.

She shook her head. "I'm fine."

Landon glanced at Buchanan. He was standing in the middle of the living room, his arms folded across his chest, a pissed-off expression on his face.

"You sure?" he asked Ivy.

"I'm sure. Go."

Landon wasn't crazy about leaving her alone with the guy, but he didn't see a way around it without making a big deal out of the whole thing. He gave her a nod, looked at Buchanan—who was still glowering—then walked out. To say Ivy had shitty taste in friends was an understatement.

"Do you want something to drink?"

Clayne shook his head. He was wearing his dark hair longer. It brushed his shoulders. "I'm good. Why'd Donovan think you wanted him to stay?"

She should have known Clayne's exceptional hearing would pick that up. "Because you look like you want to rip my head off."

He scowled, the muscles in his square jaw flexing. "You know I'd never hurt you."

"I know that. But Landon doesn't."

Clayne was silent for a moment. "How do you like him? As a partner, I mean."

As opposed to what? Boyfriend? She flopped down on the couch, tucking her legs under her. "He seems capable."

Clayne grunted. "I don't like him."

"You don't even know him."

"I know he's a norm. That's good enough for me."

"You know, when you say things like that, you sound just as narrow-minded as the norms who hate us because we're different than they are."

He growled low in his throat. "I'm not anything like them."

"Right," she scoffed.

He clenched his jaw. "Dammit, I didn't come here to argue."

"Then what did you come here for?"

Clayne didn't answer right away. "To ask if you wanted to grab dinner with me."

"I already ate."

His lip curled. "With Donovan?"

"Yes, with Landon." She shook her head. "God, Clayne, you make it sound like we went out for an intimate dinner at a romantic restaurant. We ate peanut butter and jelly sandwiches."

He scowled. "I just don't like the idea of you spending time with him."

Now he was jealous, too. "He's my partner, Clayne. We're going to be spending a lot of time together, especially while we're getting certified."

"That doesn't mean you have to hang out with him in your off-time," Clayne argued. "Why do you want to spend time with him, anyway? He's a human. You know as well as I do how fast their kind can turn on our kind."

She knew, only too well. But she didn't despise everyone who wasn't a shifter because of it. Clayne clearly didn't feel that way. But then his emotional scars went deeper than hers. If she so much as mentioned his ex-partner's name, it would only piss him off even more.

"I'm human, too, Clayne," she said softly. "And whether you want to admit it or not, so are you."

He let out a snort. "Don't remind me."

She was too exhausted for this. "I'm not going to sit here and fight with you. I'm tired and all I want to do right now is go to bed. I've got to be up early for training."

Hurt flashed in his eyes. He shoved his hands through his hair and blew out a breath. "This wasn't the way I wanted this to go. I just thought we could have dinner together. Hang out like we used to, you know?"

Ivy wished they could do that, too. She missed hanging out with Clayne. But going out for something as simple as dinner was hard when one of them wanted to be more than friends and the other didn't.

She uncurled herself from the couch. "I've got an early day tomorrow."

His mouth tightened. "Which is your way of saying you're not interested. I get it." When she didn't say anything, he stalked across the small apartment to the door. He yanked it open, then turned to face her. "I just want to know. Would you be willing to go out with me if I wasn't a shifter? Say I was—I don't know—a norm like Donovan?"

She felt her face color as she remembered the not-so-innocent fantasy she'd had in the shower. "Landon and I are partners, that's all."

"Yeah?" Clayne snorted. "Well, you two seem damn chummy for partners."

Chummy? Who the heck said that? Not that it mattered because she and Landon weren't chummy. They weren't anything but partners. Ivy opened her mouth to tell Clayne that—again—but he was already gone.

Chapter 5

IVY SHIFTED IN HER SEAT, TRYING TO GET COMFORT-able as the helicopter careened through the night sky. She might be part cat, but she felt more like a donkey with all the gear she was carrying. She wasn't looking forward to hoofing it through the jungles of Venezuela with all this weight. Hopefully, the copter would drop them close to their target.

She'd been surprised when Kendra had called early that morning and told her and Landon to report to the DC office immediately for a mission briefing. Just minutes before, Ivy'd been filling Landon in on the weeks and weeks of grueling training they had ahead of them before they were certified for field duty. Lock picking, safecracking, electronic surveillance and wiretap procedures, computer hacking, security systems bypass, diving, weapons and demo training, close quarter combat, hand-to-hand combat. The list was long and exhausting.

Yet here they were sitting on a Black Hawk heli-copter flying over Colombian territory about to embark on what was essentially a final certification exercise in Venezuela. This was unheard of. John had told them that due to her experience and Landon's demonstrated mili-tary expertise, senior management decided they were more than ready to handle this challenge. She hadn't bought it and, from the look on their faces, John and

Kendra hadn't either. That meant only one thing—Dick Coleman, the DCO's resident rat, was up to something.

Dick was the DCO's deputy director under John. At least that's how it showed up on the organizational flowcharts. But everyone knew his real job was to be a mole for the Committee. As far as she and every other operative knew, the Committee was a subpanel of the House and Senate Intelligence Oversight Committees. Like everything in Washington, it was full of politicians with their own agendas, and Dick made sure they got what they wanted. Ivy didn't know why John put up with his crap.

Right now, she didn't have time to worry about the man or his machinations. She was more concerned about being out in the field with Landon so soon. If things went wrong on the op and she got compromised, would he try to help her or just carry out orders and kill her? Heading out on a mission with that big unknown hanging over your head wasn't a comforting thought.

Their mission was simple enough—retrieve evidence linking several high-ranking officials in the Venezuelan government to the Colombian drug trade. The DCO wasn't exactly sure what form the evidence would take—though they suspected it was most likely on a laptop. But they knew for certain that said laptop was in the home of Julien Calballero, a man famous in the drug trade. He had a well-established system in place for moving drugs from Colombia through Venezuela to the Caribbean and to the United States. He'd accumulated a lot of money and power over the years, and killed a lot of people to keep it. And he had a small army of men guarding his compound.

Ivy's stomach lurched as the helicopter suddenly tipped and she had the pleasure of watching trees pass by below her. This was one of those rare times she really didn't appreciate her perfect night vision. She gripped the side of the open door more tightly. She could barely stay on the flimsy nylon seat with the way the pilot was flying, even with her seat belt on. Either the Colombian pilot was trying to show off for the hot American chica—his words, not hers—by cavalierly flying a hairsbreadth above the top of the tree canopy, or he was trying to make her puke.

Then she saw the tracer rounds zipping past the Black Hawk, and the crazy flying technique suddenly made a lot more sense. Landon had told her this part of Colombia was completely overrun with FARC fighters. Apparently, the Revolutionary Armed Forces of Colombia enjoyed shooting at helicopters in the middle of the night. Even if they didn't know who was on them.

Landon's head was lolling from side to side as he slept through the combined roller-coaster ride and fireworks display. He'd come in late last night and looked like shit during the mission briefing. If she had to guess, she'd say he'd been out with a woman all night, though she never smelled anything on him.

She cringed as a bullet hit the Black Hawk.

The shooting only got worse, or maybe just more accurate. The pilot went into overdrive, zigging and zagging to keep the chopper from getting hit again.

Beside her, Landon was awake now. Or maybe he'd never been asleep. He tightened a few straps that had come loose on his backpack.

"We might be getting off early," he shouted over the deafening noise in the cabin.

The original plan was to get as close to the Venezuelan border as they could, but that didn't look like it was going to be happening now. No sooner were the words out of his mouth than the pilot yelled something in Spanish over his headset to the crew chief, who gestured alternately at the jungle below and the fast-rope bag sitting on the floor near him.

Landon leaned close. "You good?"

She nodded. Unbuckling her seat belt, she scooted closer toward the open door and fast-rope line.

The Black Hawk stopped jerking and dropped to hover a few feet above the top of the trees. The crew chief tossed the fast-rope bag out and she watched it disappear into the jungle, laying out their descending line as it went.

Fast roping out of a helicopter wasn't so bad—definitely not as bad as jumping out of a plane. All she had to do was slide down the line and let go once she reached the ground. But in this jungle? The idea of getting dragged through the trees while she was halfway down because the helicopter started taking fire didn't thrill her. Worse, she'd have no way of knowing if the line was all the way down to the ground. It could be too short or it could get hung up in the tree branches on the way down.

She reached for the line, but Landon caught it first. "We don't know what's waiting for us down there. Let me go first."

Ivy opened her mouth to tell him she didn't need protecting, but he was already gone, sliding down the fast-rope line into the trees below. That pissed her off. Typical military grunt—didn't think a woman could handle herself.

Tracers zipped past the Black Hawk from a nearby

ridgeline, and the helicopter bucked as the pilot tried to avoid them. Ivy tightened her hold on the doorframe. If Landon were still on the line, he could get seriously hurt thanks to this jerk.

Ivy shot the pilot a venomous look. "Hold it steady!"

She had no idea if the man could understand English, but the Black Hawk steadied. The crew chief smacked her on the shoulder, yelling something in Spanish. Taking that as her cue to get off, she grabbed the thick rope in her gloved hands, then clenched her booted feet around it and slid down the line.

Bullets whistled over her head as she dropped, and she swore under her breath, instinctively ducking. She hoped the rope went all the way down to the ground and wasn't wrapped around a tree branch. Unfortunately, she couldn't see anything in the branches, even with her shifter night vision.

The rope suddenly swung wildly through the air, flinging her sideways through the trees. The pilot was freaking out. Any second now, he'd pull up—dragging her back up through the trees—or just say the hell with it and release the entire fast-rope assembly.

She wasn't going to wait for either.

Taking a deep breath, she let go of the rope and immediately felt dizzy from falling.

She caught sight of the ground a split second before she hit. Not tensing was hard, but she forced herself to roll through her points of contact—calves, thighs, butt, back—just like she would if she was doing a parachute drop. The big backpack she'd complained about earlier sucked up a lot of the impact, making her fall a lot less painful than it might have been.

Landon was at her side before she came to a stop.
"You okay?"

She did a quick self-check. Everything felt like it was
in working order. "I'm good."

She ignored the hand he offered and got to her feet.
The muscle in his jaw flexed, but he said nothing. Instead
he focused his attention on the helicopter above them.

"Damn jackasses," he muttered. The helicopter
disappeared in the distance, but the sounds of gunfire
remained. "We better get out of here. They're going to
come looking for whoever the helicopter was dropping,
and we don't want to be here when they do."

He had that right. She could already hear the faint
sound of soldiers moving through the brush. They were
still at least a mile away, but they were getting closer.

"Avoiding these assholes might be good for our health.
Are your kitty cat talents any help in this situation?"

Ivy blinked. Her first partner hadn't been as guilty
of it as Dave, but even Jeff hadn't liked to rely on her
shifter abilities, especially in a potentially dangerous
situation. And they definitely hadn't called her shifter
skills by such an endearing name.

"I can pick up scents if I'm downwind of people, and
I can hear them moving from a pretty good distance no
matter where they are. Sometimes I get a…"

He frowned in the darkness. "You get what?"

She chewed on her lower lip, not sure if she wanted
to mention this part. It was sort of supernatural. The
bullets whizzing through the trees decided it for her.
"Sometimes I get a…hunch, I suppose you'd say. I just
know when things are going to go bad."

Landon regarded her in silence, as if debating

whether he wanted to put his faith in something as flimsy as a hunch.

"Okay," he said as he strapped on his NVGs. "Sounds like you're on point then. Get us out of here without a firefight and I pay for the first beer when we get back."

Landon was actually going to let her take the lead. That was an absolute first for her. Not waiting for him to change his mind, she took off into the jungle, heading due east.

Landon followed twenty feet behind as she navigated the dense jungle. It would have been hard enough moving quickly through the thick foliage during the day. At night—with a heavy pack—it was even more difficult. But Ivy ignored the weight and concentrated on hiking as fast as she could. She glanced over her shoulder frequently, checking to make sure Landon was keeping up. He never wavered from his position behind her.

An hour later, Landon let out a soft whistle. Ivy immediately stopped and turned around.

"You hear anyone behind us?" he asked when he caught up.

"Not in the last thirty minutes."

He handed his canteen to her, then got out the map and GPS so he could figure out where they were. He swore under his breath.

"How bad?"

"Bad." He put his finger on the map. "We're here, more than thirty miles from the Venezuelan border. In this thick crap, it's going to take probably more than twenty hours to get to the border, then another two or three hours to get to the compound. That puts us at the target early in the morning day after tomorrow. Too late to hit Calballero's place, so we'll lose more time waiting for dark so we can go in."

Ivy groaned. They'd be worn out before they even got to their target. Worse, they'd miss their rendezvous with the tourist group that was supposed to be their cover for getting out of the country. If she and Landon didn't make that pickup, they were going to have to hike through the jungle all the way back to Bogotá.

Landon folded the map and put it away. "If we want to stick to the plan and get to Calballero's place by midnight tomorrow, we're going to have to lighten our load and haul ass."

Landon pulled out extra gear and put it in a pile. Ivy didn't complain about the extra energy rations he unloaded. They tasted like crap and wouldn't be needed if they didn't have to hike back to Bogotá. They could find something in the jungle to eat. The sleeping net was another matter.

"We're going to get eaten alive by mosquitoes while we sleep if we don't have that," she said.

"I doubt we're going to sleep much, plus I know of some local plants we can smear on us to repel the bugs." He looked at her questioningly.

At least he'd asked. "Toss it," she said with a sigh.

The blocks of plastic explosives were a little more difficult for Landon to part with. Ivy almost laughed at the forlorn look on his face as he set most of them aside. He'd wanted to have plenty in case they had to take down the wall around the compound. They'd just have to make do with less.

She had to sacrifice most of the concussion grenades, leaving all but two behind. The plan was for her to go into the house on her own while Landon provided cover with his silenced sniper rifle. If anything went wrong, she could have tossed half a dozen of those high-blast babies in her wake and dived out a window in the confusion. Guess they'd have to make sure nothing went wrong.

Landon wrapped the abandoned gear in the sleeping net and buried it, then locked in the location on the GPS.

"If everything goes to hell in a handbag and we have to come back this way, we can stop and grab it," he told her.

Good thinking. But she really hoped they didn't have to do that.

———

Landon hadn't spent much time agonizing over dropping their excess gear. It had been necessary. By midmorning of the next day, he knew they'd made the right decision. It was only 0900 and it already felt like a sauna under the stifling canopy of trees. By midafternoon, it'd be like they were in a convection oven.

He swore as he hacked his way through the dense jungle behind Ivy. After spending the majority of the last ten years in Afghanistan and Iraq, he'd forgotten how tough it was to claw through undergrowth so thick it felt like the damn stuff was physically wrapping its arms around you.

Ivy had saved their asses more than once already with her kitty cat senses and those little "hunches" that told her trouble was just around the next bend in the trail. This part of the border region was crawling with FARC soldiers and guerilla forces. If he'd been with his Special

Forces Team, they probably would have been involved in a half dozen firefights already.

In his book, a partner with skills like hers was worth more than a backpack full of C-4 and a thousand extra rounds of ammo.

It got to the point where he trusted those skills so much that his mind wandered and stopped at the mission briefing they'd received yesterday. More precisely, the conversation he had with Kendra before he and Ivy left. Kendra had pulled him aside and told him that some moron in the DCO named Dick Coleman had been the one who'd decided to yank them out of training and put them in the field early. Since Landon was this great Special Forces warrior with tons of training and experience, and Ivy had been through the training twice, Coleman felt they didn't need any more training. It might have been a compliment, but the truth was that this guy was hoping they'd fail. And if they failed, Landon was going back to Special Forces, Ivy was out of a job, and the DCO was going to have one hell of a black eye.

"Why would this guy want one of his teams to fail?" Landon had asked.

"Because some of the people on the Committee would love to see the EVA program get canned."

Landon had been trying to figure out what Committee she was talking about when Kendra continued.

"Look, none of that is important. All I'm asking is that you cut Ivy a little slack. She's had a string of shitty partners, which has led to some trust issues," Kendra told him, then added, "But you two have what it takes to be an amazing team. She just needs you to trust her."

He'd wanted to tell Kendra the trust thing was a little difficult. He didn't know the first thing about Ivy, other than she was a cat shifter and had better hearing, eyesight, and sense of smell than he did. And—as he'd learned a little while ago—she had *hunches*. He was used to putting his life in other people's hands—you did that every day in Special Forces. But he didn't know what kind of training she'd had or what her instincts were like in a gunfight. Putting his life in her hands wasn't easy.

But he knew what it was like to have people want you to fail. When he'd gone from enlisted to officer, a lot of people had wanted to see him fail out of the program. That was reason enough to help Ivy—even if she didn't fully trust him yet.

"I'll try," he told Kendra.

Ivy motioned and they both slid into the dense jungle alongside the trail. A few seconds later, a troop of twenty-five ragtag soldiers stomped past their hiding place. She *was* good.

As they knelt there, something else Kendra'd said came back to him—about the difficulty Ivy had with previous partners. Kendra was the third person—fourth if you counted Buchanan—who had mentioned the problems Ivy had with her previous teammates. He'd discounted everything Foley had said, but Kendra got him thinking, especially after the little run-in he'd had with Buchanan as he was leaving the dorms that morning. Ivy had already left for the DC office and he'd been moving fast to catch up. He'd seen Buchanan, but since the shifter had brushed past him without so much as an "excuse me" the first time they'd met, Landon decided to return the favor, ignoring the man as he headed for his truck. But Buchanan grabbed his shoulder.

"Where's Ivy?"

Landon had the urge to tell him to fuck off, but instead simply told him the truth. "She's headed to the DC office."

Buchanan's eyes narrowed. "You think you're hot shit, don't you?"

Landon clenched his jaw. The jerk acted like he was the reason Ivy wasn't interested in his sorry ass. "What the hell is your problem, Buchanan?"

"You're my problem." His lip curled. "You and every other norm. You're not good enough to pick up her trash from the curb much less be her partner."

It would have been so easy to introduce Buchanan's face to his fist. After the visit he'd had with Jayson the night before, he was certainly angry enough. But that'd only be playing into Buchanan's hands and make the people in charge think he had impulse control problems.

"Yeah. Well, the DCO disagrees." He grinned. "So does Ivy. In fact, I'm sure we'll make a damn good team."

Buchanan took a step closer, a growl low in his throat. "I'm warning you right now, if you ever try and pull the shit her previous partners did, I'll rip your throat out with my bare hands."

Snarling, he held up his hand and slowly let his fingernails extend until they were long and ragged—far more dangerous than Ivy's. Those nails could do some serious damage. But if Buchanan thought that was going to scare him, he could forget about it. Landon refused to even flinch.

"I don't know what happened with Ivy's previous

partners, and I don't give a rat's ass. I take care of my teammates, so back the hell off, shifter."

Buchanan's lips curled back to reveal sharp canines. "You're telling me to back off. That's funny."

"I don't see you laughing." Landon closed the distance between them until he was inches from the other man. "Just so you know. The fact that you're Ivy's friend isn't going to keep me from kicking your ass if you get in my face again."

"I'd like to see you try."

With a growl that turned into a laugh, Buchanan turned and walked off.

Landon ground his jaw at the memory. Before he and Ivy got back on the trail, Landon found some of the plant he'd been looking for all morning. The bugs were really getting to be a nuisance.

"Crush the leaves and smear them on your exposed skin," he told Ivy. "It'll keep the bugs away."

She followed his suggestion without comment. He hadn't been able to bring up the subject of her former partners at any point during their flight to Colombia, and last night had been out of the question. But maybe it was time to ask Ivy about them. If Kendra had gone out of her way to warn him and Buchanan was willing to kill him over something they did to her, there must be more to the story.

He moved closer to Ivy. "Any bad guys nearby?"

"No. I think we're clear."

"Good. Because there are a few things I think we need to get out in the open, and the first among them is what the hell happened with your first partner. A couple people have brought up this Jeff guy, but I'd rather hear the real story from you."

When she didn't answer, he figured she wasn't going to tell him.

"He tried to assault me."

Landon did a double take. He hadn't seen that coming.

"The official story according to Jeff's old friends, like Foley and his camp, is that I'm a cock tease who tried to cover up my incompetence by getting Jeff to sleep with me." Her voice was unusually soft in the stillness of the jungle, as if she were almost speaking to herself. "When Jeff turned me down, I used my shifter abilities to attack him and leave him for dead. Then I ran back and whined to management that I'd been sexually assaulted. According to their version of the story, the DCO believed me over an honorable and decorated military hero because I was one of their EVA pets."

"That must make it hard to work in a place when so many people hate you."

"You get used to it."

She clearly hadn't.

"Of course Foley goes out of his way to make sure every new person in the department gets his version of the story before they meet me." Ivy looked back at Landon. "I have to admit, I was a little worried that first day when I saw him talking to you. I figured you'd buy his crap since you were both in the military and all."

"And all? What, because I have a penis?" He laughed. "Trust me, Ivy. I smelled shit the second Foley opened his mouth."

Now that he'd gotten her talking, he wasn't about to let her stop. "How long did you and Jeff work together before he tried to attack you?"

"A little over a year." She glanced at him. "It worked out okay at first. I mean we were never a high-speed, well-oiled team by any stretch of the imagination, but at least he didn't think I was a freak of nature."

"What was the problem then?"

"He always wanted to do things one way, and I wanted to do them another. One of us had to compromise, and it usually ended up being me. Maybe that's why he thought I'd give in when he wanted to have sex. Because I gave in on everything else he wanted to do."

Landon knew where this was going, and he didn't like it. "Ivy, whatever happened wasn't your fault."

"Not directly. But I hung out with him outside of work. I thought it would make us a better team. He thought it should make us bed buddies." She made a disparaging noise. "I should have known there was a problem when he stopped calling me Ivy and started calling me babe. I mean, I had sexual harassment training for heaven's sake. But I thought it was completely innocent on his part, so I let him get away with it. Until he copped a feel of my ass."

"I take it you didn't report him?"

She stopped long enough to open her canteen of water and take a sip. "No. I thought I could handle it myself. I told him if he did it again, I'd break his hand. Jeff acted like the injured party, saying he'd done it accidentally and that it wouldn't happen again."

"What happened from there?" he prompted.

She recapped the canteen and started moving again. "We were on a stakeout on a rooftop in the worst part of town in Mexico City. One minute I was lying flat on my stomach looking through a telescope at a cartel drug dealer meeting with a DEA agent, and the next, Jeff was on top of me trying to rip off my clothes." She took a deep breath and let it out slowly, as if reliving the nightmare. "I was so shocked it took me a minute to realize what he was trying to do. My first instinct was to scream bloody murder, but I knew if I did I'd give away our position to not only the DEA agent and the drug dealer, but to half the street gangs in the area, too.

"My survival instincts—my animal instincts—took over and I shifted without even realizing it. Probably because I was so terrified. And so damn pissed. I kicked Jeff halfway across the roof, hoping he'd stay down long enough for me to get away, but he immediately got up and came at me again. He must have figured I didn't need to be conscious for what he had in mind because he hit me hard enough to knock out a normal woman. He forgot I'm a shifter, though. All that punch did was infuriate me more than I already was, and when he tried to pin me to the ground and tear off my clothes a second time, I clawed his face to shreds."

"If you ask me, he got off easy. What'd you do then?"

"I walked off the roof with the video of the DEA agent taking bribes from the drug dealer, and then I went back to DC and told John that Jeff tried to rape me. I wasn't sure he'd believe me since one, the bruise on my cheek from where Jeff punched was already gone by the time I left Mexico, and two, Jeff—when he finally had the nerve to show his scratched-up face—claimed I attacked him without provocation.

"Luckily, it didn't have to come down to he said/ she said. The DCO had satellite footage of the whole thing. Turned out Jeff attacked me on top of a building in the middle of one of the most scrutinized cities in North America." Her lips curved. "Nothing says sexual assault like photos taken from several hundred miles up in space. John fired him on the spot."

Landon didn't think too much of Buchanan, but now he understood why the man would be willing to rip apart anyone who did what her previous partner had done.

He glanced at Ivy. He couldn't fully see her expression, but he knew it had to have been difficult for her to talk about what happened. He felt guilty for bringing it up.

"Hey. I didn't mean to make you rehash everything like that."

She shook her head. "It's okay. It was a long time ago, anyway. Jeff is history, and I'm over what he did to me."

Was she?

Ivy was trying to act tough and hard, but he could see in her eyes she was bothered by the memories. When she looked like that, he'd never know she wasn't completely human.

He sounded like that asshole Foley. Landon had never been the type to care whether someone was Native American, Hispanic, Asian, or anything else. He wasn't going to start now. Ivy wasn't some kind of nonhuman freak, she was simply different. That was the way he was going to treat her, even if she didn't think too much of him. Ivy *was* human. Period.

Time for a change of subject. "How'd everything go last night with Buchanan? He looked pretty pissed off when I left."

Okay, he was fishing for information, but so what? There was definitely some history between her and Buchanan. Besides, they had to talk about something.

Ivy groaned. "Don't ask."

"That bad, huh?"

"Yeah." She gave him an embarrassed look. "I'm sorry he was rude to you."

"Don't be. It's not your fault."

"Actually, it kind of is. Clayne is in a bad place right now and I think I did more damage by telling him I didn't want to be anything more than friends."

"You can't control who you're attracted to." If he could, Landon wouldn't be having unprofessional thoughts about Ivy every time she walked in a room.

"I know." She held up her hand for a second, listening and sniffing the air. Apparently it was nothing, because she started again without comment. "I just hate hurting him like this. He's one of the few shifter friends I have and I don't want to lose him."

"When did Buchanan decide he wanted to go from friend to boyfriend?"

"A little while after his partner quit the DCO."

He tried to imagine a walking time bomb like Buchanan with a partner. It must have sucked to have been that guy. "Why'd he quit?"

"It was a woman, and I don't know why she left. Clayne wouldn't tell me and no one else at the DCO is talking. Not even Kendra, who knows everything about everyone. I got back from a mission, and Danica—his partner—was gone. Clayne won't admit it, but I got the feeling they were more than just partners. Which is why I think he got so messed up when she left."

The woman must be a saint to have put up with Buchanan. "Why isn't he off training with his new partner instead of harassing you?"

"Because they can't find anyone who can work with him."

Thank God they didn't pair him up with Buchanan instead of Ivy. He and the asshole shifter would have killed each other a dozen times over already.

They reached the Orinoco River dividing Colombia and Venezuela an hour before nightfall—way ahead of schedule. The river was fast moving and they had to walk a ways before they found an area below the rapids where they could cross. Once on the other side, they quickly moved into the denser part of the jungle again, checking repeatedly to make sure no one had seen them.

Ivy squeezed the water from her long braid. "That didn't take as long as we thought. Calballero's place is only a couple miles from here."

"That'll give us a chance to get some shut-eye if you want. I know I'm beat."

He and Ivy couldn't break into Calballero's until midnight at the earliest, and since neither of them had slept in close to thirty hours, they might as well take advantage of the downtime. They found a dense section of jungle well off the beaten path to set up their ponchos, then climbed inside the makeshift tent.

Eager to get out of his soaking wet clothes, Landon started unbuttoning his uniform overshirt, then hesitated. If he'd been with his Special Forces team, he wouldn't give stripping down a second thought, but he was in a tiny makeshift tent with a beautiful woman. Did the same rules apply?

Only one way to find out. He looked at Ivy.

"I was going to get out of these wet clothes, but if

you're uncomfortable with me sleeping in my T-shirt and underwear, I'll keep them on."

Her eyes glinted green as she blinked at him. "Um, no. I mean, go ahead. There's no way you'd get any sleep in wet clothes, and it'll give them a chance to dry. I was going to take off mine, too."

Landon tried not to look as Ivy got undressed, but as she stripped off her pants to reveal shapely thighs, it was impossible not to take a quick peek. Those were some long, gorgeous legs. He could just imagine them wrapped around him while he drove himself deep inside her until neither one of them could remember their own name.

His cock went hard as a rock in his boxer briefs, and he was glad it was dark so Ivy couldn't see. Then he remembered her outstanding night vision, and hurriedly rolled over onto his side so he faced away from her.

That was enough of those kinds of thoughts. Workplace romances didn't work, he reminded himself. *Just remember what happened with Erica*, he chanted like a mantra. It seemed to work.

Until Ivy lay down beside him and their bodies were touching. Then his mind was once again going to places it shouldn't. He closed his eyes, trying to think of something—anything—other than his partner's half-naked body pressed up against his. Field stripping an M4 carbine in his head worked for a while, but then she squirmed—probably to get more comfortable—and her ass brushed his, and he was back in fantasyland, having erotic visions. They played in his head like scenes from a porn movie—her on her hands and knees in front of him, his hand wrapped in her long hair while he took her from behind; her riding cowgirl, his hands cupping that perfect ass; her up against the wall, him pounding into her.

Landon stifled a groan. He shouldn't be having thoughts like this about his partner, especially after the grueling hike they'd just had, not to mention the potentially deadly mission in front of them. But he couldn't help himself. Even after humping through the jungle all day and night, her face smudged with sweat and river mud, Ivy was still the most beautiful woman he'd ever seen. The fact that she was so damn capable at her job made her even more attractive. He'd always found confidence and competence to be very sexy qualities in a woman. Ivy had those—and a lot more.

But no matter how much he wanted her, he was never going to act on it. She'd been burned by previous partners who thought working with her automatically got them a free ticket on the carnival ride. He wasn't going to be that guy.

———

Ivy wasn't sure whether to smack the person who'd hired Landon or hug them. No one could have known they'd accidently paired her up with a guy who smelled so delicious it was almost torture to be this close to him. Touching him like this, she could taste him on her tongue—which was why she was lying here in the dark with her mouth hanging open, softly panting.

She squeezed her nails into her palms as she drew in the scent of him. Sweat, river water, mud—none of it masked his pheromones. And she was getting more and more aroused by the second.

She squirmed, trying to ease the ache between her thighs, and ended up rubbing her ass against Landon's butt. Which only made her more aware of her partner—and her response to him. She froze, forcing herself to stay still. Landon was beat and needed to get some rest before they started the final phase of the operation. He couldn't do that with her wiggling around.

It would be so easy to roll over and straddle him. First, she'd kiss and nibble her way up his broad chest, then along his chiseled jaw until she came to that sinfully sexy mouth. And while she did that, she'd tease him—and herself—by rubbing against his erection. Then, when neither one of them could take it anymore, she'd slowly sink down on his cock, sheathing him all the way inside her.

It was all she could do not to reach down and slip her fingers under her panties. Where the heck was this coming from? It was like she was in heat. But that wasn't possible. Was it?

It wasn't like there was a handbook that came with the shifter gene. The only other shifters in her family were her maternal grandmother, who passed away when Ivy was in high school, and her younger sister, Layla. Her sister had never mentioned reacting to a guy like this. And unfortunately, Ivy couldn't just pull out the satellite phone to call and ask.

Ivy clenched her jaw to keep from growling. She hoped the hours passed quickly. She needed something to take her mind off her sex drive or she was going to explode.

Chapter 6

IVY DIDN'T EXPLODE. SHE CONTROLLED HERSELF RE-markably well and even managed to get a few hours of sleep. Landon, on the other hand, looked like crap.

"You okay?" she asked.

"Not really. I'm beat."

"I'm not surprised. An hour or two nap doesn't make up for days of missed sleep. You looked exhausted yesterday morning at the DCO offices, too. Not much sleep that night either, huh?"

He shook his head.

"Okay, I gotta ask. You just got to DC. How the heck did you meet a woman so fast?"

He looked taken aback. "What?"

"Well, I mean you told me you weren't from around here, but you go out the very first night in town? I put two and two together and came up with the obvious. What's the deal? Did you meet her on the plane or something?"

"I didn't go to see a girl. It was a guy."

It was Ivy's turn to be stunned and she stopped hiking to face him. "Oh. Oh! I mean…Right…A…guy… Of course you have every right to…you know…"

She stuttered to a halt. Landon was gay. She was okay with that, really. Even if it was a crime against women everywhere for a guy that hot to be gay.

He chuckled. "If you could see your face right now. Man, I wish I had a camera."

She flushed. "It's not that. I mean I have a lot of gay friends." Okay, a few. "It's just that you don't look gay." She cringed. Had she just said that out loud? "I mean… I'll stop talking now."

He laughed again, louder this time. "Ivy, I'm not gay."

"It's okay if you are. I understand…"

"Ivy, I'm not gay. Really."

She studied his face. He didn't sound like he was lying. "Oh. Where did you disappear to then?" She held up her hand. "I didn't mean to pry. It's none of my business. Sorry."

"It's okay. You're not prying." He nudged her into moving again. "One of my teammates—my assistant A-team commander—got injured in Afghanistan and is now over at the Wounded Warrior Barracks in Bethesda. I like to visit him when I can."

Now, she felt like even more of an idiot. She'd been jealous about a wounded soldier. One who must have been seriously injured if he was at Walter Reed.

"How badly was your friend hurt?"

"Pretty bad. He got a lot of shrapnel in his back. It really messed him up. He's not confined to a wheelchair or anything. Not yet, anyway. But he will be if he doesn't do physical therapy, and right now, he doesn't see the point since the army is chaptering him out." He gave her a rueful smile. "There aren't many jobs in the military for a guy who'll have to use a cane for the rest of his life."

"That must be hard."

"It is."

It seemed like it was hard on Landon, too. She still had issues with what happened to Dave, and they'd been anything but close. "What happened over there?"

Landon was silent.

"It's okay if you don't want to talk about it."

He hesitated, then cleared his throat. "We got some intel that the Taliban had been strong-arming the local police force in a small town outside of Kabul. The cops were looking for some help, so my team was assigned to go in and spend a couple weeks training them on how to stop the Taliban attacks. It wasn't supposed to be a direct action operation—we weren't expected to have to do anything more than advise and assist."

"I take it things didn't go as planned?"

He shook his head. "No. A few hours after we arrived, the head of the local police told us they found a cache of weapons in a farmhouse about a mile outside of town. He asked if I could send some of my men out with his officers to confiscate them."

"And?" she prodded.

"I should have known better. It was just too easy, too smooth. We roll into town and within a couple hours, I'm splitting my team. I should have known it was a trap."

"How could you have known?" He didn't answer. "So, you sent Jayson out with the local cops to help confiscate the weapons?"

"Yeah. Him and four other guys." He shook his head. "I was going to go, but Jayson wanted to handle it. He pulled me aside and told me to stop coddling him all the time, that he was an operator, too."

"Was he right? Did you coddle him?"

"No. I don't know. Maybe." Landon shrugged. "A little, I guess. But he was inexperienced. Hell, he was barely out of West Point. I shouldn't have let him talk me into sending him."

"What happened?"

"It was an ambush. One second the cops were guiding them through the makeshift corrals of a goat farm, and the next, they were getting lit up."

Her eyes went wide. "The police chief set you up?"

Landon nodded. "Yeah. The Taliban had grabbed his wife and daughter, and forced him to betray us. He didn't have a choice. He screwed us good. We didn't know anything had even happened until the radio started squawking."

"What did you do?"

He took a deep breath. "The rest of the team and I hauled ass to the farmhouse. By the time we got there, Jayson had already taken a load of shrapnel from an RPG round right into his back. Luckily, his flak jacket had absorbed most of the blast and frag or he would have died on the spot. The insurgents probably thought the explosion from the RPG would stun my guys and they'd be easy pickings. But they weren't. He might have been wounded, but Jayson got the team into a defensive position. He was shouting orders from flat on his stomach when the rest of us got there. He was pretty amazing."

There was pride in Landon's voice. And a lot of pain. So much of it that Ivy almost reached out and took his hand. She grabbed her canteen and took a sip of water instead.

"Were any other members of your team injured?" she asked.

"None of them were as bad as Jayson. They were all treated at the hospital at Bagram and back with us within a week. Jayson was so bad we didn't know if he'd live until the medevac bird got there. Even then, we didn't exhale until we got word through command channels he'd survived the trip to Germany and was recovering at Landstuhl."

"Whatever happened to the chief of police? Did you...I don't know...arrest him?"

"We would have. At first, it took everything I had to keep my team from shooting him where he stood. Hell, I wanted to put a bullet in him. Not that it would have mattered. The Taliban decided he didn't do a good enough job of luring us in and killed his wife and daughter anyway. He blew out his brains before we ever got around to taking him in."

She shook her head. So much heartache and death. "Well, at least Jayson made it."

Landon snorted.

"Hey, he's alive. That has to mean something."

"I'm not sure Jayson would agree with you." The muscle in his jaw flexed. "It should be me in Walter Reed. It would be if I'd just listened to my gut and gone to confiscate those damn weapons instead of sending him."

So that's what this was. Survivor guilt. "And if you had, the insurgents might have ambushed him and the other guys back in town, and Jayson would have been injured anyway."

"You don't know that."

"No, I don't. And neither do you." She climbed over a downed tree that blocked their path. "I understand where you're coming from, I really do. But what happened to Jayson wasn't your fault, Landon. He was an unfortunate casualty of war."

Just like Dave's death. She wasn't sure if telling

Landon the story now would make him feel better or worse. She'd tell Landon about Dave another time.

They arrived at Calballero's compound a little after midnight. The place looked exactly like the surveillance photos—a huge hacienda-style home surrounded by outbuildings and a high stone wall. Ivy scanned the windows for light as she crouched down in the bushes beside Landon, but the place was dark inside.

"Doesn't look like Calballero's home," she whispered.

"Or he's asleep." Landon adjusted his NVGs as he surveyed the compound. "Main guard house, one tower in front, and one in back. Two guards in each tower."

She gazed over the bottom floor. "All the lower windows have bars on them. We can't get in that way unless we use the main entrance, which is right beside the guard house."

"That's not going to work." Landon's NVGs went from one tower to the other. "It looks like the guards in the two towers can't see each other. The back one is closest to the office. We scale it and get in that way."

"Sounds like a plan."

He pulled out one of the blocks of explosives they'd kept. "I'm going to set this up by the main gate in case we need a distraction. I'll be back."

Ivy kept an eye on the guards while he was gone, listening for anything that might mean they'd spotted Landon.

Turned out, Landon was as good with a sniper rifle as he was at being stealthy. He loaded the rifle with those fancy DCO tranquilizer bullets and took out all four tower guards before they even knew what happened.

Ivy was impressed. Nice shooting.

He slung the rifle over his shoulder. "Ready to do your thing?"

Ivy didn't have to ask what he meant. She backed up to get a running start, then raced toward the wall and leaped into the air. Grasping the edge, she pulled herself up onto the top, then turned to give Landon a hand. As soon as he was beside her, she led the way to the guard tower and climbed inside, careful not to step on the unconscious men on the floor.

Landon didn't waste any time pulling out his M4 and shooting the foam-covered grappling hook over to the roof of the hacienda. Because the tower was higher than the house, the trajectory was trickier, but he nailed it in one shot. She had to admit they worked well together, and it made her forget she normally wasn't thrilled working with military types. Landon was turning out to be a lot different than she had expected.

He glanced at her as he tied the thin aircraft cable to one of the tower's support columns. "Can you really get across this?"

She flashed him a smile as she turned on her communications headset. "Do cats like milk?"

He chuckled. "I know one who doesn't."

Laughing, she climbed onto the cable and ran down it. When she reached the hacienda, she dropped onto a balcony off a third-floor room.

"So far, so good," she whispered to Landon.

She tiptoed to the French doors and cautiously peeked inside. The bedroom was empty. "I'm going in."

She probably didn't need to tell Landon that since he was already covering her with his night vision scope, but she liked keeping him in the loop.

"Be careful."

"Always," she told him.

She stopped to sniff the air when she got inside. No indication of anyone on this floor. While she trusted her nose, she still moved carefully. She didn't know exactly where the office was, so she had to check each room. Luckily, it was the fourth one on the right, which meant Landon had a clear view of her through a window.

"There's a computer on the desk," she told him. "I'm going to check it now."

She took out the gadget Oliver from the tech division had given her to decode passwords and break through firewalls, and plugged it into the USB port. She browsed through the files, but there was nothing even remotely incriminating.

"Anything?" Landon asked.

"No. I'm going to look through his desk, see if there's something in there."

That turned out to be a waste of time. Lots of junk, but nothing tying him or anyone else to drug smuggling.

Ivy looked around the room, searching for someplace Calballero might hide something he didn't want found. Her gaze locked on a painting. It couldn't be that simple, could it?

She got to her feet and walked over to it. Sure enough, there was a wall safe behind the painting.

"I'll be…"

"What is it?" Landon asked.

She quickly told him what she'd found. "The problem is, we don't have anything to open it. Except explosives."

"Which we can't use without risking destroying what's inside. Not to mention bringing the rest of the guards running."

Ivy chewed on her lip. "There's something else I can try, but it might take a little time."

"As long as you can do it before Calballero gets back, go for it. What are you thinking about doing?"

"I might be able to smell which buttons on the keypad Calballero uses most."

"No way. You can do that?"

She smiled at his words. There was no animosity there, just amazement. "Yeah. But it's going to be hard. My sense of smell isn't my strongest skill."

"Take all the time you need. I've got your back."

Ivy's lips curved. That was the first time anyone had ever said that. She leaned close to the keypad. She sniffed each key, trying to pick out which ones had Calballero's scent. This kind of wall safe used either a four- or six-digit combination. Hopefully, Calballero used a four-digit number. If not, she could be screwed.

The number four key was definitely one. And the eight. After that, it got tough. It was almost as if Calballero slid his fingers across some of the other keys as he moved around the pad.

To do this right, she needed to shift completely. She'd never done that on a mission because it was hard to notice what was going on around her when she did. Which meant she was completely vulnerable. And dependent on her partner. She'd never trusted anyone she worked with enough. But Landon said he had her back.

Confident he'd alert her if trouble closed in, Ivy closed her eyes, sinking deeper into her animal self.

~~~

Landon was so mesmerized by watching Ivy work on

the safe, he almost didn't hear the car drive up to the gate. Calballero was back.

"We've got company," he said into the headset. "Time to go."

Ivy didn't answer. Instead, she leaned closer to the safe.

"Ivy, let's go."

No answer. What the hell? Frowning, he grabbed his flashlight and pointed it at her, giving it a quick flick on, then off. No response. Like she hadn't even seen it. Was there some special code word he was supposed to say, like *here, kitty, kitty*?

Down on the ground, Calballero entered the house, along with several men.

"Ivy, come on."

She ignored him.

Landon slewed his scope away from her to scan the rest of the house. Calballero and the men looked like they were heading for the stairs.

"Get the hell out of there. Now!"

Still no answer. What the hell was wrong with her? Couldn't she hear the men coming? Another few minutes and they'd be in the room with her.

Swearing under his breath, Landon slung the barrel of his sniper rifle over the cable. Holding on to both ends of the weapon, he slid down to the balcony directly across from the tower. The friction of the wire against the barrel completely screwed up the rifle, but he didn't give a damn. Dropping it to the floor, he whipped the M4 off his back and raced into the house.

He charged into the hallway just as Calballero and the two men with him topped the stairs. They had a clear view of the office—and Ivy— from the landing, and didn't even see him. They immediately pulled their guns and aimed at her.

Landon squeezed the trigger, taking all three of them out just as one of them shot at Ivy. As the bullet hit the wall beside her head, Ivy spun around, a laptop in her hands. Wide-eyed, she gaped at the dead men on the floor, then at him.

"Dammit, let's go!" he shouted.

She obeyed, running past him into the bedroom. He followed, pulling the remote from his pocket and setting off the explosive charges near the main gate as he went. Hopefully, that'd distract the rest of Calballero's guards long enough for him and Ivy to get away.

Outside, Ivy jumped up and grabbed the wire, then pulled herself onto it and gracefully raced back to the guard tower. Landon scooped up the sniper rifle he'd discarded earlier. It might be ruined beyond repair, but he wasn't about to leave it. Praying someone wasn't below waiting to pick him off, he grabbed the cable and climbed hand over hand up to the tower. The thin cable was rough on his hands, and it took him a while to get across.

By the time he got there, Ivy had already leaped from the wall. He vaulted down after her, following as she sped toward the tree line. If he wasn't so damn pissed at her right now, he'd have seen the two guards come around the corner of the wall ready to shoot him. Luckily, Ivy put a bullet through each of them before Landon could even lift his carbine.

Swearing under his breath, he tossed one of the concussion grenades over the wall into the compound. With any luck, the other guards would get confused and think whoever had killed Calballero was still inside.

The blast rocked the ground as he and Ivy disappeared into the trees. She made a beeline for their packs. While she recovered them from the bushes where they'd hidden them, he shoved the ruined sniper rifle in the bushes. Trucks roared in the distance, echoing in the jungle.

He took his pack from Ivy, slipping his arms through the straps as he ran after her. Somewhere behind them, Calballero's guards randomly shot at them. They didn't sound like they were getting closer, but he and Ivy ran for a solid thirty minutes before stopping to rest.

Their headlong flight through the jungle hadn't done a thing to cool Landon's temper, and he immediately rounded on her. "What the hell happened back there? Why didn't you respond when I told you Calballero was back?"

Ivy flinched as if he'd hit her. "I-I couldn't hear you."

"What the hell do you mean, you couldn't hear me? I was practically shouting in your ear."

"I…"

She looked away. But not before he saw the tears shimmering in her green eyes. Another reason he was glad they didn't allow women on the A-teams. They were too freaking sensitive.

"I…" She swallowed hard. "I messed up. I'm sorry, okay?"

Landon frowned. He got the apology. What he didn't get was the way she'd said it. Like she was some timid mouse instead of the bold, confident woman he'd spent the past two days with. That Ivy would have glared and told him she'd been trying to get the information they'd come there for and wasn't leaving until she got it.

There was more going on here than just a screw-up on

her part; he'd bet his next paycheck on it. And whatever it was, it had something to do with her being a shifter. Their ability to work as a team depended on each of them knowing the other's weaknesses. If she went deaf sometimes, he needed to know about it. But the middle of the jungle wasn't the place to have that conversation.

Landon jerked his chin at the laptop she still clutched in her hands. "You think that's what we're looking for?"

Ivy lifted her head to look at him. "Probably. People don't lock up a laptop unless there's something important on it."

She had a point. "It'll be easier to carry if we rip out the hard drive."

"Yeah." She dropped to her knees, flipped the computer over and used the tip of her nail to unscrew the compartment holding the hard drive. She took it out and put it into a plastic bag, then sealed it and stowed it in her pack.

He hadn't really been concerned whether the laptop was what they'd been after. It either was or it wasn't. It wasn't like they were going to go back and look for something else. But he needed Ivy's head back in the game, so he'd wanted to kick her mind into gear. It was a long way to the extraction point and there were likely going to be patrols out looking for them. He and Ivy needed to put as many miles between them and the compound as they could before daylight.

Landon buried the laptop, then pulled out the map. "Here's where we're supposed to ditch our uniforms, weapons, and gear." He pointed at a tiny village about fifteen miles up the road. "Think you can get us past all the patrols on the road?"

Ivy didn't look at the map. "Yes," was all she said.

"Then let's go. We need to be there by daylight if we can."

Landon let Ivy take the lead again. Regardless of how unreliable her hearing was, her eyesight was still a hell of a lot better than his, especially at night. He prayed whatever had happened to her at Calballero's was a fluke. But what if it wasn't? What if it happened to her all the time? As much as he didn't want to believe that idiot Foley, maybe the man was right. Had that been what got her previous partner killed?

<center>~~~</center>

Ivy could feel Landon's eyes boring into her back all the way to the village. She glanced over her shoulder at him. His jaw was tight, as if he had to restrain himself from shouting at her. He was probably so pissed he couldn't see straight and was likely berating himself for ever getting put on a team with a whack job like her. She couldn't blame him. Her mistake could have gotten both of them killed. She wasn't sure why she should care what the hell he thought about her, but all of a sudden, she did.

Tears stung her eyes and she blinked them away. She had to face it. Landon was the best thing that had happened to her since she'd come to the DCO, and she'd just blown it. She wouldn't be surprised if he bailed on her when they got back to the States. She supposed she should be lucky he'd come to get her out of Calballero's and hadn't simply followed orders and shot her.

They reached the tiny village around midmorning, exchanged their military clothes for civilian clothes, then dumped their gear. The locals—mostly older people and small children—pointedly ignored them.

Landon didn't say anything to her as they hiked the last two miles to the extraction point in Puerto Carreño. That hurt more than having him shout at her. She wished he would yell. At least then she'd know what was going on in his head. She could hardly wait to meet up with the eco-tour group just so she wouldn't have to listen to the endless silence.

Fortunately, she and Landon got to the outpost around noon. A smiling blonde checked them in under the names Sam and Marcy Colter, newlyweds. Like she and Landon could pass for a couple on their honeymoon. He couldn't even look at her without grinding his jaw.

They sat on the shore of the river while they waited for the other tourists to show up. Ivy opened her mouth half a dozen times to tell Landon what had happened back at Calballero's and that it would never happen again. But she couldn't find the right words.

Two miserable hours later, the other tourists arrived along with their tour guides, and by then it was too late. Ivy pasted a smile on her face and did the meet-and-greet with the other people in the tour—a mix of Americans, Europeans, and travelers from nearby South American countries. As they chatted, one of the tour guides came over to introduce himself as Dean Stockton—and give the prearranged code word that identified him as their contact.

"Play it cool today, but after we stop, announce one of you aren't feeling well and go to bed early. Feel slightly better in the morning, then take a turn for the worst after the noon stop. You do your part and I'll do mine."

Right. Part of that was acting like a married couple. Something Landon must have finally remembered. He put his arm around her waist as they followed their tour guides over to the waiting rafts. His skin was warm through the thin material of her T-shirt, and she had to stifle a moan.

Ivy tried to keep up friendly chatter with the other couple who climbed into the raft with them, but it was tough to act like a newlywed when Landon was sitting beside her looking like he'd rather be anywhere else. Putting on the happy-couple act was more exhausting than hiking the thirty-five miles to Puerto Carreño, and she sighed with relief when they pulled onto a sandbar to stop for the night.

"We're not supposed to know how to do this, remember?" Landon gave her a pointed look as they set up the small tent the tour guides had provided.

It wouldn't look good for a couple from the big city to be more efficient at setting up their tent than the tour guides. So, she and Landon pretended to fumble with it for a while before they both got tired of being incompetent and just put the damn thing together. Then they gathered around the campfire with everyone else while their guides cooked the fish they'd caught for dinner.

Ivy waited until after they'd eaten before she announced she wasn't feeling well. Landon played his part, getting up when she did, concern on his face as he helped her to the tent.

Since their clothes weren't wet—wasn't that a shame?—she didn't have a reason to get undressed, so she took off her boots and socks, then unbraided her hair. The tent was bigger than the lean-to they'd slept in the other night, but not by much, and she was keenly aware of Landon sitting beside her, staring into space. Why the heck didn't he roll over and go to sleep? He had to be as tired as she was.

"Did your last partner get killed because you zoned out on him like you did on me back at Calballero's compound?"

Ivy stopped combing her fingers through her hair and looked at him sharply. She could handle his anger, even his silence. But having him think she was so incompetent she'd gotten her former partner killed? That was the worst.

She went back to running her fingers through her hair. "No. Dave didn't get killed because I zoned out."

"Then what did happen?"

She didn't want to talk about this. But not talking about it was part of the reason they were in the place they were right now.

"The DCO paired me up with Dave less than a month after what happened with Jeff. He'd heard the rumors about what I'd supposedly done to my first partner and decided they were true. He didn't trust me and wouldn't talk to me more than he had to. And forget about using my shifter skills. He'd rather die first." Bad choice of words. "I still have no idea how we made it through certification."

"Why'd the DCO put you together if you didn't function well as a team?"

"Because, even though we fought like cats and dogs, we always managed to get the job done. Which, looking back on it now, was stupid. We hated working together and if we'd failed to complete a mission, the DCO would have split us up. But we were both too pig-headed. Besides, I was afraid if I complained about

Dave after what happened with Jeff, the DCO would decide I wasn't worth the trouble of keeping around."

"So, what happened to him?" Landon prompted. "Dave, I mean."

She took a deep breath and told him, starting with why they'd gone to Grozny and finishing with Dave getting shot.

"Dave ordered me not to follow, but I did anyway. He wasn't in there five minutes before I heard gunfire. I shouted at him to answer me, but he'd turned off his headset. I didn't know if he was alive or dead or what." Which was exactly the way Landon must have felt back at Calballero's when she hadn't responded. Knowing what she'd put him through made her feel even worse. "By the time I got to him, he and the Russian were both dead."

Landon was silent for a long time. "I'm sorry. For thinking you had something to do with what happened. When you zoned out at the hacienda, I assumed..." He sighed and ran his hand through his hair. "What happened to you back there, Ivy? And don't say you couldn't hear me."

She lifted her head to see him regarding her expectantly, his dark eyes almost desperate for the truth. She owed him that much, didn't she? "Sometimes when I shift really deep—like I had to do to pick up Calballero's scent on the safe's keypad—I get lost in my animal side."

His brows drew together. "What do you mean, get lost?"

"My feline side takes charge and I take a backseat. I'm there, just not in control." That made her sound like she had some kind of split personality. She caught her lower lip between her teeth. "I heard you over the head-set. I just couldn't answer."

"How many times has this happened to you?"

"Never," she assured him, then added, "At least never on a mission. The only time it's ever happened is in intensely emotional situations."

The first time it happened had been when she'd lost her virginity. She was twenty, a sophomore in college. Getting to the point where she trusted a guy enough to sleep with him in the first place had taken a while, and when it'd finally happened, she wondered why it had taken so long. It had been incredible and as she got more and more into it, she found herself slipping into an almost trancelike state where every sensation in her body had been heightened a hundredfold. She'd been on top, completely lost in the sensations as she rode her boyfriend into orgasm when the one small part of her awareness that still seemed to be intact realized she was clawing the bed on either side of his head. The realization that she'd shifted without knowing it had jolted her back into her own body, where she'd been horrified to discover her fangs had come out. She'd immediately jumped up and run into the bathroom where she'd looked in the mirror to discover her eyes had changed, too. Thank God her boyfriend had been too caught up in his own pleasure to notice any of it.

When she finally came out of the bathroom—an hour later—she found her boyfriend sitting on the bed, completely dressed, his head in his hands. He'd been convinced it was his fault regardless of what she said. It hadn't helped that she'd broken up with him. But what else could she do? A guy might want a woman who was an animal in bed, but not in the literal sense of the word.

It was no surprise she didn't get serious with anyone for a while, and when she did, she was careful not to lose control in bed, which resulted in some very unsatisfying sex. On the bright side, she'd gotten great at faking it.

Landon definitely didn't need to know any of that. She cleared her throat.

"Up until now, I've always kept myself completely under control."

"What made this time different? You weren't emotional while you were trying to crack the safe, were you?"

"No. But while emotional situations can bring on a deep shift accidentally, I can do it on purpose if I really need to. Like figuring out which keys a person touched on a keypad. It takes a lot of concentration, and I can't do it without letting my feline half take over." She looked up at him. "I've never attempted to do anything like that on a mission before because it leaves me so exposed. I never trusted any of my partners enough to shift that deep. I never believed they'd have my back. But I really wanted to show you I could get that safe open. I'm sorry for putting you in that position."

Landon didn't say anything. He didn't have to. It was too late for excuses. And too late for apologies. It wasn't too late for self-recriminations, though. Hot tears stung her eyes. Now she was going to start crying, too. Her humiliation would finally be complete.

She tried to look away before Landon could see, but he cupped her cheek. "Hey. Why are you crying?"

"I'm not…"

Her voice broke. A tear trickled down her cheek,

making a liar out of her. Dammit. She wasn't usually so emotional. It had to be tied to her body's crazy reaction to Landon—a side effect of being in heat.

He gently wiped the tear away. "Tell me why you're crying. Please."

She sniffed. "Because you're the best partner I've ever had and I screwed it up. And because the thought of you asking John to team you up with a new partner is tearing me up inside."

Her chin quivered. She had to get out of this tent ASAP or this was going to get even more embarrassing than it already was.

She tried to get up, but Landon cupped her face with both hands, refusing to let her go. He brushed more tears away, making quiet shushing sounds. "You haven't screwed up anything. Please don't cry."

Another tear fell. "It's okay. I don't blame you for wanting another partner. I don't."

He swept her hair away from her face, shushing her again. Then he leaned forward until their faces were only inches apart. It was hard to think about crying when he was this close.

"I'm not going to ask John for a new partner, Ivy."

She blinked at him, afraid to hope. "Y-you're not?"

"No. And I'm not telling him about what happened at Calballero's hacienda, either. But we do have to make sure nothing like that ever happens again. Your animal nature is part of what makes you so good in the field, but it's not the only part. Your human side plays a part, too. You can't let one part shove the other part in the backseat. You have to be the one in control."

He made it sound so simple. "That's easy to say, but

hard to do. In some ways, I'm half human, half animal. It's not always easy to separate the two."

"Then we'll work on it together. That's what partners do. And you're my partner—period."

Partners. Her heart squeezed at the word. She wanted to thank him, but nothing she could say seemed adequate. So, instead, she leaned forward to touch her forehead to his. It wasn't their foreheads that touched, however. Not even close. She couldn't swear to which one of them initiated it, but she found her lips on his. Then she didn't care who started it.

Landon's mouth was tentative at first, but then all at once the kiss became urgent, intoxicating, his tongue finding hers and slow dancing with it. The rich emotional response she'd experienced back in the makeshift tent that first night in the Colombian jungle didn't compare to the things she was feeling now. He was like a drug she couldn't get enough of, and she kissed him back just as fiercely as he was kissing her.

Her hands found their way into his hair, twisting it between her fingers and pulling him closer. Her mouth opened with a willingness and hunger that almost shocked her. Her whole body was responding, trembling with need.

She slid her hands down the front of his chest to the bottom of his T-shirt and urgently pushed it up. Underneath, he was all smooth skin and rock-hard muscle. She moaned appreciatively as she ran her fingers over every glorious ripple. He felt as incredible as he looked.

She pushed his shirt higher, trying to take it off, but Landon interrupted her by doing a little exploring of his own. His hands found their way beneath her top and were slowly gliding up her midriff. When they cupped her satin-covered breasts, she almost purred. When his fingers caressed her nipples, that almost purr turned into a deep-throated moan.

Some tiny corner of her mind tried to tell her this was a mistake, that she and Landon shouldn't be risking their partnership for a few stolen kisses and a groping session. But pushing him away was more difficult than she ever imagined. It was like convincing her body to stop breathing.

But she had to. If she didn't, she was going to completely lose control. And that would be beyond bad.

Landon must have come to a similar conclusion, because he dropped his hands and pulled back at the same time she did. His face was flushed, his eyes smoldering in the darkness. She could hear his heart beating hard.

He opened his mouth. Closed it. Tried again. "I'm sorry." His breathing was ragged, making his deep voice even huskier than usual. "I didn't mean to kiss you. I just…"

She touched her finger to his lips, silencing him. "Stop. I won't accept apologies for what just happened. You weren't kissing me—we were kissing each other."

He caught her hand and gently pulled her finger away from his lips. "You're my partner, Ivy. I shouldn't have kissed you."

"I shouldn't have kissed you, either. But I did." And God help her, she wanted to do it again. She took a deep breath. "We can't let it happen again."

If they did, there was no telling what would happen. She'd been so close to ripping off his clothes and pouncing on him.

Landon sat back and rubbed his hand across his face. When he met her gaze again, his eyes were full of remorse. "I don't want you to think I'm going to turn into another Jeff."

The pain in his voice cut her to the core, and she wanted to reach out to cup his face but didn't trust herself. "I know you'd never intentionally hurt me." She gave him an embarrassed smile. "Besides, it wouldn't be an issue of you attacking me against my will. It'd be about me not having the will to want you to stop. In case you haven't noticed, I'm seriously attracted to you."

His mouth edged up. "Ditto. But you're right. We can't let it happen again."

"Okay, then. I won't lay any more kisses on you, and you don't lay any on me. Deal?"

"Deal."

Sleeping beside a guy like him in a tent this small would be asking a lot of any woman, but after a kiss like the one they'd shared, it was tantamount to torture. Jumping his bones wasn't an option. She wasn't going to succumb to her desires no matter how much her body might want it.

That promise would have carried a lot more weight if her lips hadn't still been tingling from his kiss.

Chapter 7

THE MOMENT THEY GOT BACK TO THE DCO OFFICES, Todd took Landon into one conference room to be debriefed, while Kendra led Ivy into another.

"I knew it! You two are good together," Kendra said. "Tell me I'm wrong."

"You're not wrong," Ivy said. "We are good. Maybe too good." She chewed on her lower lip, remembering how she'd fallen asleep on Landon's shoulder on the flight back. "In fact, I'm worried we're getting along too well."

Kendra took a seat and motioned for her to do the same. "What the heck does that mean?"

How was she going to explain it to Kendra? It sounded crazy to her. "Promise me none of this will show up in the official records."

Kendra made a face. "Do you even have to ask that?"

Ivy knew she didn't. Kendra would never say anything she told her in confidence. "I'm more than a little attracted to Landon."

"A little attracted?" Kendra lifted a brow. "I'm attracted to him and I don't even get to have the fun you do rolling around the floor with him during hand-to-hand combat practice."

Ivy blushed. "Okay, so maybe I'm more than a *little* attracted to him. In fact, it's damn near impossible to be around him without wanting to jump on him like he's some kind of kitty chew toy."

"Landon-scented catnip, huh? Now that's what I'm talking about." Kendra sat back in her seat with a grin. "I knew I picked the perfect teammate for you."

Huh? "What do you mean, *you* picked the perfect teammate?"

Kendra gave her a smug look. "You don't think running around here with a stopwatch and a clipboard is my only job, do you? I'm a behavioral psychologist in case you've forgotten. With all the problems you had with your first two partners, I convinced John to finally let me try out the interpersonal compatibility algorithms I've been working on. I put in everything the DCO knows about your skills, your personality, your strengths and weaknesses, then added in everything I know about you personally. Using that, I scoured every federal database out there to find the one guy who would match up with you perfectly. You know, the ultimate yin to your yang. My program identified that person as Landon Donovan. Of course, I had to really sell my idea in order to get John to give the okay to scoop Landon out of Special Forces, but let me tell you, he's patting himself on the back right now."

Clearly John wasn't the only one pleased with himself. "Wait a minute. Are you saying you found my new partner with a homemade package of matchmaker software?"

"Yeah." Kendra grinned. "Pretty good, don't you think?"

Ivy stared at her friend in disbelief. She thought she'd hit the lottery jackpot with Landon, but now it turned out the game had been rigged. No wonder they worked together like a well-oiled machine—Kendra was clearly brilliant when it came to understanding team dynamics.

She frowned again. "Hold on a minute. Go back to the part where you said you programmed your software with personal things you know about me. What kind of things?"

Her friend shrugged. "Normal stuff. Like the fact that you prefer tall men with broad shoulders and six-pack abs. That you go for guys with dark hair and soulful eyes. That you want a man to be a gentleman out of bed, but an animal in it—"

Ivy's face colored hotly. "I never told you that."

"Well, I had to make a few assumptions based on the things you said." A smile teased the corners of Kendra's mouth. "You probably don't realize it, but you let some revealing stuff slip now and then. Did I get any of the parameters wrong?"

Actually, her friend was right about all of them. But Ivy wasn't going to tell Kendra that.

"So, how the heck do you scan a federal database for information on whether a guy is an animal in bed or not?"

"That took a little extra work," Kendra admitted. "Let's just say that you can learn a lot about a man from hacking into his social networking sites, and those of every person that has ever met him." She said that last part like even she was surprised at what she'd done. "You can learn even more by seeing what their flings and exes have to say about them. According to them, Landon has mad skills in bed."

The thought of Landon with another woman sent an irrational surge of jealousy through Ivy. She immediately stomped on it. Sitting back, she folded her arms.

"Well, just because you seemed to have found the perfect partner for me, it doesn't mean I'm going to be sleeping with him."

"Why not? And don't tell me it's because of that silly DCO rule about partners not getting romantically involved." Kendra shook her head. "John uses that same lame excuse every time I bring up the subject of allowing teammates to get together on a more meaningful level if they want to. All of the data supports my hypothesis that teams work at their most efficient and optimal level when they're compatible in every way, and that includes sexually. If an operative is attracted to his or her partner, it's completely natural for them to have sex with each other. Denying something so instinctive and primal isn't only impossible, it's foolish."

Giving in to it would be foolish. But what if she couldn't control herself? What if Kendra was right, and it was instinctive and primal?

"Even if I wanted to sleep with Landon, I can't. I don't trust myself with him."

"What do you mean?"

Ivy sighed. "All we did in South America was kiss and—"

Kendra bolted upright. "Wait a minute. You kissed?"

"Yes, we kissed. And I just about tore off his clothes." Which just about scared the hell out of her.

"And that's a bad thing?"

"It is when you can't control yourself. When your eyes glow green and your claws come out." Ivy ran her hand through her hair. "Do you know how many men I've slept with since college? Three. They were all one-night stands and the sex was terrible. Why? Because I couldn't let go with them. I was terrified if I did, I'd turn into an animal in front of them."

Kendra's lips curved. "Every man wants an animal in bed."

Ivy frowned. "You're not helping."

"But Landon already knows what you are. You don't have to hide it from him." Kendra reached over and covered her hand. "According to my compatibility software, you're perfect for each other."

"Your software is wrong. Just because I'm a shifter doesn't mean I'm an animal who does things based on instincts and primal urges alone, you know. I have a say in what I do and how I act." She folded her arms, pinning her friend with a look. "Let me ask you something. Have you ever tried this wonderful interpersonal compatibility software out on yourself to find your perfect partner?"

Kendra's face colored and she looked away. "Of course not. That would be completely unprofessional."

Ivy had no doubt Kendra used the software program to see if she and Clayne were compatible. She'd love to see what the computer had to say about that particular pairing.

Landon had been debriefed many times, but none like this. Apparently, the hard drive he and Ivy had recovered was everything the DCO had been looking for and more. While John was thoroughly impressed, Dick, sitting on the other side of the table from Landon, was pissed.

Apparently, Kendra was right when she warned Landon about Dick—he sure acted like he wished they'd failed. While John praised their ability to adapt when the Black Hawk dropped them earlier than anticipated, Dick pointed out they wouldn't have had to adapt if they'd had a better plan to begin with. He also wasn't pleased that Calballero and some of his men had ended up dead.

Landon had to bite his tongue to keep from telling Dick to shove it up his ass. He recognized a desk-bound warrior when he saw one. It was obvious this jerk had never seen any real action. The most danger he'd probably faced was getting a paper cut. "While the goal was to get in and out without hostile action, the ultimate objective was to get the information—whatever the cost."

Dick couldn't say much about that. They'd been John's exact words during the mission briefing. Undoubtedly, there was a tape somewhere.

"That guy is such a moron," Landon muttered to Ivy as they walked down the hall a little while later.

She looked like she was about to wholeheartedly agree, but stopped, a frown creasing her brow. She cocked her head to the side as if listening to something.

"What's up?" he asked.

She put her fingers to her lips and motioned him closer to the conference room where he'd had his debriefing earlier. Landon didn't need Ivy's super hearing to pick up the raised voices inside, even with the door closed.

"Accomplishing a single mission doesn't mean Halliwell and Donovan are certified," Dick said loudly. "I think they need more training."

"Wasn't it you who insisted they were so experienced they didn't need all that training?" John countered. "You were obviously right. They got the mission done."

"Barely."

"But they got it done and that trumps every rule in your silly-ass book."

Dick made an impatient sound. "Those rules were put into place by the top people in the organization. People who fund the DCO, I might remind you."

"You don't have to remind me where the money comes from, or the strings attached to it. I notice you didn't seem to have a problem breaking those rules when you forced me to put Halliwell and Donovan in the field. Well, they got the job done, and now, according to your bureaucratic rules, they're certified. Which is a good thing. If the intel we have on this guy Stutmeir is good, we're going to need every operative we can get, especially with Tate's team already on a mission in Washington state."

"Okay, so they're certified," Dick snapped. "But aren't you the least bit curious why Halliwell gets along with Donovan when she couldn't stand either of her previous partners?"

"Besides the fact that you selected them for her? No, I'm not."

"I sure as hell am." A pause. "I think they're sleeping together."

Landon slanted Ivy a sharp look. He could tell from the panic on her face she was thinking the same thing — that the next words out of Dick's mouth would be an order to split them up.

In the conference room, John swore. "You're just making up shit to wreck this team, aren't you? Just like you did the last time two of my operatives performed so well the heat finally started to disappear off the shifter program."

"I'm not making up anything," Dick ground out. "On the contrary, I'm doing my job."

"And which job would that be?" John demanded. "The one the DCO pays you for or the one your friends up on the Hill tell you to do?"

"If I were director—"

"You're not," John reminded him. "The Committee put me in charge."

Dick sputtered, but John cut him off. "I let you split up one team because you thought they were sleeping together, and I'm still dealing with the fallout from it. There's no way I'm letting you do the same thing to Ivy and Landon. They're too good to break up."

"It's not up to you," Dick said. "It's up to the Committee, and I'll be giving them a full report on your new team, including my suspicions."

"Knock yourself out, Dick," John told him. "You're not the only one with friends in high places, you know. I'll be giving full reports of my own. And something tells me that my words will carry more weight than yours when it comes to field operations."

Landon smirked. He would've hung around to hear what else the two men said, but Ivy grabbed his arm and pulled him away. She dragged him around a corner just as Dick stormed out. Okay, so his hearing still wasn't as good as hers.

"Why does that asshole have such a hard-on for the field teams?" he asked Ivy.

She peeked around the corner to make sure Dick was gone, then started for the front entrance. "It's not all the field teams. Just the ones with shifters on them. He hates us. He thinks we're all a bunch of animals that should be locked up in a zoo."

"Good thing he's not in charge then."

She let out a snort. "Tell me about it. If he was, he would have canceled the shifter program already. And if he couldn't manage that, he wouldn't be recruiting them off the streets."

Landon frowned. "What do you mean, off the streets? What were you doing before they recruited you?"

"I came over from the FBI. But Declan was a forest ranger. And Clayne was…" She made a face. "Let's just say he wasn't exactly on the right side of the law when they recruited him. And Lucy—you haven't met her yet—used to be a public defender in Boston."

A lawyer? Landon wondered if she was part shark. He wasn't surprised about Buchanan, though. He'd love to know the story behind that one. But even more, he wanted the story about Ivy's FBI background. She was so graceful he thought for sure she must have been a dancer or something. Now that he thought about it, though, it made sense. While she looked like a ballerina, she carried herself like a cop.

"Anyway," she said. "Who cares what Dick thinks? John has our backs, so as long as he's around, we're okay."

Chapter 8

WHEN THEY GOT TO THE TRAINING AREA THE NEXT day Landon found Todd and Kendra as well as a few more training officers and a dozen other operatives—including Buchanan—gathered around a pit filled with mulch. A telephone pole was mounted horizontally across it, and pugil sticks lay on the ground on either end. Since he didn't think they were going to be playing a game of *American Gladiators*, the stick meant the next best thing—combative training. Which was just another term for *beat the shit out of each other*. Landon noticed there weren't any protective helmets or gloves lying around. Hardcore. Hooah. Man, he hadn't done this kind of thing since infantry school—or was it during some down time at language school? It'd been so long since he had combative training, he couldn't remember when it was.

Todd separated them into two groups, one on either end of the log. Landon and Ivy were on the same side, along with Buchanan. Damn. He'd been hoping to square off against the shifter.

"You spar until one person ends up in the pit," Todd announced. "Standard rules—no face shots, no nut taps."

Beside Landon, Ivy rolled her eyes. "Leave it to a man to come up with that silly rule. Concussions are fine, but please don't hit me in the balls. You'd think it was the only important part on a man's whole body."

Todd gave her a stern look. "I'm serious this time, Ivy. No more of your *oops, my bad.*"

She held up her hands. "Okay, okay. I'll be good. Promise."

The first two combatants grabbed the pugil sticks and carefully moved toward each other, which was difficult to do on something the size of a balance beam. Todd waited for them to get their balance, then blew the whistle.

Both men were intent on taking out their opponent with one hit—not something you could easily do while balanced on a log. They got in a few good pops, but after a few swings—and misses—they both ended up in the pit, victims of their own aggression.

The next matchups were more of the same. There was some strategy, but mostly it was all brute force. Landon cheered along with everyone else. It might be ugly to watch, but it was entertaining.

Landon was next. As he hopped onto the log, a blond-haired man did the same. Before his opponent could step forward, however, Buchanan hopped into the pit and stalked over to the man. The shifter climbed onto the log and yanked the pugil stick out of the guy's hand.

"What the hell?"

Buchanan threw him a glare. "It's my turn."

The man wanted to argue, but then shrugged, muttered something that sounded like "whatever," and walked over to take the empty spot Buchanan had left.

Landon met the shifter's cold eyes. *You want to fight, asshole? Fine with me.*

Todd blew the whistle.

Buchanan attacked immediately, leading with a

vicious overhand swing. Landon jerked his stick up just in time to block the blow—and keep the shifter from taking off his head. The son of a bitch was using the bare part of the stick instead of the padded end.

You want to play dirty? I can do that, too.

Landon aimed a vicious shot at Buchanan's left hand and heard a satisfying crunch. The shifter didn't react to the pain. Instead, he smiled. That's when Landon noticed Buchanan's canines were longer than before. And that his eyes weren't their usual brown, but gleaming yellow.

Ivy knew the sparring match wasn't going to end well the moment Clayne climbed up on the log. She hadn't thought the idiot would shift, though.

Crap.

She couldn't believe Clayne was going to beat the hell out of Landon—or try to—simply because she wouldn't give him the time of day. It was childish and stupid.

She darted a quick glance at Kendra, who looked as nervous as Ivy was. Todd and the other training officers, on the other hand, were practically salivating at the matchup. What the hell was wrong with them? Anyone watching could see this wasn't going to be a simple sparring match. Both men looked ready to cause some serious damage.

Clayne growled low in his throat as he swung his pugil stick again and again. Landon followed every block with a counterstrike, going after Clayne as ferociously as Clayne went after him.

"Hey!" Todd shouted after an especially savage hit from Clayne. "Take it easy."

When Landon and Clayne ignored him, he blew his whistle. Like that was supposed to stop them. Neither one was following standard sparring rules. What the heck made Todd think they were going to pay attention to a whistle? This fight would only end one way—with someone going to the hospital. If they were lucky.

Unless she stopped it first.

Ivy took a deep breath and extended her claws, ready to jump into the fray, when Clayne abruptly tossed his pugil stick aside and launched at Landon with a deep, rumbling growl. They hit the pit in a twisting heap, fists and claws flying everywhere. Todd blew his whistle again, yelling for them to break it up as Clayne raked his claws across Landon's chest. Ivy's heart seized as the scent of blood filled her nose.

Landon didn't flinch. Instead, he swung his fist, hitting Clayne in the side of the head hard enough to knock him senseless. While Clayne was still reeling, Landon shoved him onto his back and climbed on top, cocking his fist back for another punch.

Ivy dove into the pit, latching on to Landon's arm with all her strength. Beneath him, Clayne lunged, canines flashing as he went for Landon's throat. Ivy instinctively moved to put herself between them when someone landed hard on Clayne's chest, knocking him back. It took Ivy a moment to figure out who it was and when she did, she blinked, staring at Kendra in astonishment. There were nearly two dozen men standing around, but the only one willing to help was another woman.

The guys must have realized how that made them look because Kendra's interference was finally the signal to get their asses off the sidelines and separate

Landon and Clayne, who were still trying to get at one another. It took some hard work, but with the men's aid, Ivy and Kendra managed to drag them away from each other. Then it became a war of words, complete with a lot of cussing, name calling, and growling.

"Calm the fuck down!" Todd ordered. "Both of you!"

Clayne bared his teeth at the training officer. Todd rounded on him. "You better get it under control, Buchanan, or I'll have you thrown in lockup and hosed down."

Landon let out a self-satisfied snort. "Serves you right, asshole."

Todd turned his glower on Landon. "And don't think for a minute I believe this was entirely Buchanan's fault, Donovan. You're just as much to blame. Unless you want to get locked up in a detention cell for a day or two alongside him, cool your jets."

Landon's jaw worked, but he wisely kept his mouth shut. Ivy let out the breath she'd been holding.

Todd looked from one man to the other. "You're both in anger management for the rest of the week." He glanced at the men restraining Clayne. "Take him to the clinic to get checked out and make sure he doesn't have a concussion. And send a medic down here to look at these scratches on Donovan."

Clayne sent one more low growl Landon's way, but allowed the men to escort him out of the training area. Kendra left with him, but not before giving Ivy an exasperated look. She turned to find Landon scowling at her.

"What the hell were you doing, getting between Buchanan and me?" he demanded. "He could have ripped out your throat."

A simple thank-you would have been nice. "I was

trying to stop you two from killing each other. What was that about?"

His jaw tightened. "I reckon that was Buchanan's way of saying he doesn't think much of me being your partner."

"Yeah, that much is obvious." She didn't even want to think of how Clayne would have reacted if he knew about the kiss in Venezuela. "What I want to know is why you were spoiling for the fight."

Landon stopped examining the scratches on his chest to scowl at her. "What are you talking about? I was only defending myself."

Right. Ivy wasn't naïve enough to think this was a case of boys being boys. Clayne had tried to lay claim to her, and Landon had told him what the shifter could do with that notion.

Ivy shook her head and moved Landon's hand out of the way so she could get a look at the damage Clayne had done. She lifted Landon's shirt, trying to ignore the way his chiseled muscles flexed as she ran her fingers over the scratches. They weren't as deep as she'd feared, but Clayne's ragged claws would probably leave a few scars.

"Damn him," she muttered.

"What the hell kind of shifter is Buchanan anyway, a Tasmanian devil?"

She couldn't stop her lips from twitching. "Just your plain, garden-variety timber wolf."

Landon snorted. "More like a freakin' werewolf."

"Well, it's a good thing he's not." Ivy flashed him a grin. "Then I'd have to worry about you turning into one and we'd have to deal with the whole cats and dogs thing."

Ivy didn't want to even think of the animal attraction there'd be between them then.

---~~~---

After two straight days of anger management classes, Landon wanted to punch somebody. He'd come close when Coleman, who'd been there the first day, made some snide comment about Landon being at the DCO to help keep the "animals" in line, not become one himself. Not to defend Buchanan, but Ivy. Because he knew Coleman had included her in that remark just to get a rise out of him. He hated that man.

The only thing that made sitting in an uncomfortable stuffed chair opposite Marlon the shrink bearable was knowing the big, hulking, paranormal asshole Buchanan was being forced to go through the same torture.

"Does that idiot doctor even realize he works for an organization that kills people and blows things up on a regular basis?" Landon glanced at Ivy as he shoved clothes in his duffel. She'd already been packed and waiting for him when he got back to their room, and was now leaning against the doorframe. "He actually told me it was okay to get mad at people, but it wasn't okay to yell at them, call them names, or—heaven forbid—hit them. Forget Buchanan and I were in combative training using pugil sticks on each other when the fight started. Or that the rabid wolf attacked me first. He gave me a placating smile and told me if I resort to violence, I'm no better than the other person."

"What'd you say?"

He zipped his bag. "That turning your back on an enraged werewolf had to be the dumbest idea I've ever heard."

Ivy's lips curved. "I'm with you on that. How'd that go over with Marlon?"

Landon opened his mouth to answer, but his cell phone cut him off. He swore as he dug in the pocket of his jeans. If it was Todd saying he needed another session with Doctor Doofus, he was going to throw the phone through a wall.

He didn't bother to look at the call display. "What?"

"Whoa. Someone got up on the wrong side of the sleeping bag this morning. Hello to you, too, dude."

"Angelo, how the hell are you, man? You back from deployment?" Landon grinned. It was good to hear that voice.

"We got in a couple days ago. With both you and LT gone, the battalion considered us nonoperational and sent us home."

"Everyone?"

"Roger that. We're all in one piece."

Landon breathed a sigh of relief. "That's good to hear."

"So, what the hell'd you do, sleep with some general's daughter and get demoted to pushing papers at the Pentagon?"

Landon chuckled. "Nah. Believe it or not, I got transferred to the Department of Homeland Security. Or at least an organization within it."

"No shit. Well, damn. We're thinking of going up to DC this weekend. You want to grab a beer with the guys and me?"

"I don't want you guys burning up your leave on me."

"It's a few days. And we were heading up there to see LT anyway. Besides, Diaz grew up in the DC area and says there are some sweet clubs up there."

Landon shook his head. Diaz. Should have known. "Since you're coming up anyway, why the hell not? When do you want to get together?"

"How about tomorrow night around 2000 hours at this place called DC Scandals?"

Landon cupped the phone with his hand and looked at Ivy. "You ever heard of DC Scandals?"

She nodded. "I've heard of it, but I've never been there. I know where it is, though."

"Who are you talking to?" Angelo asked.

"My partner."

"Invite him along so we can meet him."

Landon's mouth twitched. "He's a she."

Angelo made a sound that was a half laugh, half snort. "Well, then definitely invite her."

Landon hesitated. After the kiss, they'd both agreed to keep things purely professional, and going to a place with a name like DC Scandals screamed anything but professional. It wasn't as if they were going alone, though. If he knew his team, they'd all be there.

He cupped his hand over the phone again. "Some of the guys from my old team are coming up this weekend. You want to go out for a drink with us?"

Her lips curved. "Sure. Sounds like fun."

There was no good reason why her answer made him want to pump the air with his fist, but it did. He resisted the urge—barely—and told Angelo they'd both be there.

~~~

At the risk of making it sound like a date, Landon offered to pick Ivy up, but she said she needed more time to get ready and would meet him at the club. Finding Angelo and the guys wasn't difficult. They'd clearly picked two tables where they could easily scope out the door, and shoved them together. They waved him over the minute he walked in. Angelo and Diaz were there, along with Marks, Deray, Griffen, Tredeau, and Mickens. Almost his entire team. It was good to see them.

"The rest of the guys would have come, but the battalion didn't want the whole team on block leave at the same time." Angelo caught the waitress's eye and gestured for another round of beers. "So, tell us about this Homeland Security gig."

Griffen finished what was left of his beer in one swallow. The guy had to have gills hiding somewhere. "We spent the whole drive up here speculating."

Landon was about to say he couldn't tell them very much, but the waitress appeared with the round of beers Angelo ordered. She gave Landon and the rest of the guys a smile, her gaze lingering on Deray as she reminded them they knew where to find her if they needed anything. The dark-haired engineer gave her a wink.

"Okay, spill," Angelo said when she left.

Landon took a swig of beer. "Not much to tell. I work for an organization that's under the Department of Homeland Security."

Tredeau grabbed a handful of pretzels from the bowl in the center of the table. "What kind of work are you doing?"

"Can't really talk about it." Which bothered the hell out of him since these guys were like family. "All I can say is that it's closer to CIA shit than Special Forces work."

Deray leaned forward, one hand on his beer bottle. "Tex-Mex said you have a female partner? What's that like?"

Landon chuckled. "It took a little while to get used to, but outside of you guys, there's no one I'd want covering my ass more than Ivy."

"Where is she, by the way?" Angelo ran his hand through his shoulder-length hair as he glanced at the door. "You said she was coming."

"She'll be here in a bit. Enough about me. What happened with you guys after I left?"

He wanted to change the subject. He'd been caught off guard by Ivy the first time he'd met her. No reason Angelo and the other guys shouldn't be, too. Besides, he'd driven himself crazy for weeks now wondering what happened to his team.

"We went back to Qari's place with Bennett. Used a BLU-129 to take out the tango, then went in and collected up all the intel we could." Angelo snorted. "Battalion wanted to temporarily dissolve the team to fill shortages in the other A-teams, but Johnson wouldn't put up with that shit. He made such a fuss they shipped us back the next day."

Landon should have known Master Sergeant Johnson would take care of the guys. Johnson could get away with damn near anything.

"Whoa," Angelo breathed, his dark eyes going to the door. "Hot babe at two o'clock."

Landon turned to see Ivy sauntering in. His mouth fell open. He'd seen her in everything from the black DCO uniform to a tank top and pair of panties, and thought she looked sexy as hell in all of it, but tonight, hot babe was the only way to describe her. In a short, sleeveless dress with makeup accentuating her exotic, dark eyes and her long, usually straight hair hanging down her back in soft waves, she was perfection on a pair of high heels.

He got her attention and waved her over, then glanced at his friends. "That's Ivy."

Someone at the table—make that a few of them—choked on their beer.

"That's your partner?" Deray asked. "Do they have any more openings in this organization? If they do, I'm requesting a transfer the minute we get back to Campbell."

"I'll just skip the transfer and go straight to the third date, thank you very much," Diaz said.

Landon chuckled. "Careful, boys. She can rip out your guts in a heartbeat."

"It'd be worth it," Mickens said.

Landon wasn't sure if he was jealous or proud. Probably a bit of both. And because he knew he could trust his teammates not to mess with his partner, he'd concentrate on being more proud than jealous.

He made the introductions, starting with Diaz and finishing with Angelo, who grinned and told Ivy she wouldn't be paying for anything she ordered from the bar.

"The guys and I have you covered."

They also regaled her with every embarrassing story they had about Landon—and there were a lot. When they launched into the one about the time their operating base had been attacked in the middle of Landon's weekly shower and he'd run out wearing nothing but a flak jacket and a pair of combat boots while carrying his M4, he decided things were getting a bit too personal.

"Okay," he said. "That's the end of the stories. That's an order."

Ivy laughed. "But I want to hear what happened."

Landon liked the way her eyes sparkled when she laughed. He chuckled. "I fired my weapon until I was out of bullets. End of story."

In the back corner of the club, the DJ put on a song with a dance beat. It sounded like Justin Timberlake. At least Landon thought it did—with back-to-back deployments he hadn't really kept up with who sang what.

Beside him, Ivy sat up straighter. "I love this song. Who wants to dance with me?"

She was looking at Landon as if she expected him to be the one to offer. He wanted to. God, how he wanted to. But dancing with Ivy could be dangerous. Correction—it would most definitely be dangerous. And yet if he didn't, he'd be kicking himself later. Unfortunately, by the time he got his tongue loosened from the roof of his mouth, everyone else at the table was already on their feet.

"I'm junior in rank," Diaz pointed out. "So, you guys can suck it up. Take care of your troops, remember?" He came around the table and held out his hand to Ivy. "Lead the way, fine lady."

She gave Landon a small smile, then took Diaz's hand. Landon didn't join in when the rest of the guys cheered Diaz on. He was too busy kicking himself.

Ivy danced the same way she did everything—gracefully. She swayed to the sexy beat, lifting her arms above her head as she moved her hips, and it was all Landon could do not to groan. Dragging his gaze away from her, he picked up his beer and took a long swallow, hoping it would cool him off. On the other side of the table, Mickens eyed him thoughtfully. The medic had an uncanny way of knowing what other people were thinking. That was great when it came to the enemy. When it came to him, not so much. All he needed were his friends figuring out he was lusting after his partner.

"Be real, Captain," Mickens said. "No freakin' way is that woman dancing with Diaz your partner."

Meaning how the hell did he get paired up with a hot number like Ivy. The guys were all looking at him— when they weren't sneaking peeks at her on the dance floor—like he'd won the lottery. He'd think so, too, if it wasn't for that lame rule he had about not getting involved with someone he worked with ever again. "I'm shootin' straight here. She's my partner."

"And she does Homeland Security stuff, like go after terrorists and shit?"

Landon chuckled. Good to know he wasn't the only one who underestimated her. "Yeah, she goes after terrorists and shit." That raised more than one eyebrow. "Look, what I'm going to tell you is for your ears only. Got it?" They nodded. "Ivy's qualified with more small arms weapons than you can name. She's had as many airborne jumps as any of us. She's a trained diver and explosives expert. She can break into a safe one second and hack a computer the next. I've watched her hump a heavy rucksack through deep bush for twenty-four hours straight without so much as stopping to take a breather. The first time we met, she dropped me in hand-to-hand combat like a toilet seat. On top of that, she's killed men while covering my back. She might look like a Victoria's Secret model, but she can kick some ass."

They were silent, their gazes going to Ivy again. She waved when she saw them looking her way.

"Damn," Angelo breathed. "All that and she can dance, too? Sure this organization of yours isn't hiring? I could definitely see myself working there."

Landon laughed. Leave it to Angelo to pick out the most important skill.

"Speaking of dancing, Diaz has been out there long enough," Deray complained. "It's time I pulled rank."

Mickens pushed back his chair. "Me, too."

Marks, Griffen, and Tredeau clearly didn't want to wait their turn, either. They followed Deray and Mickens onto the dance floor, leaving Landon alone with Angelo.

"So, you and Ivy are just partners, huh?" his friend asked.

Landon picked up his beer. "Yeah."

"It looks like more than that to me."

For a guy who looked like he could get a job as a bouncer in a biker bar, Angelo could be damn perceptive. "Well, I'm trying to make sure it's not."

Angelo flicked him a glance as he absently rubbed his thumb up and down the label on his beer bottle. "What's Ivy have to say about that? Because from where I'm sitting, she's clearly got a thing for you."

"Ivy feels the same way I do." Which only made not giving in and taking her to bed even harder.

"You're both playing with fire, Landon. You remember the last time you got involved with a woman you worked with."

He didn't need a reminder. "I know. Which is why Ivy's off limits."

"Then you won't mind if I make a move on her."

Jealousy immediately shot through Landon. He scowled at his friend, unable to help it.

Angelo grinned as he got to his feet. "Relax, dude. I'm just going to dance with her."

Landon watched Angelo make his way over to Ivy, trying not to notice the dazzling smile she gave him. It didn't help that the rest of the guys picked that moment to decide to come back to the table for another round of drinks, leaving the two of them alone on the dance floor. If Ivy was going to hook up with anyone on his former team, it'd be Angelo for sure. Even he had to admit they looked good together. Friend or not, if Angelo and Ivy ended up leaving together, he was going to kill the guy.

Two songs of them gyrating on the dance floor was about all Landon could handle before he went out there and cut in on Angelo. The big Texan didn't seem surprised. Flashing Ivy a grin, he gave Landon a knowing look, then turned and went back to the table.

Ivy smiled at him as she wiggled her hips to the new beat. "I was worried you were one of those guys who thinks it's not cool to dance."

He followed her moves, picking up the rhythm. "Normally, I wouldn't, but I'll make an exception for my partner."

Watching Ivy dance from across the room had been one thing. Being out here on the floor dancing with her was another. If he thought her moves had been sensual before, that didn't compare to the heat coming off her now. Not letting it bother him was tough given her body was almost touching his. They might have promised to keep things professional, but that promise apparently didn't extend to the dance floor. What they were doing was about as far from professional as you could get.

And as close to sex as you could get in public without being arrested.

Thank God they were in a club or he might have done something seriously stupid, like kiss her again. The memory of how sweet her lips had been was nearly enough to make him ignore the people around them and pull her into his arms to kiss her. Which would be a bad idea because then he'd want to see if her breasts felt as soft as he remembered. And from there, who knew what would happen? He'd never felt this out of control around a woman in his life.

He wasn't sure if he was relieved or disappointed when Diaz showed up to cut in. "You've had her long enough, Captain. Time to share."

Landon didn't feel like sharing. And he sure didn't feel like letting Diaz cut in. But he needed to get away from her, if only to get control of himself.

Thankfully, no one back at the table noticed what had been going on out there on the dance floor between him and Ivy. No one except Angelo. Landon avoided looking at him and reached for his beer.

"Oh shit," Griffen muttered.

Landon looked up to see Tredeau jerking his head toward the dance floor.

"Diaz is being his usual charming self."

Something about the way Tredeau said the words made Landon stiffen, and he whipped around to see Diaz facing off against three big, burly guys. Ivy stood beside him, frowning. Landon might not be able to hear what the men were saying to the slightly less than average-sized Diaz, but he figured it out from their body language. They wanted to know what a guy like Diaz was doing dancing with a woman like Ivy and probably assumed they could intimidate him into walking away. Unfortunately for them, Diaz had a chip on his shoulder bigger than the state of Texas.

Tredeau pushed back his chair, but Landon held up his hand. He wanted to jump up and defend both his ex-teammate and his new one—Ivy more than Diaz—but she was more than capable of dealing with this. She wouldn't appreciate him coming to her rescue in front of his friends.

"There's only three of them," he told Tredeau.

"But they're big," Mickens pointed out. "Like head-and-shoulders big above Diaz."

Landon opened his mouth to tell him Diaz would be offended by that statement, but all that came out was a curse as one of the guys shoved Diaz out of the way while another grabbed Ivy by the arm.

Diaz clocked the one guy across the jaw while Ivy took hold of other guy's wrist and bent his arm back until he dropped to his knees. Someone screamed. The DJ cut the music. And the crowd on the dance floor moved away to give Ivy, Diaz, and the three men space.

The third guy evaluated the situation, his eyes darting from his two buddies on the floor to Ivy and Diaz. He must have decided he couldn't fight them by himself because he backed up, hands up in the universal gesture of surrender.

Movement in the crowd caught Landon's attention. Eight guys pushed their way through the onlookers and stomped onto the dance floor, the expressions on their faces leaving no doubt of their intentions. Landon didn't care if Ivy got mad at him for coming to her rescue or not. There was no way he was going to sit there while she fought an entire football team.

He glanced at Tredeau "Okay. Now we help."

Tredeau and the rest of the guys immediately jumped up and charged onto the dance floor with him. Anyone who wasn't interested in a fight quickly got out of their way—which was pretty much everyone. That'd make it easier to pull Ivy and Diaz away from the fight, then get everyone out of there. Unfortunately, the assholes who'd started it weren't down with that plan and closed in on Landon and his teammates like some kind of unarmed infantry charge.

Landon slugged the first guy rushing him, then did the same to the next, putting both men on the ground. They were big and brawny, but they didn't have the hand-to-hand combat skills to compete with trained Special Forces soldiers. He and his teammates were black belts in one type of martial art or another, from ju-jitsu to tae kwon do. Depending on their preferred styles, they either sent their opponents sliding across the slick floor by using the men's own aggression against them or laid them out by kicking them in the face.

Ivy and Diaz were standing back to back, defending themselves until Landon and his teammates could get to them.

"You okay?" he asked her as he punched a curly-haired guy in the jaw.

She flashed him a grin. "Never better."

Her eyes were shining like crazy. As if the animal inside was just waiting to get out. He hoped people assumed it was the strobe lights.

She executed a perfect roundhouse kick, hitting a big, beefy guy in the stomach and sending him flying. "Cops are on their way. I heard the bartender say he called them."

Landon loved that bionic hearing of hers. He threw a

glance over his shoulder at his teammates. "Cops will be here soon. Ten blocks west and rally in the first parking lot you come to."

They immediately dropped the nearest opponent and headed for the door. Landon hung back long enough to make sure none of his guys were left behind, then grabbed Ivy's hand and pulled her out of the club.

She gestured over her shoulder as they ran. "My car is parked in a lot on the other side of the building."

He didn't stop. "We'll come back for it later."

Mickens and Tredeau piled into the backseat of his truck cab, while Ivy climbed in the front. Diaz threw himself in the bed, stretching out so no one'd see him. Landon scanned the parking lot for anyone who hadn't caught a ride. When he saw it was clear, he pulled out just as cop cars poured in.

He drove west for ten blocks, praying there was a parking lot around. By pure luck, there was a pharmacy on the corner. Angelo's SUV was already there, Griffen's fire-engine red Charger parked beside him.

Angelo grinned as he and the others sauntered over to Landon's pickup. "Everyone came out alive, so I'd call that a successful mission."

"Just like old times." Mickens gave Ivy a wink. "But with much better looking company."

On the street, two police cars sped past, sirens blaring. The pharmacy wasn't one of those twenty-four hour ones, so hanging around in the parking lot at 0200 hours was bound to get them noticed.

"We better split before someone at the club describes us to the cops and they come looking for us," Landon said.

"I know this other club. Killer DJ." Diaz grinned. "And it's still early."

As much as Landon enjoyed hanging out with his teammates, he didn't know what would happen if he gave in to temptation and danced with Ivy again. Kissing her was a definite possibility this time. What was he going to say? That he'd rather go home and go to bed? They'd think aliens had kidnapped him and replaced him with a replicant.

"Another time, Diaz," Angelo said. "We need to get some shut-eye if we expect to head to New York City early tomorrow."

Since when did Angelo need sleep? The guy could outlast any of them when it came to pulling guard duty in the middle of the night. Then Angelo gave him a meaningful look and Landon knew exactly what was behind his charade. He had to admit, he was grateful.

Mickens laughed. "It's only four or five hours."

"Yeah, well I'm doing the driving, and I'm tired," Angelo grumbled. "So is Griffen. He looks beat."

Griffen opened his mouth to argue but shut it again at the pointed look Angelo sent his way. Rank had its privileges.

After giving Landon the requisite man hugs, his teammates crowded around Ivy to hug her, too. They extended an open invitation to party with them anytime she wanted, anywhere she wanted.

"One night with her and the guys are ready to drag their asses across broken glass just to stand next to her in a fight." Angelo slanted him a look. "I can see why you're attracted to her. If you do something stupid, no one here would blame you. Just be sure it's what you really want to do—before you do it—because it'll change everything between the two of you once you do."

"Weren't you the one who told me an hour ago that I should steer clear of her?"

"That was before I saw you dance with her."

Landon shook his head. "Forget it. I learned my lesson with Erica."

Had he? If Ivy gave him the go-ahead, he'd be all over her in a second, DOC rules and ex-girlfriends be damned.

"If you ever need anything, give me a call," Angelo said. "And I mean anything."

Landon grinned. "I will. Give me a call on your way back down to Campbell and we'll get together again."

"Will do."

Ivy waved as they drove off, a smile on her face. "I haven't had that much fun in a long time. I'm glad you invited me."

"Yeah, me too."

They locked eyes for a moment before she looked away. "Do you think it's safe to go back and get my car yet?"

He glanced at his watch. It'd only been fifteen minutes since they'd left the club. "Maybe we should give it a little while longer. I saw a coffee shop a couple blocks back that looked like it was still open. Want to grab a cup?"

That should be a completely safe activity.

She smiled. "Sounds good to me."

The coffee shop was empty except for the gray-haired barista behind the counter and a twenty-something couple dressed in club clothes sitting at a table near the window. Landon and Ivy ordered coffee, then sat down at a table in the back corner.

Ivy sipped her latte. "So, how come everyone calls you Captain, but Angelo calls you by your name?"

"You noticed that, huh? Because we both used to be enlisted. We went through Infantry School and Special Forces training together. After that, we both got assigned to the 5th Group. That history gives him some perks."

She frowned. "Wait a second. I'm confused. I thought you were an officer."

"I went to Officer Candidate School when I was an E5. It's where enlisted guys go to become officers," he added, then chuckled. "Angelo's actually the one who talked me into going green to gold. Thought I'd be good officer material. At the time, I wasn't sure if I should be offended, but he turned out to be right."

Her lips curved. "Obviously. Wasn't it a little weird for you guys when you went back to the 5th as his commander, though?"

"It was at first, but Angelo's an amazing troop. He played it square. Never even let on we were friends."

"Why didn't he become an officer, too?"

"I tried to talk him into it, but he's just not programmed to be an officer."

"What do you mean?"

"An officer has to be able to put up with a lot of politics and bullshit. Angelo prefers to call it like he sees it and shoot anything that looks like it needs to be shot." Landon glanced at her over the rim of his cup. "It's selfish of me, but I'm glad he didn't. If he had, he would have gotten assigned to another team and he's a damn good soldier."

She smiled. "A damn good friend, too."

A good enough friend to point out how much Landon would lose if he screwed up this partnership with Ivy. Which was exactly what he'd needed to hear right now.

Chapter 9

KENDRA INTERCEPTED IVY IN THE LOBBY THE MOMENT she got to the DCO offices on Monday. "John wants you and Landon in the conference room ASAP. I'll go round up your partner."

Ivy opened her mouth to ask what was up, but Kendra had already darted down the hallway. Sighing, she went into the conference room and took a seat.

Landon came in five minutes later, a cup in one hand and a brown paper bag in the other. "Hey."

"Hey." At least he'd been smart enough to grab coffee. Could she get to the break room and back before John came in?

Landon sat down across from her, then opened the brown bag and pulled out a monster-sized cream-filled donut with chocolate on top. Her stomach growled, reminding her she hadn't eaten breakfast.

"Want half?"

Ivy lifted a brow. "Are you serious? That thing probably has enough calories to feed a small nation."

He chuckled. "I thought you might say that, so I bought you this instead." He pulled out a muffin covered in rolled oats and handed it to her. "The woman behind the counter said it was healthy."

Ivy stared down at the muffin. Wow, a guy who realized she probably wanted to eat something other than a cream-filled time bomb. Or a can of cat food, like her previous partner had brought her. The jerk would drop it in her lap and make some snide remark about making sure he got something with a pop top since the store didn't sell can openers. It had annoyed the hell out of her.

"The muffin okay?"

She looked up to see Landon regarding her curiously. She smiled. "It's great. Thanks. That was nice of you."

He flashed her a grin. "I'm a nice guy. Which is why I brought you this to go with it." He reached into the bag again and pulled out a small cup of coffee. "No milk."

Before she could get too enamored by him, he dipped into the bag one more time and brought out a blue ball of yarn, then rolled it across the table to her. If Dave had done something like that, it would have been condescending, but with Landon, it was touching.

"Very funny."

Just then John and another man walked into the conference room. She barely had time to snatch the offending ball of string and hide it under the table on her lap.

Landon let out a soft chuckle. "I knew you'd like it but didn't figure you'd get so possessive about it already."

John came around to the head of the table and turned on the computer that was hooked up to the projector. "What was that?

"Nothing, John." Landon gave her a roguish smile. "We were just talking about a toy I bought for my cat."

His cat? Ivy knew she shouldn't, but for some ridiculous reason, she liked the way that sounded. It probably had something to do with how much fun she had dancing with Landon at the club the other night. As embarrassing as it was to admit, it was the closest she'd been to sex in a long time, and she'd been turned on like crazy. If Diaz hadn't interrupted them, she might have done something she would have regretted. Like slid her hand down his chest to the obvious bulge in his jeans.

She wasn't the only one who'd been aroused. For all his cool, professional demeanor, Landon had been horny as hell—she could smell it. Her partner put off a particularly scrumptious pheromone when he was turned on. It wasn't fair for him to smell that good.

John looked up sharply, a frown creasing his brow. "You have a cat?"

"Oh, yeah. An exotic long-hair beauty." Landon sent another grin her way. "But she's picky. Never likes anything I buy her."

Ivy kicked him under the table hard enough to make him grunt.

Thankfully, John didn't notice. He introduced the man who'd come in with him as Evan Lloyd from the intel branch, then clicked the computer keys. Two photos appeared on the screen. One was of a pretty woman in her thirties with long, blond hair. The other was of a slightly older man with gray touching the sides of his hair and sprinkling his well-trimmed beard.

"The woman is Doctor Zarina Sokolov. She works at the Minsk Institute of Research in Moscow. She's an expert in DNA splicing and manipulation, among other things too technical for me to understand. The man is Doctor Jean Renard. He works for a French pharmaceutical firm outside of Paris called Pharmaceutiques Nouveaux. His specialty is in the emerging science of..." He looked at his notes. "Segment-specific nucleases."

"Nucleases are enzyme proteins that break down select portions of the DNA strand," Evan said.

Landon looked from the intel guy to John. "Outside of working in the same field, how are Zarina Sokolov and Jean Renard connected?"

"They both disappeared over four months ago," John said.

Ivy peeled the wrapper off her oat muffin. "And you assume foul play?"

"Not at first. The cases were a thousand miles apart, being investigated by separate local police agencies who thought both Sokolov and Renard had some kind of midlife crisis. That they simply left home and never came back. But Renard's wife had a friend in INTERPOL by the name of Giraud and got him to dig deeper."

Landon took a big bite out of the cream-filled donut. Ivy licked her lips. It might be fattening as hell, but it looked damn good.

"Giraud discovered Renard's disappearance had similarities to Sokolov's, which sent up a red flag," John continued. "Even though they worked in the same field, they'd never met. There's nothing to indicate they'd even heard of each other."

Ivy nibbled her muffin and took a swig of coffee. Somehow Landon had known exactly how she took it — plenty sweet.

"But then Giraud stumbled on something interesting," John said. "Sokolov and Renard were both approached by the same headhunter a few days before they disappeared. No one knew about it because both doctors turned down the offers, but Giraud found a business card for the headhunting agency in Renard's office. It turned out to be a dummy corporation. Giraud dug through fake documents of incorporation and email traffic until the trail led to this man."

Another face appeared on the screen. Middle-aged, he had close-cropped hair and eyes so cold they made Ivy shiver. He was the kind of man who looked like he enjoyed pulling the wings off butterflies.

"This is Keegan Stutmeir, former East German Stasi Secret Police and currently wanted on a couple dozen international arms dealing charges. We're not sure what use he'd have for Sokolov and Renard, and unfortunately, Giraud was murdered before he could uncover anything else."

Stutmeir was the guy she and Landon had heard John mention the other day.

Landon unscrewed the cap from the bottle of milk. "Stutmeir?"

"Almost certainly," John said. "Giraud's apartment was ransacked, and his field notes and laptop were missing. Fortunately, he kept all his notes backed up on an INTERPOL server, which is how we know about Stutmeir."

Ivy reached across the table and grabbed the milk from Landon's hand so she could add some to her coffee, then gave it back to him. "Where do we come in?"

"Two more DNA experts went missing here in the U.S. about six weeks ago," Evan answered. "Both within a few days of each other. Same as Sokolov and Renard."

Landon frowned. "Why are we just hearing about it now?"

John sighed. "The Department of Homeland Security

threat recognition software picked up on the data pattern, but no one knew what to make of it."

"Intel finally filtered down from Canada that Stutmeir had slipped into the States through their border. We think he's behind the latest kidnappings." Evan pressed a key on the computer and two more faces joined the rest on the screens. "Sarah Beacon, one of the top researchers for the Human Genome Project, and Mitch Dowling, a senior scientist studying genetic adaptation of pathogens for the Centers for Disease Control."

"Dowling is the one who finally tripped the alarm," John said. "Every expert at the CDC is red-flagged. Something happens to them, we know about it."

"So a high-tech arms dealer is kidnapping DNA, genetic, and disease control experts," Ivy said. "That kind of points to a bioweapon, right?"

John glanced at Evan, his mouth twitching. "Told you we could skip the ramp-up and get straight to the point." He turned back to her and Landon. "It's your job to find Stutmeir and confirm if he's holding the scientists prisoners and whether he's developing a bioweapon. If you can figure out whom he's planning on selling it to and when, that's a plus. But be careful. If the information out of Canada is correct, Stutmeir has a sizable group of mercenaries with him.

"Once you find Stutmeir and have ascertained the situation, it'll be your call on how to handle it. You'll have access to anything you need, be it a hostage rescue situation or a complete destroy and sanitize mission." He gave them a meaningful look. "I'm giving you a lot of leeway on this because we don't have a clue about exactly what's going on. No matter what else happens, you are not to allow Stutmeir to develop and put a high-grade biological weapon on the black market. You're authorized to do anything to stop it—including killing the scientists he's holding hostage."

Ivy saw Landon's jaw flex at that, but he didn't say anything. She didn't like the idea of killing innocent people any more than he did, and she prayed it didn't come to that.

John and Evan discussed a few more key points, then left. The moment they walked out, Ivy pulled the ball of yarn out and tossed it at Landon. He caught it in one hand.

"What? You don't like the color?"

Smiling, she took the top folder off the stack John left and opened it. Zarina Sokolov gazed back at Ivy, the woman's blue eyes smiling. Ivy quickly looked away and focused on reading Sokolov's file. She and Landon might have to kill the doctor. Getting personally attached to her would only spell trouble.

"Man, Stutmeir is one mean bastard," Landon muttered. "Have you found anything to suggest he's part of a larger syndicate?"

"He surrounds himself with a lot of muscle, but I haven't seen anything to indicate he's working with anyone. Check this out, though."

Landon came around the table to read over her shoulder, and suddenly, Stutmeir's known associates didn't seem so interesting anymore. She found herself taking several deep breaths to get more of his scent into her lungs. Which completely distracted her. He drove her crazy.

"Looks like a lot of ex-KGB and former Warsaw Pact Special Forces types."

"A couple sound downright nasty." She tilted her head to gaze up at him. Bad idea. She clenched her hands into fists to resist the urge to run her fingers over the trace of stubble on his jaw. "Any thoughts on what our first move should be?"

"Beacon and Dowling are the most recent abductees, so I say we start there."

They grabbed the folders and left the conference room so they could talk to Kendra about plane tickets and badges. As they rounded a corner, she saw Clayne coming down the hall toward them, scowling.

Another fight was all they needed.

Landon looked more than ready to oblige him, too. He stepped half in front of Ivy, his body tense.

Clayne held up his hands. "I'm just here to talk to Ivy."

Landon shifted just enough to see her face without turning his back on Clayne. When she nodded, he moved farther down the hall. That didn't stop him from keeping an eye on them.

She glared up at Clayne. "What do you want? We're kind of busy, so make it fast."

Clayne hesitated, his eyes going to Landon. Her partner was standing there, arms folded across his chest, watching them.

"He can't hear us, Clayne. He's not a shifter, remember?"

Clayne looked at her sharply. "I remember. That's why I'm here. To tell you what you already know—that you're making a mistake getting close to him."

She tightened her grip on the folders, clutching them to her chest. "I'm not getting close to him."

Liar.

"Try that again, only this time with more feeling. Maybe I'll believe it."

She flushed. "I don't care if you believe it or not. Look, you've already said everything you have to say—more than once. That crap you pulled at the pugil pit the other day spoke loud and clear. I don't want to hear it anymore."

Clayne lifted his hands like he wanted to take her by the shoulders, but whether it was to shake her or pull her into his arms, she'd never know because he ran his fingers through his long hair instead. When he lowered them to his side, his face was a mask of calm.

"I just want you to know one thing."

"What's that?"

Clayne moved closer, his eyes a swirl of gold and brown, as if he was on the verge of shifting. "That when things go to crap with Donovan—and they will—I'll be there for you. All you have to do is call me and I'll be there. Wherever there is."

She opened her mouth to tell him he was wrong about Landon, but he'd already turned and walked away.

Landon came over. "What was that about?"

"Nothing," she said. "Absolutely nothing."

Chapter 10

THEY WENT TO MITCH DOWLING'S PLACE FIRST, BUT IT was a bust. Other than learning from his brother that Dowling worked on how pathogens adapt to their environment so the CDC could understand why some people reject vaccines, they found nothing.

They went to see Sarah Beacon's husband next. The man was too distraught to be much help, but he did mention Sarah's work on gene therapy required a very specific type of computer—a very large, expensive one you couldn't get at the local Best Buy.

While Landon found them someplace to have dinner, Ivy called the DCO and told John what they'd learned, then asked him to see if anyone recently had purchased a computer like the one Sarah Beacon used. John got back to them before the waitress even brought their food.

"A man by the name of Arnold Doyle ordered a similar computer a month ago, paid up front for it, and had it delivered to a warehouse outside of Atlanta. I'm sure it's an alias, but I've got someone trying to track him down anyway. In the meantime, I'm sending the address of the warehouse to your phone. I don't want you two taking chances, though," John warned. "Check the place out and if it looks suspicious, call for backup."

It was dark by the time he and Ivy got there, but Landon saw enough of the sign illuminated by the lone streetlamp to know the abandoned warehouse had once been a distribution center for an organic food supermarket chain. There didn't seem to be anyone around, but they scouted the perimeter just to be sure.

"No one's been here for a while." Ivy's voice was soft in the darkness as they entered the building. "Three weeks, maybe a month."

The first room they came to looked like whoever had been there used it as a break room, but the food wrappers and empty pizza boxes could just as easily be from vagrants as from Stutmeir and his men.

Ivy sniffed the air, her nose wrinkling.

"What is it?"

Her mouth tightened. "Blood."

"Fresh?"

She shook her head as she led the way down the hallway into the main part of the warehouse.

As they drew nearer, even Landon picked up the smell. It was metallic and pungent. To Ivy's heightened senses, it must be a hundred times more potent.

Landon wasn't sure what he expected to find, and he was surprised when he stepped into a makeshift medical clinic. On top of the bright lights and ghastly wall color, there was surgical tape and bloody gauze. Used needles and empty IV bags, too.

"What the hell is this place?" Ivy breathed.

"I don't know. But this stuff doesn't exactly look like standard-issue equipment for making a bio-weapon." He looked around. "Let's check out the rest of the building."

There were several rooms in the back that looked like they might have been offices at one time. Two of the doors had padlocks on the outside. Landon cautiously pushed open one of them. It was empty except for a pile of blankets on the floor.

Landon glanced at Ivy. "Prison cells for the scientists, you think?"

"Maybe." She walked in and sniffed the air, then the blankets. "Mitch Dowling and Sarah Beacon were definitely here."

Landon opened the door to the other room and immediately reeled back at the foul stench that hit his nose. Didn't need a super sense like Ivy's to pick up that odor. Or to know that it came from something dead.

Beside him, Ivy made a face. "It's coming from there."

There was a walk-in freezer big enough to hold a dozen dead bodies. And judging from the way it reeked, the unit clearly wasn't turned on.

"Rock, paper, scissors?" Ivy just gave him a look. "Yeah, I didn't think so."

He tightened his grip on his Glock and opened the freezer door.

There were at least fifteen bodies strewn across the floor, wrapped in plastic and twisted up in what looked like a seriously painful death. Except for one—a well-dressed man in his mid-fifties with a bullet hole through his forehead.

"Mitch Dowling," he said to Ivy.

She scanned the other bodies, a worried frown knitting her brow. "It's probably a little late to ask, but do you think they're contagious?"

Damn, he hadn't even thought of that. "I don't think so. The bodies are all in different stages of decomposition. That means they were dumped in here one or two at a time over a period of a week or so. Plus, there's blood outside the freezer. That's not the way someone who's worried about getting infected treats dead bodies."

She relaxed a little at that. "You're right. But I'd feel better if we call it in."

John agreed about taking precautions and immediately had Kendra work on getting a CDC decontamination and survey team there.

"Once you're cleared—which I'm sure you will be— we'll get the CDC to examine the bodies. We need to figure out what Stutmeir is up to. If he's come up with something that can kill people so horribly without infecting others nearby, then I'm really worried. It'd be the perfect bioweapon."

Landon had to agree.

While he and Ivy waited for the decontamination team to arrive, they snooped around some more. She found a trail of dried blood leading to the back door, and a whole lot more—or what was left of it at least—on the concrete outside.

Ivy kneeled down and put her nose close enough to do a sniff test. "It's Dowling's."

"You can ID blood that old?"

She nodded as she got to her feet. "But only because I smelled the body a few minutes ago. He must have tried to escape." Ivy chewed on her lower lip. Something she did when she was thinking. "I wonder if his work was done, or whether he bailed before they could make him do what they wanted."

"From what we saw in that freezer, Stutmeir's weapon is coming along nicely, with or without Dowling's help."

"Unless whatever Stutmeir is up to is even worse than what we've already seen."

Landon didn't want to think about that possibility. His cell phone rang, echoing in the huge, empty building. It was John calling to tell them the CDC was on its way with an emergency decontamination team. Landon put him on speaker so Ivy could hear.

"So, either Stutmeir killed Dowling because he didn't play ball or because he'd outlived his usefulness." John sighed heavily on the other end of the line. "Wish we knew which, so we'd have some idea if Stutmeir is finished making the weapon."

"Our guess is that he's not," Landon said. "If he was, he would have killed the other scientists, too."

"Good point. Which means Stutmeir might be hunting for more experts. I'm going to get analysts to put together a list of people who might have Dowling's same skill set—just in case they go after someone to replace him."

Ivy frowned. "Dowling's been dead at least two weeks. Stutmeir could already have gone after someone else."

"We would have heard about it," John said. "Intel has been monitoring every missing person and possible kidnapping out there related to doctors and scientists. There haven't been any since Dowling and Beacon. If there's another expert out there, we'll find him. Hopefully, before Stutmeir does."

Landon hoped so, too.

The decontamination team from the Centers for Disease Control arrived fifteen minutes later dressed in standard-issue space suits. Without asking a single question, they introduced themselves, then quickly and efficiently set up tents for a decontamination line. Landon expected them to run him and Ivy through separately, but in an emergency response like this, there wasn't time for modesty. Landon did the gentlemanly thing and turned his back so he could give Ivy some privacy, but he couldn't help catching the occasional glimpse of those perfect breasts and long legs as the techs stripped her down. Watching the techs lather her up was way more X-rated than it should have been considering the freaky suits the CDC workers were wearing, but with that body, it was hard not to have pornographic thoughts, even with the whole they-might-have-been-exposed-to-a-contagious-disease thing hanging over their heads.

He lifted his head to make sure Ivy hadn't caught him looking and found her giving him a rather frank appraisal in return. She didn't even bother to hide the interest in her eyes. He thought he saw them glimmer green for a second. They went back to their normal brown before he could be sure. He stifled a groan. It was good the water the techs hosed him down with was cold, otherwise his erection would have been a lot more blatant. And a lot more embarrassing.

<center>~~~</center>

When she and Landon had been sufficiently decontaminated, the techs drew blood, took some DNA swipes, handed them bathrobes, and led them to yet another tent. This one had two folding chairs in it and a small table. Sitting around wearing nothing but a robe was strangely erotic. Probably because she was still a little turned on from the impromptu strip show earlier. A lot of women would pay money to see a hot guy like Landon stripped naked and lathered up in foam. Her included. She only wished it wasn't because they might be infected with something that might kill them in an awful, painful way.

She looked at Landon. He was sitting back in his chair, looking as relaxed as he always did. Why didn't he look as terrified as she was?

Because he was a guy, and guys never worried about anything. At least not in front of a woman.

She sighed and looked around the tent for something to take her mind off the tests the CDC was running—and the fact that Landon was naked underneath his robe—when a light dancing on the floor caught her eye. She lifted her head to see where it was coming from and saw Landon flicking the laser pointer from his pistol around the floor in front of her feet.

"What are you doing?"

"Giving you something to do besides worry about whether we're infected or not." His mouth quirked. "Cats like to chase lights around a room, right? It's supposed to be an involuntary reflex or something."

She gave him a wry smile. "Very funny."

It *was* funny. She liked that he could joke about her being a shifter, even if he was only doing it now so she wouldn't obsess about whether they'd been exposed to whatever Stutmeir had cooked up. It meant he was comfortable with her being part feline. That was all she'd ever wanted in a partner—and a man.

"Ivy, it's going to be okay."

Coming from him, she believed it.

She took a deep breath. "Since I'm not going to chase a light around on the floor—no matter how much it might amuse you—you're going to have to do something else to distract me. Talk to me."

"About what?"

"You." She smiled. "I hardly know anything about you. Other than that you were in Special Forces and worked with some great guys. Tell me about your family."

"Not much to tell." He set the laser pointer on the table. "My old man liked to smack us around for fun, which was whenever we did something he didn't like, which was pretty much all the time. Mom was an alcoholic and refused to walk away from him even after he almost killed her. And my sister, Laci, decided I was the reason Dad was such an asshole."

Ivy didn't know what to say. She'd grown up in a wonderful family with parents who loved her and the best sisters in the world. She sometimes forgot other people weren't so lucky. Hearing about a stranger coming from an abused home was different than knowing someone it had happened to.

"That must have been terrible for you," she said when she'd finally found her voice.

"It was what it was." He shrugged. "When I got big enough—and strong enough—to fight back, I did. But every time I tried to protect Mom and Laci, they'd blame me for making it worse. Like it was my fault. Finally broke my old man's jaw when he came at me with a baseball bat. That asshole was trying to kill me and Mom threatened to have me arrested for assaulting *him*. I walked out that day and never looked back."

"My God." She imagined him as a scared kid having to defend himself against his father—the person who was supposed to love and protect him. She wanted to reach out and put her arms around him, but didn't. "How old were you?"

"Sixteen."

"That made you what, a junior in high school? Where did you live?"

"On the street at first, and when it got too cold for that, I'd sneak back into the high school after class and spend my nights there. I already had a part-time job, so I had enough money to cover food, and I had extra clothes in my locker. It wasn't so bad."

It sounded bad to her. "Didn't your parents report you missing?"

He snorted. "You kidding? They were glad to get rid of me."

"What about the school? No one figured out you weren't living at home?"

"I showed up to class. That was all that mattered. The only person I told was my best friend, Steve. He finally convinced his mom and dad to let me sleep on the couch. They wanted to get child services involved, but I talked them out of it."

"Why?"

"Because they wouldn't have been able to do a damn thing. It was my word against my old man's, and my mom and sister would have backed up whatever story he told. Knowing that bastard, he probably would have taken it out on them. With me out of the picture, maybe he stopped abusing them."

She frowned. "You don't honestly think you were responsible for what he did, do you?"

"No. I'm not a martyr, Ivy." The muscle in his jaw flexed. "But when I stopped by the middle school to check on Laci a few weeks after I left, she said Dad hadn't hit her or Mom since I took off. That could have been because he was too doped up on the pain meds he was taking for his broken jaw to bother, I guess, but who the hell knows? Laci could have been lying to protect him."

"Or to protect you. Maybe she and your mom always took your father's side because they were afraid for you."

He let out a harsh laugh. "Yeah, right."

She knew that idea wouldn't go over well. "It's possible. I'm guessing you got the worst of it by always coming to their defense. Maybe they figured if they sided with him, he'd leave you alone."

He sat back and folded his arms across his chest. "Well, whatever. I guess we'll never know. My old man drank himself to death a few years after I went in the army, and my mom died last year."

"What about Laci?"

"Last time I talked to Steve, he said she was married with two kids."

"You don't talk to her?"

He shook his head. "I joined the army the day after graduation and never went back. Never looked back. That just shoots my nice guy image all to hell, doesn't it?"

"You're image is still intact." She gave him a small smile. "I think it shows how strong and courageous you are. To come from that kind of life and be where you are now says a lot about the man you are."

"What, sitting around a decontamination tent in a bathrobe, telling my life story to a woman I've known for a whole week?"

"There are worst places to be."

"Don't I know it."

The pain in his voice told her the wounds were still deep even after all these years, and she hated that she'd been the one to reopen them. Curiosity might not always kill the cat, but it could sure make her feel bad. "So, what made you pick the military?"

"I wanted to get someplace far away from where I was. I didn't have the money for college, so it was either that or work on an oil rig somewhere. I figured I had a better chance of going to college if I went in the military."

She was glad he hadn't chosen oil rigging. "Why Special Forces?"

"The recruiter showed me a video of these guys doing cool stuff like jumping out of planes, shooting machine guns, and blowing shit up. What more could a guy want?"

"What more indeed?" she said dryly.

"It's a guy thing. How about you? What made you join the DCO?"

She shrugged. "I was tired of riding a desk at the FBI."

Landon sat back in his chair. "How long did you work for the Bureau?"

"Almost four years."

"And they never put you in the field?"

"No. Which annoyed the hell out of me." She rolled her eyes. "My glass ceiling was set at the first floor in the FBI. You're lucky you don't have to deal with crap like that."

He was silent for a moment. "What about family?"

"My parents live in Virginia with my three sisters."

"Are they shifters, too?"

"Only one sister—Layla. We're the first in my family

since my great-grandmother. Something my other sisters are still bummed about. They complain Layla and I got all the good genes."

The tent flap opened and one of the CDC techs walked in. He'd taken off his protective suit and was carrying their clothes. That had to be a good sign.

"You're in the clear." He set their clothes on the table. "At least as far as we know."

That didn't exactly inspire confidence.

Landon exchanged a frown with her. "As far as you know?"

The man shrugged. "Homeland Security ordered us to forward all the results from your samples directly to them without any review on our part. They're the ones who made the call that you're clear."

Because the CDC techs would take one look at her blood and know she was different. She should have realized the DCO wouldn't let anyone get a look at her blood.

Landon turned his back while they dressed to give her privacy. Ivy did the same, but not before taking a quick peek at his ass. He was built, all right.

She was just sliding her feet into low-heeled pumps when her cell phone rang. She picked it up, putting it on hands-free when John's name came up on the call display.

"Are you out of quarantine yet?"

She slipped her gun holster on her belt. "We just got cleared."

"Good. I need you two on a plane to New York five minutes ago. Evan got a hit on a geneticist in Pittsburgh who was killed a week ago during what was assumed to be a kidnapping gone bad. She fits our profile of the kind of expert Stutmeir would be after."

Landon shrugged into his suit jacket. "Then we were right about Stutmeir looking for a replacement for Dowling."

"Looks like it. Evan and his team have generated a list of the top twenty candidates, and all teams not already in the field are on their way to secure and protect the targets. Your assignment is a biologist from the Genetic Institute of New York City by the name of Phil Bosch. Your plane leaves from Hartsfield-Jackson in an hour. I'll dump all the information we have on Bosch to your phone."

Landon picked up his gun. "An hour isn't a lot of time to get to the airport from here. Making our flight is going to be tough."

"Kendra already instructed them to hold the plane for you."

Ivy almost laughed at the surprise on Landon's face. "Another perk of working at the DCO."

"So I see. New York City here we come."

Chapter 11

IT TOOK ALMOST AN HOUR IN NEW YORK CITY TRAFFIC to get to Bosch's Manhattan apartment, then another ten minutes to find a place to park.

"This is insane. How the hell does anyone live here? Look at that psycho over there."

Landon jerked his head at a car as he and Ivy walked up the steps and into the apartment building. The driver had parked practically perpendicular to the street, one front wheel up on the sidewalk, the back of the car still sitting out in the street.

He glanced around as they crossed the fancy lobby to the elevator. "Can you believe a place this nice doesn't have a doorman? I reckon a couple thousand dollars a month in rent doesn't buy what it used to."

She shook her head, but didn't smile at his joke.

He pressed the button for the fifth floor. "What? I'm just saying."

They stepped out on the fifth floor just as the doors to the other elevator closed. Ivy stopped, her eyes narrowing at the barely discernible thump coming from inside. Landon stopped, too.

"Problem?"

She stared at the second elevator for another moment, then shook her head. As they headed for Bosch's apartment, she kept glancing back at the elevator.

"Something's not right," she said.

Landon didn't ask for clarification. He pulled his pistol and ran down the hallway. The door of Bosch's apartment was ajar, the frame splintered. Beside him, Ivy pulled her weapon and gave him a nod.

He pushed the door open the rest of the way and moved quickly into the room, covering the far left and right corners of the living room. Out of the corner of his eye, he saw Ivy checking the blind spots behind him. He was about to say the room was clear when he heard sobbing coming from the other side of the couch. He exchanged looks with Ivy, then crossed the room, gun lowered but still at the ready.

A young girl kneeled over an unconscious woman. Bosch's wife and daughter. The girl—What was her name? Ivy had read it off her phone on the way— Abigail—was trying to stanch the flow of blood from a head wound near the mother's temple with her hand. She lifted her head, letting out a piercing scream when she saw him and Ivy.

"It's okay. We're with the police." Ivy holstered her gun and hurried to the girl's side to check the mother's pulse. "Where's your father?"

Abigail stared at Ivy in confusion. Was she so traumatized she couldn't talk? Couldn't even remember what had happened? He'd seen it often enough in combat zones.

But the girl wiped the tears from her cheeks. "Men broke in and took him. Why did they take him? Why did they hurt my mom?"

Ivy put a gentle hand on the girl's shoulder. "Your mother's going to be okay, and we're going to get your father back. I need you to be calm and call the police for me. Can you do that?"

Abigail nodded, her blond curls bouncing.

Ivy pulled out her iPhone and handed it to the girl. "Do you know how to use this?"

A sniff. "Yes. I have one just like it."

"Good. Call the police and tell them what happened." There was a cardigan on the back of the couch. She grabbed it and pressed it into Abigail's free hand. "Hold this against the wound until the paramedics get here, okay?"

The girl nodded.

Ivy got to her feet and came over to him. "That must have been who was in the other elevator. Dammit!"

"It's okay." Landon was careful to keep his voice low so Abigail couldn't hear. "They only have about thirty seconds on us. If we hurry, we might get lucky and stop them down on the street."

"Get downstairs. I'll try to cut them off if I can."

Cut them off? "How…?"

But Ivy had already opened the sliding glass door to the balcony and was vaulting over the railing. His gut clenched. Shit, they were five floors up. He started for the railing to make sure she was safe, but stopped himself. Ivy wasn't suicidal. She wouldn't have jumped if she didn't know she could handle the fall. Besides, she was depending on him to get downstairs and cover her.

Landon swore under his breath and turned for the door, only to stop at the shocked expression on Abigail's tear-streaked face. The girl had seen Ivy jump. People didn't do things like that. Not normal people anyway.

"She's going to get your dad. I promise we won't let anything happen to him." He jerked his chin at the iPhone in her hand. "Call the cops like she asked, okay?"

At the girl's nod, he left, hitting the hallway at a dead run.

He took the stairs instead of the elevator. On the bottom floor, he discovered why there hadn't been a doorman in the lobby when he and Ivy had come in earlier. The guy was slumped in one corner of the stairwell, out cold. At least Landon hoped he was only out cold—he didn't have time to check. It had been at least twenty seconds since Ivy jumped from the balcony. That was a long time to go without backup. Especially when they had no idea how many bad guys they were up against.

Landon heard a gunshot the moment he raced out of the stairwell. He swore and ran across the lobby but slowed when he got to the glass doors. Across the street, two men crouched behind the sedan he'd seen on the curb earlier. They were firing their weapons toward someone out of Landon's field of vision off to the right.

Ivy.

She was hiding behind a parked Escalade half a block down the street, and as he watched, she put a round into the sedan the men were hiding behind. She didn't hit either of them, but that wasn't her intent. She was simply keeping them occupied until Landon arrived, but a lucky shot could still take her out any second. He didn't have much time.

Landon burst out the door and dived behind a big, concrete flower box in front of the apartment building. He crouched and quickly peered around the edge, looking for Bosch, but didn't see him. He hoped Stutmeir's goons hadn't stashed the biologist in the trunk of the sedan Ivy was targeting.

Landon put a round in the kidnapper closest to him.

The second guy immediately turned and darted behind the cars parallel parked along the curb before his colleague even hit the pavement.

Landon stayed where he was, waiting to see if the guy would take up another defensive position. But the schmuck was too smart for that. He kept his head low and took off running down the sidewalk away from him and Ivy.

Landon threw a quick glance at the Escalade and saw Ivy give him a nod. Trusting her to cover him, he raced across the street to check the sedan. Bosch was curled into a ball on the floorboard of the backseat, his arms protectively over his head. He looked up hesitantly when Landon poked his head in. The biologist's wire-rimmed glasses were a little cockeyed but otherwise he looked fine.

"I'm a federal agent. Stay put," Landon ordered, then turned and took off down the street, keeping the cars between him and the fleeing attacker. Behind him, he could hear Ivy's barely audible footsteps as she raced to catch up.

<hr />

Ivy cursed as she ran after Landon. She'd felt that nagging little voice in her head the moment they walked into the lobby of the posh high-rise. But it wasn't like her kitty cat alarm had been screaming at her, so she'd ignored what it was saying. It wasn't until they were in the elevator and Landon made the comment about the doorman—or lack of one—she realized she'd made a mistake. By then the elevator doors had opened and everything had gone wacky. First the noise on the second elevator, then the sound of Abigail's sobbing, followed by the unmistakable smell of fear. There'd been too many sensations coming at her all at once, and she couldn't separate what was important and what wasn't. If she'd listened to her instincts downstairs, they might have stopped the kidnapping altogether.

That was probably why she'd recklessly jumped off the balcony without knowing what was waiting for her below. Fortunately, she'd landed in the middle of a grassy community outdoor living space and not on top of a jungle gym.

Landon glanced at her as she pulled even with him. "Let's take this guy alive if we can."

Good idea. But hard to do when the guy was firing a gun in their direction. Fortunately, he wasn't very accurate, but she was still worried about innocent bystanders. She yelled for them to get to safety as she and Landon gained on the suspect.

The guy ran out of ammo, tossed the gun aside, and kept going. Now that they didn't have to worry about him shooting back, she picked up speed. Beside her, Landon did the same.

Up ahead, the man darted down a side alley. She slowed, coming to a stop at the entrance. She darted her head around the building for a quick peek, then looked at Landon.

"He's hiding behind a Dumpster on the left-hand side about halfway down the alley. I can see his foot sticking out."

"Can you jump over it?" Landon asked.

"The Dumpster? Yeah."

"I'll cover you. If he pops up his head, I'll fire."

Giving her a nod, he ran down the alley, putting a single round through the Dumpster so the man hiding behind it wouldn't even think about returning fire—if he even had another weapon.

Ivy followed, hugging the left wall of the alley so the man wouldn't see her coming, then hurtled the Dumpster. If she didn't do her part—and quickly—Landon'd be standing square in the middle of the alley with nowhere to duck and cover. She tucked her knees and somersaulted into the air. She landed hard so Stutmeir's man would hear her. When he craned his head around to look, she punched him square in the nose. He went down just in time for Landon to tackle him, which was unnecessary since she'd already knocked the guy out. But she let him have his fun.

He lifted the unconscious man and hoisted him over his shoulder, then grinned at her. "Nice work."

She grinned back. More like nice teamwork.

The NYPD and paramedics were on the scene by the time she and Landon got back to Bosch's apartment. The biologist, however, wasn't in the back of the sedan where Landon had ordered him to stay. Something that pissed off her partner.

"His wife was hurt. You didn't expect him to stay in the car, did you?" Ivy asked.

Landon only grunted.

Ivy frowned as they neared the patrol cars. Two cops were checking out the bullet-riddled car, while another was crouched beside the body of the man Landon had shot. No doubt there'd be more cops on the way, which meant they needed to take control of the situation. She flashed her badge, identifying herself and Landon as Homeland Security, then explained they needed to leave the man they'd apprehended in the back of a police cruiser until their backup got there to take the guy in.

The cops looked uncertain for a moment, then shrugged. "Yeah, sure." One of the officers glanced at her as he led the way to one of the squad cars. "Who is that guy? A terrorist or something?"

"Let's just call him a person of interest for now," she said.

Landon dumped the unconscious man in the backseat, then slammed the door. "When your duty captain gets here, let him know my partner and I are up on the fifth floor in apartment five twelve."

Ivy had been right about Phil Bosch. He was sitting on the couch with his wife and daughter. A red-haired paramedic was tending to his wife Deidre's wound. Upon seeing her and Landon, Abigail jumped up and ran over to hug Ivy. She almost laughed when the girl threw her arms around Landon next. He looked like he'd been attacked by a small creature from Mars. He had no idea what to do. Finally, he hesitantly put an arm around the girl.

Abigail beamed up at him. "I knew you'd save my dad." She handed Ivy her iPhone. "I called the police, just like you told me to."

Phil Bosch murmured something to his wife, then stood and came over. "I have to thank you as well. Though I have no idea who you are or who those people were who tried to grab me."

Landon told him they were with Homeland Security, then added, "Just doing our job."

Ivy glanced at Deidre. "How is your wife?"

"She says she's fine, but I still want a doctor to take a look at her. She might have a concussion." His eyes were clouded with concern when he turned back to them. "You said you're with Homeland Security. Were those men terrorists?"

"We can't give you details at this time," Ivy said. "All I can tell you is that those men were interested in you because of what you do for a living. We'll be able to explain everything later, but for now we're going to have to ask you to play stupid when the NYPD asks you anything."

He gave her a wry smile. "That shouldn't be difficult since I have no idea why the kind of work I do would interest anyone, much less prompt this much violence. I'm just glad you showed up when you did."

Ivy's cell phone rang. "Excuse me." She moved off to the side and held it to her ear. "Halliwell."

"It's John. A team is on the way to pick up your prisoner, as well as another one to debrief Bosch and his family and take them to a safe house. When they arrive, I want you and Landon on the next flight back to DC. I want to move on Stutmeir as soon as his guy talks."

She made a face. "If he talks."

"That's not going to be a problem," John assured her.

Ivy pocketed her phone and turned to find Landon beside her. She was about to fill him in when Abigail came running over. She didn't want the girl knowing about the safe house until they'd talked to her parents.

"I wanted to thank you again," Abigail said.

Ivy smiled. "You're very welcome. We're glad we got here in time."

Abigail glanced at her parents, then lowered her voice conspiratorially. "I didn't tell my mom and dad."

Ivy frowned. "About what?"

"About you jumping off the balcony. I figured that was supposed to be our secret."

Ivy looked at Landon, stunned. She hadn't even thought about the girl seeing her when she'd done that. Rule one in the Shifter Rule Book—Don't Let Anyone See You Shift. And if someone did, deny it. Something told her Abigail wasn't going to buy that. Better to not make a big deal of it.

"Thank you, Abigail. I appreciate it."

"I wanted to ask you something." The girl hesitated, looking suddenly unsure of herself. "I was wondering… are you a superhero? You know, like in the movies?"

The way the girl was looking up at her all wide-eyed with admiration made Ivy blush. She'd never thought of herself as a superhero.

Landon grinned. "Yeah, she's a superhero."

Ivy did a double take.

Abigail's smile was smug. "I thought so." She looked at Landon. "Are you a superhero, too?"

He chuckled. "Me? Nah. I'm just a sidekick."

The girl nodded. "Being a sidekick's cool, too. And don't worry, your secret's safe with me."

Giving them a wave, Abigail hurried back to her parents.

Ivy leaned in close to Landon. "Sidekick, huh? You, Agent Donovan, are so much more than that."

Leaving him standing there, she turned and walked over to talk to Phil and his wife about moving to a safe house.

Chapter 12

"WANT TO COME OVER FOR DINNER?"

The words were out of Ivy's mouth before she could stop them. She wished she could chalk it up to being tired—she and Landon hadn't had more than a catnap (he'd teased her so much about that stupid word she'd almost hit him) on the flight back to DC that morning, which had been followed by a ridiculously long debriefing—but she couldn't. She never thought she'd say it, but she liked spending time with her partner. And since they'd already demonstrated they could be alone with each other without tearing off one another's clothes, she didn't see a problem.

"Want me to grab takeout?" he asked.

"I'll make something." She smiled. "Have to get some use out of that fancy kitchen of mine."

But cooking dinner—even if it was for a partner she had a completely platonic relationship with—made it feel suspiciously like a date. And if that didn't, standing in front of her closet wondering what top to pair with the jeans she had on sure did. Muttering under her breath, she grabbed a fluttery flower-print retro shirt and slipped into it just as the doorbell rang.

Landon was at her door, a bottle of wine in his hand.

"My contribution to the meal." His mouth curved. "I didn't know whether to get red or white."

"Red's terrific." She stepped back, opening the door wider. "Come in."

He'd showered and changed before coming over, and she had to keep from taking a big whiff as he walked in. She closed the door, then led the way into the kitchen.

"This is nice."

"Thanks." She glanced over her shoulder at him. "Where did they put you up?"

Now that they were done with training, they didn't have to stay at the complex down at Quantico.

"An apartment down in Alexandria. It's nice, but not this nice."

Probably meaning it had a bed, a television, and not much else. "The bigger square footage comes as part of the EVA benefits package. There are some really good home decorating stores around here. If you want, I could go with you and help pick out some stuff, spruce up your place."

The words were out of her mouth before she could stop them. *Great, Ivy. Way to put some distance between you and your partner.* Who looked even more scrumptious than usual in a pair of jeans and a T-shirt. She gave him a sideways look and saw him flash her a grin.

"I just might take you up on that. My decorating skills are limited to figuring out where the TV goes."

"Dinner's almost ready." She set the bottle on the counter. "There's a corkscrew in the top drawer if you want to open the wine."

As she took the lasagna out of the oven, Ivy tried not to watch him work, but the way the muscles in his forearms flexed as he uncorked the wine was mesmerizing. His hands were pretty fascinating, too. Big with long, tapered fingers. The kind of hands that would feel so good on her naked body.

She gripped the edge of the casserole dish tightly as she carried it to the table. Even the lasagna couldn't mask the pheromones Landon was emitting.

"This table looks like it's an antique," he remarked as they sat down. "Is it?"

Not exactly where her mind had been going, but talking about her dining room table was much safer dinner conversation than what she'd been thinking.

"You have a good eye." She dished out the lasagna. "I picked it up in an antique shop when I was in Italy a few years ago. It was pretty beat up, but I fell in love with it anyway. At the time, I didn't know how much work it'd take to get it in shape, but it was worth it."

He lifted a brow. "You refurbished it yourself?"

"Clayne helped, but I did most of it."

"I'm impressed."

It was silly to feel so darn pleased by the compliment—it was only a table—but she did. She'd put her heart and soul into refurbishing it, along with a heck of a lot of sweat and hard work. Knowing Landon appreciated her efforts made them even more worthwhile.

But putting so much worth into what Landon thought was dangerous. The more comfortable she got with him, the harder it was to convince herself not to give in and do what her body was screaming for—lean across the table and kiss him until their clothes happened to fall off.

It didn't get any easier when they'd moved into the living room after dinner. Even though he sat on the other end of the couch, Landon's scent was driving her wild. He might as well have been lying on top of her. Like she needed *that* image in her head. She stifled a moan.

She reached for her wineglass, only to freeze when she saw her claws were out. Crap. She hadn't even felt them extend.

"Are you okay?" Landon asked.

She quickly retracted her claws before he could see. "Yeah. Why?"

"Because your eyes are glowing."

Damn. She forced them back to their normal color. Could she play it off as a natural response to the lowered light in the room? Landon might buy it. That would be a lie, though, and a lie of any kind between them felt wrong. But she couldn't be honest with him, either.

She picked up her nearly empty wineglass. It was easier not to give in to her animal urges if there was some distance between them. "I'm going to get a refill. I'll grab you another beer."

She hoped Landon would leave it at that, but she should have known better. He followed her into the kitchen and gently put his hand on her arm. His touch was electric on her skin and she had to bite back a moan.

"Whatever's wrong, you can talk to me about it. You know that, right?"

She kept her gaze fixed on the bottle of wine, afraid if she didn't, she'd do something crazy. She knew this was stupid, but she couldn't stop herself. Maybe it was time to give in to her animal instincts. Maybe if she had sex with him, she'd finally get it out of her system once and for all.

"Remember when I told you my feline side comes out whenever I'm feeling any intense emotion?"

"Yeah."

"Well, it doesn't have to be just fear or anger. It can be any powerful emotion—hatred, happiness." She looked up at him. "Arousal."

He said nothing, but his eyes suddenly smoldered. "So, if I had to guess which of those emotions you're feeling right now and I said arousal…?"

Her pulse quickened. "You'd be right."

Something flared in his eyes. "Back in South America, we both said we weren't going to do this. Go where this is heading, I mean."

Landon stepped closer even as he said the words and Ivy breathed in his scent. He was as aroused as she was. She could smell it. And damn did it smell *good*. "My head keeps reminding me of that, but my body won't listen. Being so close to you every day and not touching you… It's driving me crazy."

He brushed her hair back from her face, his fingers gentle. "It's been like that for me, too. You don't know how badly I've wanted to kiss you again. It's all I've thought about since we came back from Venezuela."

She swayed toward him, her lips parting. "Me, too."

"If we do this, there won't be any going back, Ivy. One night of sex with you won't be enough for me," he said softly. "I'm okay with that. Hell, I'm more than okay with that. Are you?"

He was giving her a chance to change her mind, to put a stop to this before things went too far. If she did, this would end right here and he'd likely never bring it up again. But for the life of her, she didn't want it to end here. She wanted it to end somewhere else. Preferably in bed. Although the kitchen counter was fine, too. She pictured him sweeping everything off the granite with one arm, then lifting her up on it and taking her right there. Heat pooled between her thighs.

It would be off-the-charts amazing.

"I couldn't be more okay with it."

She wrapped her hand around the back of his head and pulled him down for a kiss. This time, there was no hesitation on Landon's part. His mouth was hot and demanding on hers, his tongue almost desperate. He tasted just as delicious as she remembered. Maybe more. She buried her fingers in his hair, holding him tightly and plunging her tongue into his mouth. She could get drunk on him.

He slid one hand in her hair, kissing his way along the curve of her jaw and down her neck, making her moan. She could feel his cock pulsing against her through both their jeans. Her pussy clenched in response.

She wasn't sure which of them started it, but their clothes came off at the same time, her undressing him while he undressed her, jeans and underwear hitting the floor one after another until they were both finally naked.

She ran her hands over his shoulders, then down his muscular chest and six-pack abs. The one taste she'd had of his body in Venezuela hadn't been nearly enough. To be able to touch him like this again after hours spent fantasizing was pure heaven, and she murmured her appreciation against his mouth as she traced every chiseled inch. He was absolutely perfect.

Landon touched her everywhere, his hands palming her breasts and teasing her nipples for one long, delicious moment before sliding down to cup her throbbing sex. His finger dipped into her moist pussy just long enough to fan the flames even hotter than they already were before sliding back out. His roaming hands found every one of her most sensitive erogenous zones and lingered there before moving on to ones she didn't even know she had. What he was doing gave new meaning to the words *hot and bothered*. She thought she might actually spontaneously combust.

"God, Ivy. You're driving me crazy." He dragged his mouth away from hers, his breathing ragged. "Where's the bedroom?"

She clung to him, her knees like Jell-O. "At the end of the hall."

He closed his mouth over hers again in a fierce, possessive kiss, then he swung her up in his arms and strode down the hall. Ivy was so spellbound by Landon she didn't even realize they were in her room until he set her down in the middle of the bed.

She barely had time to catch her breath before he bent to kiss his way down her body. His mouth was molten on her skin, setting her on fire everywhere he touched. She gasped as he stopped to take one of her nipples in his mouth and suckle greedily on it. He swirled his tongue around the tip, playfully letting it slide out of his mouth before capturing it again. He repeated the move until she was on the verge of going insane. Then he moved to the other nipple and did it again. By the time he kissed his way down her stomach then to the juncture of her thighs, she was practically dizzy. She needed this so bad.

Landon cupped her ass in both hands and buried his face in her pussy like a starving man. She arched against him, grabbing fistfuls of his hair in both hands as he lapped hungrily at her clit. She'd had guys go down on her before, but none of them had been this talented with their tongue. Landon knew exactly what to do to make her come and wasn't shy about doing it. He slid the tip of his tongue up one wet fold to linger on her clit, making lazy circles around it. Then, just when she felt herself start to build toward orgasm, he pulled his tongue away to tease her folds again. She'd never been with a man so patient when it came to oral sex.

But Landon continued tormenting her until she was writhing on the bed. And then, when he had her right on the edge, he slid a finger in her pussy and fucked her with it. The combination of his soft tongue and firm thrusting set her off like a rocket. She arched off the bed, letting out a long, low moan that echoed off the walls.

When she came back down, Landon was grinning up at her from between her legs.

"So, you really do purr." He pressed a kiss to her inner thigh, then climbed up beside her. "I've been wondering about that."

She blushed, suddenly self-conscious of the animal sounds she might make. She bit her lip and turned her face away, but he cupped her chin and gently turned her face back to his. He leaned forward and covered her mouth with a consuming kiss. By the time he was done, she could barely remember what it was that had made her embarrassed in the first place.

"Don't you dare try to rein yourself in." Landon's voice was husky in the near darkness. "I think those purrs and growls are sexy as hell."

His erection pulsed against her thigh, heavy with need, and she knew he wasn't just saying that stuff to make her feel better. She turned him on as much as he did her. She reached down to wrap her hand around his thick cock. He sucked in a sharp breath.

Then swore.

She jerked her hand away. Had her claws come out? Had she hurt him? "What is it?"

"I don't have a condom."

She almost laughed. That she could deal with. "Not a problem. I have some. I just hope they aren't expired." She opened the bedside drawer and took one out, then handed it to him with a sheepish look. "It's been a while since I've slept with anyone."

He looked at her in surprise. "Me too. I've been on four back-to-back deployments. What's your excuse?"

She gave him a wry smile. "It sort of kills the mood if I have to concentrate on keeping the shifter inside."

Landon caressed her cheek. "I said you don't have to hide any of that from me, remember?"

"I know." She reached up to cover his hand with hers and kissed him hard on the mouth, trying to communicate how important his trust was. "You have no way of knowing what that means to me."

"Why don't you show me what it means." Letting out his own sexy growl, he rolled them both over on the big bed until she was lying beneath him. Capturing her wrists in one hand, he pinned them to the pillow above her head. "Just be careful with these claws of yours if you don't want me to tie you up."

Ivy purred. On purpose this time. "That might be kind of fun."

The glint in Landon's eye as he rolled on the condom told her he thought so, too.

Bracing himself on his forearms, Landon rubbed his

shaft up and down her slit, teasing her with the head. He wasn't even inside her and it was already amazing. She might just pass out when he slid in.

She didn't, but when he finally entered her, it was close. If she thought she'd been in heaven before, that was nothing compared to this. Landon was hot and hard inside her, his cock touching her in places she never knew existed until now. How was it possible to fit together with anyone so perfectly?

She didn't know the answer to that. And right then, she didn't care. All she wanted to do was enjoy how good he felt inside her. She wrapped her arms and legs around him, lifted her hips to meet his, and pulled him in deep as he slowly started to thrust.

"Harder," she demanded. She wasn't in the mood for slow and gentle. She wanted urgent and animalistic.

Landon's mouth closed over hers as he pumped into her hard and fast. She felt her body tighten and knew with all her heart that the approaching orgasm was going to be the best she'd ever had.

But then Landon flipped over, taking her with him. She wasn't sure how he did it so smoothly. One minute she was underneath him, and the next, she was on top, his cock buried deep inside her. While she liked this new position just as much as the first, the move had slowed down her climax, and she growled in frustration.

"Ride me," he commanded.

Her growl dissolved into a throaty sigh at that. She eagerly obeyed, placing her hands on his chest and slowly moving up and down on him.

"Damn, that feels amazing," he breathed.

Yes, it did. She could already feel her orgasm building again.

Landon grasped her ass in both hands, urging her to go faster. She rotated her hips more, clenching her pussy around him every time she came down. She rode him hard, wanting him to love it as much as she did.

"That's it," he urged hoarsely.

She leaned forward, grabbing his shoulders as she picked up the pace. His thrusts matched hers, and her pussy quivered around him.

She cried out as her climax surged through her and kept going. Somewhere in the throes of passion—possibly between orgasm number three and number four—she thought she dug her claws into Landon's back, but she wasn't sure. She didn't care. Because he didn't care. For the first time in her life, she had permission to enjoy sex. And she was going to enjoy it. In every way possible.

"You know." Landon's voice was a deep rumble beneath her as they lay there panting afterward. "If we're going to get that rough every time, you might want to invest in some Kevlar sheets."

She lifted her head to see him surveying the bed—and the damage her claws had done. Her five-hundred-thread-count sheets were ruined.

"Yikes."

He chuckled and pulled her back into his arms. "Forget about it. It just means we had a good time."

She smiled, tracing her finger over the Special Forces tattoo on his chest. "We did, didn't we?" She paused on the sword between the crossed arrows. "You don't regret it, do you?"

"Regret the best night of my life? No way." He put his fingers under her chin and tilted her head up. "Do you?"

"Of course not." She bent to kiss him, opened her mouth to say something, then kissed him some more before finally coming up for air again. "You know we're going to have to be careful, right? That rule the DCO has about partners not dating is stupid, but if anyone finds out, we're done."

A smile tugged at the corner of his mouth. "Necking in the hallway between training classes is out then?"

She made a face. "Landon, I'm serious."

"I know. So am I." He reached up to tuck her hair behind her ear. "No one is going to find out, Ivy. We work for the Department of Covert Ops, remember? We're good at being covert."

She laughed. She loved the way his mind worked. "Good point."

He pulled her on top of him. "Then enough about someone finding out and let's see if we can go for round two. Only this time I think I will tie you up."

―∿∿∿―

"I thought cats didn't like water," Landon said.

Ivy grinned at him from beneath the spray pouring down from the showerhead. "Well, this is one cat who has no problem getting wet."

She said things like that to purposely turn him on, didn't she? Not that it took much with her naked and wet and standing there looking like she was just begging to be fucked. His cock snapped to full attention.

He pulled her into his arms, then reached down with one hand and slipped a finger deep in her pussy. "So I noticed."

He muffled her gasp with a kiss, urging her back against the wall. He wasn't sure how many times they'd had sex last night, but he already wanted her again. And that was after making love less than an hour ago when they'd woken up around noon. It was crazy what she did to him.

He slid his hands down to cup her ass, all set to lift her up so he could bury himself in her wetness, but before he could Ivy dropped to her knees in front of him.

He liked where this was going.

Ivy placed her hands on his thighs, then leaned forward and slowly ran her tongue up his shaft from base to tip before swirling it around the head. He sucked in a breath. The feel of the water pouring over him combined with the warmth of her mouth to become one mind-blowing experience.

She looked up at him, her eyes iridescent green. That was sexy.

"Good?" she asked.

He chuckled. "Better than good. Don't stop."

She let out a soft purr. "I'm just getting started."

She bent to take him in her mouth again, but when she wrapped her lips around him this time, she moved up and down, taking him deeper and deeper with each bob of her head until he felt himself finally slide down her throat.

He let out a low groan. If she took him any deeper, he was going to lose it for sure. But she backed off before the sensation became too intense, and pressed gentle kisses to the head of his cock instead. Then, once he calmed down, she deep-throated him again, this time massaging his balls.

She established an intoxicating rhythm, sometimes licking only the head, sometimes taking him so far down her throat he thought he would explode. Then she'd do it all over again.

Oh, shit. If she kept this up, he wasn't going to last long enough to make it to her pussy. Which he wanted to do.

Landon slid his hand in her wet hair, urging her to her feet before she could deep-throat him again.

She gave him a hurt look. "Hey! I wasn't done."

He groaned. "I know, but much more of what you just did and I would be."

She grinned. "I don't have a problem with that."

"Normally I wouldn't, either, but there's something special I want to do in this shower."

Turning her around so that her back was to him, he reached around to slide his hand down her stomach into the downy curls between her legs. He found her clit and fingered it gently. Ivy rotated her hips in time with the movement, rubbing her ass against his erection. If he thought his cock was hard before, that was nothing compared to how it felt now. Ivy's ass had that power.

"Bend over," he ordered hoarsely.

She did as he told her, spreading her legs and placing her hands against the wall, giving him not only a tremendous view of her heart-shaped ass, but the pink folds of her perfect pussy, too. He wasn't sure he could even keep it together long enough to take her the way he intended. But he was sure going to try.

Grabbing her hips in both hands, he plunged into her in one thrust. She was so tight and wet he thought for sure he was going to detonate on the spot. He squeezed his eyes shut, afraid to move. Maybe if he took it nice and slow? He gave it a try but could only last a minute like this. Maybe two.

But then Ivy shoved back against him. That was his undoing.

He tightened his hold and pounded into her so hard he almost lifted her off the floor. The sound of his hips slapping her ass echoed around them like an erotic soundtrack, but the noise was quickly drowned out by Ivy's screams of pleasure.

He opened his eyes to watch her come. He loved watching her orgasm. Her face was pressed against the tiled wall, her hands spread wide to either side. She had her claws extended and was digging into the porcelain tiles like a kitty on catnip. He knew from last night that was a sure sign she was coming—and coming hard.

The knowledge that she was climaxing was all he needed to finally let go, too. Pulling her back against him, he buried his cock in her heat. His orgasm surged through him, making his legs so weak he was sure he was going to collapse to the floor of the tub.

Breathing ragged, he braced one hand on the wall and leaned forward to bury his face in the curve of Ivy's neck. He wasn't sure he could move after that. Or whether he even wanted to. But one of them was going to have to turn off the water sooner or later. They'd run the apartment complex dry if they didn't.

"The pizza guy's here."

Landon frowned but didn't lift his head. "What?"

"The pizza guy. Remember we ordered it before we came in to take a shower? He just rang the door-bell again."

He knew she had stellar hearing, but damn. How could she concentrate enough to hear that?

Landon reluctantly straightened up. Calling for pizza had seemed like a good idea when they'd rolled out of bed and had both been starving. But now that the delivery guy was at the door, he suddenly wasn't hungry anymore. Not with Ivy looking at him like she was ready for round two. When he tried to kiss her, though, she gave him a playful shove.

"Answer the door." She picked up the bottle of shower gel and squeezed some into her hand. "I promise I'll let you wash my back if you do."

Landon groaned at the mental picture of Ivy lathering herself up, white suds running down her perfect body. Dragging his gaze away from her, he quickly dried off, then went into the bedroom and grabbed his jeans. The doorbell rang again as he pulled them on.

"Keep your damn shirt on. I'm coming."

The faster he got rid of the pizza delivery guy, the faster he could get back to Ivy. He knew he had a stupid grin on his face, but he didn't care and opened the door.

And found himself face to face with Buchanan.

Shit.

The shifter was the last person Landon needed finding him at Ivy's. Even someone as thick as Buchanan could put two and two together and come up with the obvious.

Buchanan stared at him, his eyes narrowing at Landon's damp hair, bare chest, and telltale lack of shoes. "What the hell are you doing here?"

"Not that it's any of your business, but Ivy offered

to let me use her washing machine since the one in my apartment building is broken."

Damn, that was a good lie. At least he thought it was until Buchanan leaned close and sniffed.

What the fuck…?

Buchanan's nostrils flared, his eyes going from dark brown to gleaming yellow. He advanced on Landon with a snarl. "You slept with her, you bastard."

Shit.

He hated backing up, but he needed to put some space between him and Wolverine before Buchanan went crazy. "I don't know what you're talking about. I didn't—"

Buchanan growled, canines flashing. "Liar! I can smell her musk all over you."

Damn. Why the hell did the jealous wannabe boyfriend have to have such a keen sense of smell?

Maybe he could talk Buchanan down.

The shifter's claws came out.

Or maybe not.

The fight in the pugil pit showed he wasn't a match for the shifter—not without a weapon. Landon dodged Buchanan's claws and leaped over the back of the couch, hoping it would slow the shifter down long enough for him to find something to defend himself with. He should have known better. Buchanan jumped over the couch like it wasn't even there, grabbed Landon by an arm, and threw him across the room.

Landon hit the antique table Ivy had painstakingly refurbished with a resounding crash. It crushed like kindling beneath him and he fell to the floor hard. Knowing what destroying Ivy's beloved table would do to her was worse than any pain he felt, and he wanted to kill Buchanan for hurting her.

What if Buchanan turned his rage on Ivy and physically hurt her, too? The thought scared Landon.

When Buchanan came at him this time, Landon kicked the shifter's legs out from under him. He fell with a thud that should have slowed him down for at least a few seconds, but he immediately scrambled to his feet and charged.

Landon launched himself at the shifter, driving Buchanan into the wall so hard his head cracked the plaster before bouncing off. Buchanan snarled and swung at Landon, gouging four deep furrows across his chest.

Landon ground his teeth against the pain. It felt like he'd been sliced open by a piece of barbed wire.

He didn't have time to think about it, though. Buchanan was already coming at him again. Landon swore, ducking before the shifter could rip out his throat. Landon immediately retaliated, delivering a solid punch to Buchanan's jaw and following it with an elbow to the solar plexus. Unfortunately, all that did was piss off Buchanan even more. He let out a roar that shook the walls, then grabbed Landon and flung him across the room like he was a rag doll.

This time he landed on the countertop in Ivy's kitchen. The impact with the granite, not to mention the cabinet the back of his head smacked into, hurt like hell. Ignoring it, he grabbed the biggest carving knife from the block and rolled off the counter, then backed up until he was against the pantry door.

Even with the knife, Landon wasn't sure it was a fair fight. He had a weapon and skill, but Buchanan was an animal acting on pure instinct. His human side—the only part that might have made him think twice about killing—looked like it was gone. He wanted blood, and once he got it, there'd be nothing to keep him from going after Ivy next. The only way to stop the shifter was to put him down for good. Providing Buchanan didn't get him first.

The shifter barely glanced at the blade as he vaulted over the counter and advanced on Landon.

Landon shifted his weight to his back foot, ready to duck and lunge the second the shifter swiped at him with those claws. If Landon timed it right, he'd have a free shot at Buchanan's heart.

Buchanan lifted his arm, claws extended.

Landon got ready.

Shit, this was going to be bad.

Suddenly, a white blur hurtled over the counter and smacked into Buchanan, sending him crashing to the floor.

Ivy.

She landed lightly on her feet in the center of the kitchen. Dressed in a short robe, her long hair still dripping from the shower, she looked small and fragile standing between him and Buchanan.

The shifter rose to his feet, eyes blazing. Landon immediately moved to step in front of Ivy, but she kept herself between him and Buchanan. A low growl emanated from his throat. Ivy growled back, her hands whipping out to either side, her curved claws fully extended.

Buchanan snarled, lips pulled back from his fangs as he took a threatening step forward.

Landon reached for Ivy so he could pull her out of harm's way, but the sound she unleashed stopped him in his tracks. Half human cry of rage and half pure cat hiss, it was unlike anything he'd ever heard in his life. It stopped Buchanan, too. It probably would have stopped a charging bull.

The fury disappeared from Buchanan's face, his claws retracted, his eyes returned to their normal color.

Landon moved to stand beside Ivy, but she put her hand on his chest, keeping him where he was. That was when he realized her feline scream wasn't the only thing that had shocked Buchanan back to his senses. Her face was a mask of rage, her eyes pure green, her fangs long and glistening. And that rage was aimed squarely at the man in front of her.

She glanced at Landon, let out a sound that was half snarl, half plea as she nudged him back. Don't get between her and Buchanan. Period.

He gave her a nod but didn't step back. The threat from Buchanan might have passed, but he still wasn't going to let her stand up to the shifter alone.

Buchanan stared at her in shock, taking in her protective stance as well as the sharp claws that were still extended and ready as if he couldn't quite believe what he was seeing.

"My God, Ivy. I can smell him all over you. Do you have any idea what that does to me?" The shifter's voice was filled with pain. Unfortunately, Landon couldn't seem to summon any pity for him. "How could you sleep with him?"

Landon ground his jaw. He wanted to tell Buchanan who Ivy slept with was none of his damn business, but that would only start another fight.

"I slept with him because I…" She broke off, her

voice throaty and rough. "Why I slept with him is none of your business, Clayne. I can see I hurt you, and I'm sorry. But who I sleep with is my choice."

He let out a low growl. "What about us?"

Ivy cut him off with a hiss. "There is no us. Not like that. There never was. I made that clear to you over and over, but you wouldn't listen. We're friends. And if you still value that friendship, you'll respect my decision."

Buchanan regarded her in silence for a long time, then turned without another word and stormed out.

Ivy sighed, the sound loud in the suddenly quiet apartment. Landon set the knife down on the counter and gently touched her arm.

"Hey. You okay?"

She turned to face him. Her claws were in, her eyes were back to their normal color, and her fangs were gone. She was definitely far from being back to normal, though. She was hurting, he could see it on her face.

"I'm sorry," he said.

She reached up to cup his cheek. Her hand was warm and gentle. "You have nothing to be sorry about. That fight with Clayne has been coming for a long time. You just happened to be the final straw."

"But I can still be sorry I was that last straw. And I'm sorry about your table."

She made a face. "Forget about the table. I'm glad he didn't hurt you."

"It'd take a lot more than razor-sharp claws and fangs the size of railroad spikes to hurt me." The joke wasn't as funny when he said it out loud. "Ivy, you and Buchanan were friends for a long time. I didn't mean to come between that."

"He came between that, not you. What's done is done, and I wouldn't have acted any differently if I had it to do over again."

He caught the hand she was resting on his cheek and pressed it to his lips. "I'd rather you promise me you'll never do anything as crazy as jumping between me and a psycho like Buchanan again."

"That's a promise I can't make. If someone or something I care about is in danger, nothing will stop me from protecting them."

"Protective I understand. Just temper it with a little caution, okay? I thought Buchanan was going to hurt you."

"I was more worried about what he was going to do to you." The corner of her mouth curved into a rueful smile. "Besides, it's not like I had a choice about putting myself between you and him. When I ran out and saw you two fighting—not just fighting, but ready to kill each other this time—I zoned out again like I did in South America."

"I thought we talked about you trying to control that instinct, so that didn't happen again."

"I know. But keeping my animal side in check takes a lot of control, and I lost that when I saw Clayne was about to rip out your throat. I would have killed him if it meant protecting you. I'll do anything to protect the people who are important to me."

Landon didn't even want to think about Ivy fighting Buchanan. He brushed her damp hair back from her face. "Can you at least let me know when your shifter side feels like it's going to take over so I can be prepared? If for no other reason than to protect you from yourself."

She nodded a little too quickly, as if she was agreeing simply to placate him. But she started fussing over the scratches on his chest before he could call her on it. She wet a dishtowel with water and gently dabbed at the wounds, carefully washing away the blood.

"Damn him. The last claw marks hadn't even started to heal yet."

Landon looked down at his chest. After the initial pain, he hadn't thought much about the scratches, but now he saw they crossed over the ones Buchanan had given him in the pugil pit a few days ago. The new set was deeper, but nothing that wouldn't heal on their own.

"But they'll leave scars," Ivy protested when he said as much.

"I've gotten worse." He grinned. "Besides, these will be a reminder of what I had to go through to earn your affection."

She rolled her eyes. "Sweet talker."

He chuckled and bent to kiss her. He slid his hand in her hair, cupping the back of her head, and suddenly remembered that shower they were going to finish. Unfortunately, it was going to have to wait a little longer. He reluctantly lifted his head.

"Do you think Buchanan will tell the DCO about us?"

Ivy's face was thoughtful as she ran her fingers over the claw marks on his chest. "I hope not, but I honestly don't know. I want to believe Clayne wouldn't deliberately hurt me like that, but after what he did today, I realize I don't know him nearly as well as I thought."

He tilted up her chin. "Whatever happens, we'll deal with it."

Behind them, someone knocked on the door. Landon forgot Buchanan had left it open.

He jerked his head up to see a teenager standing in the doorway, a red warming bag in his hand. The kid's gaze went wide as he took in the destruction in front of him.

"Um, you the ones who ordered the large, double meat pizza?"

He'd forgotten about the pizza, too.

Ivy slid her arms from around Landon's neck. "Yup, that's us."

Reaching around, she pulled the wallet out of his back pocket, then walked over to the door. Thanks to the scuffle with Buchanan, the top of her robe had come a little undone and was gaping open slightly. The teenage boy's eyes went wide as he realized she wasn't wearing anything underneath, but he kept his cool long enough to take the cash and pull the pizza box out of the bag and hand it to her.

He swept the apartment again, his gaze lingering on the demolished dining room table before going to the hole in the wall. Brow furrowing, he looked pointedly at the scratches on Landon's chest, then at Ivy.

"Um, everything okay?"

She cracked the lid on the pizza box to make sure the kid had gotten the order right. "We were renovating the dining room and decided to stop and have sex."

The kid's eyes practically bulged out of his head. He looked around the room again, surveying the damage in a whole new light. No doubt he was wondering how much of it had come from the renovation and how much from the sex.

Realizing Ivy was waiting for him to leave so she could close the door, the kid turned to go. Then he stopped to eye the four deep scratches slashed across Landon's chest again. Landon waited for him to ask how they got there, but the kid must have a good imagination because he grinned at Landon and said, "Dude!" before giving him a thumbs-up and walking out.

Ivy laughed as she sauntered into the kitchen. "That was bad of me, wasn't it?"

Taking the pizza box from her hand, Landon set it on the counter. He then pulled her close by the belt of her robe, which made it fall open a bit more. "Yeah it was. But that's okay. I like when you're bad."

Chapter 13

"HAVE YOU SEEN CLAYNE THIS MORNING?"

Kendra looked up from her computer as Ivy perched on the edge of the desk. "Earlier. Why?"

Ivy sipped her coffee, trying to look as casual as she could. "Just wondered if you saw him talk to John. Or Dick."

Since no one had raked her and Landon over the coals when they'd gotten to work, she didn't think so. But she'd relax a lot easier if she were sure.

Kendra frowned. "What the hell would he talk to Dick for? He hates Dick."

"I don't know. I was just wondering." She took another sip. "Do you know if Clayne's around?"

"He bailed in a pissed-off mood. He only came in long enough to tell me he was taking leave." She pushed her reading glasses up on her head and sat back in her chair. "When I asked him where he was going, he practically bit my head off. I have no idea what's with him."

Ivy looked away before Kendra could read anything on her face.

Kendra bolted upright. "Wait a minute. You know something, don't you? That's why you want to talk to him. Okay, spill it."

She should have known she couldn't hide anything from Kendra.

"Clayne came over yesterday and found Landon at my place."

"So?" Kendra's eyes went wide. "No way. You and Landon...?"

Ivy nodded.

Kendra grinned. "It's about time."

"Well, Clayne doesn't share your enthusiasm, and now I'm afraid he's so pissed off he'll tell John—or worse, Dick—just to get us split up."

Kendra shook her head. "Clayne wouldn't do something like that."

"You didn't see how angry he was when he realized what was going on. He and Landon got into this huge fight. They came close to killing each other."

"You're not serious."

Ivy nodded. "I ended up siding with Landon to end it."

She didn't mention she would have fought Clayne to the death to protect Landon if she had to. She was still freaked out by that. Having sex with Landon hadn't gotten him out of her system. It made her want him even more.

"Which must have infuriated Clayne." Kendra nodded.

Ivy nodded. "Now, I'm worried he's going to destroy both our careers to get back at us."

The phone on Kendra's desk rang. She answered it, had a cryptic conversation with whoever was on the other end of the line, then hung up.

"That was John. He wants you and Landon in the main conference room. The guy you apprehended in New York finally talked." When Ivy moved to get up, she grabbed her arm. "Don't worry. I'll find Clayne and get him to calm down. I'll make sure I get through to him."

Ivy hoped so, but she wasn't going to hold her breath.

Landon was already in the conference room when she walked in. They'd ridden the Metro together that morning but came into work separately, so they wouldn't raise any eyebrows.

She yawned as she sat down across from him. They'd stayed up most of the night repairing the damage to her apartment. The hole Landon and Clayne had put in the wall was easy to fix. So was replacing the chandelier. However, her beautiful antique dining room table was history. There wasn't enough glue in the northeast to put that poor thing back together. Landon swore he'd find her one that was as close as possible to the one he'd help demolish. She didn't have the heart to tell him not to bother. It had been a once-in-a-lifetime find. But then, so was he.

Which was why she'd felt the need to show her appreciation for all his hard work when they'd finally stumbled into bed at two in the morning. That had kept them up for another hour, but it had been worth every sleepless moment.

Ivy was about to tell him about Clayne taking leave when John walked in. His face looked haggard, like he hadn't gotten much more sleep than they had.

"The man you apprehended in New York disclosed Stutmeir's location." He set down a folder on the table. "As of a few days ago, Stutmeir was holding the medical experts in a private mountain lodge located in the Cascades in Washington State, north of Chelan. Unfortunately, the guy has no idea what Stutmeir's doing with these doctors and scientists. Apparently, that kind of information is reserved for Stutmeir's inner ring of soldiers. As it turns out, you picked the least informed of the two men to capture. He wasn't much more than a driver."

"Next time we'll make sure to ask for a résumé first," Landon said dryly.

Ivy picked up her mug. "Do you believe the guy?"

"Trust me, he wasn't of a mind to tell any lies at that point." John's face was grim. "All he knows is that they were supposed to kidnap Bosch and bring him to the ski lodge."

Landon took a swallow of coffee. "What do we know about the place?"

"At the moment, not much." John sighed. "It was built to be a ski resort just after World War II, but apparently that didn't exactly thrive. So, in the early fifties, it was picked up by a doomsday group sure the USSR was going to launch nuclear missiles at the United States. Since then, it's gone through several hands and is currently owned by a software company out of Seattle that uses it as a private retreat for its board members. We found some brochures from the last time the place was used as a ski resort, but that was back in the eighties." He opened the folder and slid two brochures across the table. "They only show enough to tell you it's a big stone structure with a lot of rooms, built into the side of a mountain ridge. The satellite imagery we have of the area doesn't show much either. It's heavily wooded and the mountain peaks keep it shrouded in cloud cover during most of the year."

Landon looked up from the brochure. "You're

kidding? I can get detailed satellite pictures of any mud hut in Afghanistan I want, but getting a clean shot of a place right here in the good old US of A is asking too much?"

"Take it up with the intel branch."

"What about the company that owns it?" Landon asked. "Any connection to Stutmeir?"

"None that we found. He's most likely using the lodge without their knowledge."

Ivy flipped the brochure over to read the back. Two ski bunnies with eighties big hair stood in front of the ski lodge, smiling brilliantly for the camera. "Have we considered the possibility Stutmeir chose the place because he knows we're closing in on him?"

"We thought of that, yes, and I don't think so. The timeline suggests Stutmeir already moved to the lodge before anyone in the U.S. was even aware of his presence. The guy we interrogated said Stutmeir never stayed in one place more than a month or so until he got to the lodge. Whatever weapon he's making, he's almost certainly making it there."

"So you need us to get in there and snoop around?" Landon asked.

"Yes. And fast. We have the preliminary report back from the CDC on those bodies you found in Atlanta, and they're completely stumped. They have no idea what killed those people. Or more precisely, what killed them first. Every one of the victims shows signs of massive heart failure, severe brain damage, organ failure, tearing of all the major muscle groups, even broken bones. We have to find out what Stutmeir is brewing up there. The last thing we need is this getting into al-Qaeda hands."

Ivy didn't even want to imagine something like that happening. "Were we able to identify any of the victims?"

John frowned. "Most of them were homeless veterans. We were able to ID them by DOD dental records. We're still working on the others."

Damn, she didn't know what bothered her more—that Stutmeir had experimented on homeless veterans or that there were homeless veterans in the U.S. in the first place. "Please tell me we're going in as part of a larger team," Ivy said.

John gave her an apologetic look. "As much as I wish I could give you backup, right now I can't. We have about fifteen scientists we're still covering just in case Stutmeir tries to grab someone to replace Bosch."

Landon shrugged. "So put the FBI on the protective details."

"If I wasn't confident you two could handle the recon on your own, I'd consider it." John exhaled loudly. "Look, I know it's not the answer you want to hear, but until we can confirm Stutmeir is in that lodge, I can't pull any of the other teams. The people up on the Hill can't make a decision until the threat is ready to smack them in the face."

The muscle in Landon's jaw worked, but he didn't say anything. Ivy knew what he was thinking. She was thinking it, too. She didn't like the idea of going in there without backup.

"Isn't Tate's team in that area?" she asked.

"At last contact, two weeks ago, they were more than a hundred miles south of there."

"Two weeks ago?" Alarm bells went off in Ivy's head. "They haven't checked in since then?"

"No, but there's nothing to be worried about. They confirmed the person who killed those hikers is a shifter, and they're tracking him. He's turned out to be more difficult to apprehend than they thought. Tate said they were going to be deep in the mountains and that contact would be sporadic. I'm sure they're fine."

Then why did John look so concerned?

"Okay." John's favorite word when he wanted to end a conversation and move on. "Once you two get to the lodge and confirm Stutmeir is there, I'll be free to pull the other teams and send them in to back you up. Whatever you do, don't take any unnecessary risks. Understood?"

"Hooah." Landon's favorite word for most everything. Ivy was pretty sure he'd even said it after she'd given him a blow job during their marathon sack session. Though it had come out much raspier. "When do we leave?"

"Right after you pack," John said. "Kendra already has you on an afternoon flight to Seattle. You'll have everything you need to outfit an entire attack team, including weapons, ammo, and explosives. It's already been prepositioned in a storage unit outside of Seattle. You'll be ready to hit the ground running as soon as you get there."

Ivy groaned. So much for talking some sense into Clayne before they left.

It took her and Landon more than three hours to get from Sea-Tac Airport to Chelan. That included the short stop at the self-storage facility to pick up weapons and any other equipment they thought they'd need. John hadn't been kidding. There'd been enough stuff in the unit to start a war. Hopefully, they wouldn't have to use all of it.

As Landon drove, Ivy looked up at the snow-capped mountains surrounding them. They were absolutely breathtaking. "I had no idea it was so beautiful out here."

"You've never been here?"

"No. Have you?"

"The team came out to Fort Lewis for training a few times. We got lucky enough to have some downtime to go hiking and mountain climbing."

"You shouldn't have mentioned that part about the hiking. Now I'm officially jealous."

Landon chuckled. "After this op, we should come back." He gave her a sidelong glance. "Do some hiking. Check out Seattle. Go whale watching and stuff."

She smiled. "I'd like that."

The thought of coming back here—or going anywhere with Landon—made her heart backflip. She'd shied away from relationships for so long, she almost forgot what it was like to do the things normal people did. Being with a man who knew what she was and accepted her—claws and all—was something she'd given up on. Until now.

"Which trail is closest to the lodge on that map we bought?" Landon asked.

Ivy spread out the map on her lap so she could read it easier. "It looks like Cutthroat Pass is going to be our best bet. We can head off the trail about ten miles in, which'll probably put us at the lodge by nightfall."

When they got to the trailhead, Landon double-checked their packs to make sure they had everything they'd need while she stowed their wallets, IDs, and cell

phones under the seats. They left a note on the dash saying which trail they'd taken and when they'd be back.
There were similar notes on the other vehicles, only in
their case, the info was bogus. It'd keep the park service
from getting curious if they noticed the Jeep sitting unat-
tended for a day or two.

Despite the other cars around, she and Landon didn't
run into any other hikers on the trail. Ivy inhaled deeply,
letting the scent of pine fill her nose. When she'd been
at the FBI field office in Anchorage, she spent almost all
of her free time hiking. That was harder to do now that
she lived in DC, but as the fir and spruce trees closed in
around them, she remembered what she'd loved about it.

Ten miles in, she and Landon left the trail and headed
cross-country. The landscape was rougher, which slowed
them down, but since they couldn't do any recon until
after dark anyway, that wasn't a problem.

Ivy glanced over her shoulder at Landon. "I'm going
to check in with Kendra."

Unfortunately, the mountains were playing havoc
with the signal of the satellite phone, so it was fifteen
minutes before she finally got through.

"That happened with Tate, too," Kendra said when
Ivy mentioned it.

"So John said. If we lose contact, don't freak out. It
probably means we don't have a signal."

"Just be careful. I saw the photos of what Stutmeir
did to those bodies in Atlanta. I'm going to have night-
mares for a week."

"We'll be careful." Ivy chewed on her lower lip.
"Have you talked to Clayne yet?"

Kendra sighed into the phone. "Not yet. But I've

left a message on his cell every hour on the hour to call me. When he does, I'll talk him down. Don't worry about it."

Easy for her to say. Kendra's life wasn't about to blow up in her face. Ivy sighed as she put the phone in her pack.

Landon handed her an energy bar. "Problem?"

"Clayne is still MIA."

"Good. That means he can't rat us out."

She tore open the paper and bit into the energy bar savagely. "Just because he hasn't said anything to John yet doesn't mean he won't."

"It's his word against ours, Ivy."

She chewed slowly. "This isn't a court of law. The allegations will be enough. If the DCO splits us up, I'm handing in my resignation. I won't work with another partner who doesn't trust or respect me. Been there, done that, and I won't do it again."

He didn't say anything.

"What about you? Will you go back to Special Forces?"

"Unless you don't want me to."

She hadn't thought about him going back to the army because she didn't have any reason to. Now that getting fired from the DCO was a real possibility, it made sense he'd go back to his former career. The idea of him putting himself in harm's way on a daily basis over in Afghanistan terrified her so much she could barely breathe. But how could she ask him to give up something he loved?

"I don't know how to answer that, Landon." This was so not the time—or the place—to be having this conversation. "I know how important the army is to you."

He reached out to gently push back the hair that had come loose from her braid. "You're important to me, Ivy. If I went back into Special Forces, I'd be gone more than I'd be home. That kind of life is hard on a relationship. Trust me, I know."

Hearing him say how much she meant to him did funny things to her heart. If they weren't in the middle of a mission, she would have jumped into his arms and kissed him until neither one of them could see straight. But they were talking about his career here.

"It's not fair of me to ask that of you, Landon."

"You're not asking. I'm offering." He cupped her cheek. "Being partners outside the DCO works the same as it does on the inside. We don't do things or make decisions without talking to the other person first. If you don't want me going back into Special Forces, I won't. As long as we're together, you come first. We'll just figure out where we go from the DCO."

Her breath caught as she finally figured out what the funny feeling in her heart meant. She was crazy in love with Landon. She'd started falling for him that first day when he'd saved her from falling on the confidence course and hadn't stopped since, no matter how hard she'd tried to fight it.

Was it a shifter thing? Did her animal side somehow recognize him as her perfect mate? What other explanation did she have for falling in love with a man she'd known less than a month?

Unless this wasn't love at all. What if it were simply another side effect of being in heat? The idea that the things she felt for Landon might be purely the result of feline hormones made her want to cry.

She might have given in to tears if Landon's mouth hadn't closed over hers. The kiss was thorough and possessive, claiming her mind, body, and soul, and when he lifted his head, it took her a minute to remember where she was, much less what she'd been going to say.

"We'd better get moving." Landon's voice was low and rough. "It'll be dark soon."

Ivy reached for him when he pulled away, then stopped herself. She needed to know the things she felt for him were real before she said anything.

Resigning his commission was something Landon never thought he'd do in a million years. But he'd give it up in a heartbeat if Ivy asked him to. *Because* she would never ask him to. He'd had exactly four girlfriends since joining the army (not counting Erica) and every one of them had tried to get him to quit the military. He'd told all of them the same thing—hell no. As expected, they'd walked out. It had hurt, sure, but he'd gotten over it. If Ivy walked out of his life, it would leave a hole not even his career in Special Forces could fill. Which was why he was going to do everything he could not to let that happen.

But he'd worry about that after taking down Stutmeir.

Landon swore as he took in the massive stone structure. As evil lairs went, the lodge was intimidating. Eight stories high and built into the side of the mountain, it looked like a fortress. The perfect place to film a World War II movie.

He scanned the top of the high wall that surrounded the building on three sides. It was wide enough to serve as a walkway, but no one was prowling around up there. Why would they? It wasn't like they were expecting him and Ivy. He hoped.

He jerked his head at the mountain. "What do you think about climbing that? It'd give us a great view of the grounds."

Ivy chewed on her lip as she considered it. Her green eyes were bright in his NVGs. "I don't know. The stone up there looks really loose. If we try to climb it, we could start a rockslide."

Which would be a dead giveaway to anyone inside the lodge that someone was there.

"Plan B, then," he said. "We hike back into the hills to see if we can get a look over the wall."

He followed her up the slope, stopping when she did. It didn't give them the kind of view the mountainside would have, but it was safer.

There was only one way in and out of the property, a set of wrought-iron gates wide enough to accommodate a tractor trailer. A flash of movement caught his eye and he shifted his gaze to see two men standing off to the side. One was leaning back against the wall, a cigarette casually dangling from his fingers. The other held a Styrofoam cup in his hand. Landon narrowed his eyes, searching for signs of a weapon on either man, but he couldn't see any.

"Do you think those are Stutmeir's men?" Ivy asked.

"Neither of them are carrying weapons, so it's hard to say. They could work for the company that owns the lodge and be up here on some kind of retreat."

He took the night vision scope from his pack and slewed it from one end of the lodge to the other, hoping to see Stutmeir through the windows.

"Anything?" Ivy asked.

Landon shook his head. "The only way to be sure is to get inside and look around." He looked at her. "You up for that?"

"If you are."

They didn't have much choice. John wanted confirmation Stutmeir was there and what the situation was. That meant going in.

Landon handed her the scope and jerked his chin at the part of the building he'd scanned earlier. "That side of the lodge looks deserted."

She put the scope to her eye, then frowned. "If Stutmeir's here, wouldn't he have guards patrolling the property?"

"You'd think so. It seems sloppy for someone with his reputation. Your kitty cat senses telling you anything?"

Ivy shook her head. "Not much. There's a background hum that's always there in situations like this, but it doesn't seem like there's any serious danger." She lowered the scope. "Maybe Stutmeir doesn't have enough men to cover the scientists he's holding prisoner and guard the property."

He snorted. "We should be so lucky."

Landon put the scope away, double-checked to make sure he had everything he needed in his tactical vest, then hid both their packs under the thickest foliage he could find. The plan was simple—get in, recon the situation, and then get out without being seen. After that, they'd call in the cavalry.

Piece of cake.

Chapter 14

THE WALL WASN'T HARD FOR IVY TO CLIMB. AT THE TOP, she cautiously peeked over to make sure no one was around, then leaped over the railing and motioned for Landon to follow. The plan had been for her to lower a rope down to him, but the roughly stacked stone had cracks and crevices large enough for him to use as handholds, so he could climb it as easily as she could. When he got to the top, he stretched out on his stomach beside her.

"Still no sign of anyone," she whispered.

Even the two guys who'd been outside had gone back in. Ivy chewed on her lip thoughtfully as she surveyed the lodge. The place was dark except for a few lights on the first floor. That was good for her and Landon.

She glanced at him. "I don't see anyone on the top floors. If we can find a way in from up here, we won't have to climb down into the courtyard."

He pointed. "It looks like the wall meets up with the top floor. Even if it doesn't go all the way, it'll at least get us close enough to access one of the windows."

Fortunately, the wall went all the way to the building. Unfortunately, the door at the end was locked.

Landon shifted impatiently behind her as she picked the lock. No doubt he would have preferred to kick in the door, but that'd get them a lot of unwanted attention. The lock was unsophisticated, so he didn't have to wait long for her to pick it.

Making sure Landon was ready to cover her, Ivy took out her SIG 9mm and cautiously opened the door.

Ivy expected the inside of the lodge to be as cold and unappealing as its rough-hewn exterior, but though the interior was rather dark, it was still obvious the place was intended to be warm and inviting. The atrium that extended all the way from the ground floor to their level probably had a lot to do with that. Thankfully, the place seemed to be deserted—at least the level they were on.

She walked over to the railing separating the walkway around the top level from the open-air atrium and looked down. She didn't see anyone all the way to the ground floor. There was a dim glow coming from a hallway down there, though. That must have been the lights she and Landon had seen from outside. She strained her ears but didn't hear anything.

Landon jerked his head toward the far end of the floor. "The stairs are over there."

As she turned to follow, a blood-curdling scream echoed off the walls. It was followed by a long, drawn-out howl that turned into a deep-throated roar before finally tapering off and leaving an eerie silence.

Ivy spun around, every hair on her body standing on end. Her fangs elongated. Her claws came out. Her animal instincts screamed at her to run and hide at the same time they demanded she attack and kill. The classic fight or flight response, only a hundred times more powerful, and it made her entire body tremble with the need to do something.

"What the hell was that?" Landon's question was a hoarse whisper.

She didn't answer. There was only one thing in the world that could make a sound like that.

"Ivy?" Landon put his hand on her arm and turned her to face him. "What is it?"

She bit back a growl. "A shifter."

The shifter roared again, the sound lower and filled with unimaginable pain. Ivy's stomach churned. What was happening to him?

The fight or flight response hit her again even harder than before, and this time she couldn't ignore it. Unable to stop herself, she pulled out of Landon's grasp and vaulted over the railing to the atrium five floors below. The fall brought her to her knees and knocked the breath from her lungs, but she barely noticed as she jumped up and raced toward the screams.

Landon shouted into her earpiece, telling her to wait, but she barely registered his voice. She wanted to stop but couldn't. Nothing mattered but finding the shifter and helping him.

She let her feline senses take over and lead her through the maze of hallways and down two flights of stairs to a door that stood ajar. The air coming from the room beyond was filled with the scent of blood, pain, and terror so strong it almost made her cry.

She slowed her steps, nostrils flaring as she neared the partially open door. She'd thought she smelled one shifter, but now she realized there was more than one. A lot more. Ten, maybe fifteen.

Were they all being tortured? Growling low in her throat, Ivy moved forward, her hands working as she imagined rending the flesh of whoever was hurting one of her kind. It was only then she remembered she was holding a weapon. She almost didn't recognize it. Tightening her grip on the pistol, she pushed open the door.

Unlike the hallway, the room was brightly lit, and she blinked as it momentarily blinded her. When she could see again, she discovered she was in some sort of make-shift medical clinic terrifyingly similar to the one in the warehouse in Atlanta. Except this one wasn't empty.

A group of men were clustered around one of the beds, their backs to her. A shifter was strapped down to the bed, a heart rate monitor and a bunch of other things she didn't recognize hooked to his naked chest. She cringed as his body contorted in obvious pain. His claws and fangs came out and went back in over and over as if he couldn't quite complete the change. After one more gut-wrenching howl, he stiffened, then went still, his body limp.

The men murmured something among themselves, but Ivy didn't hear it. She was too busy trying to figure out which of them was responsible for the shifter's death so she could tear him to pieces first.

She tensed, ready to launch herself at them when the shifter bolted upright, breaking the straps securing his wrists to the bed as if they were tissue paper. He flexed his fingers, studying his claws as if he'd never seen them before. They didn't hold his interest for long as his nose picked up a scent. He jerked his head up to look at her, his eyes glowing red.

Ivy took an involuntary step back, shock breaking the control her feline side had wrestled from her. Rational thought slowly returned as she looked at the…thing on the bed. Shifters didn't have red eyes. Not normal shifters anyway.

Alerted to her presence, the men surrounding the bed spun around to look in her direction. She was stunned to see that most of them were the same red-eyed kind of shifter that was sitting on the bed. They smelled like shifters, but there was something off about them. She didn't know quite what it was, but the way their eyes blazed with excitement and hunger scared her.

That fear broke the final hold her feline half had on her. Perversely, she'd finally stumbled on a way to break herself out of the shifter zone when it took over—fear. But right now, she couldn't let that emotion take charge, either. Something was incredibly wrong here.

Stutmeir wasn't making a bioweapon in this mountain retreat—he never had been. He was making something far more terrifying.

She had to warn Landon.

"I'll be damned. That's her—the one I told you about."

Ivy recognized the man's voice but couldn't remember from where. She was still trying to wrap her head around what Stutmeir was doing.

"Take her alive," another man ordered.

Instinct took over again, only this time, the instinctive action came from years of training, and Ivy was the one in control. Lifting her weapon, she fired off what she hoped were enough shots to slow down the shifters, then turned and ran.

They followed immediately, growling like rabid dogs as they chased after her. She fired her pistol behind her, but either her aim was worse than she thought or they were bulletproof because not a single one went down.

She made it to the second set of stairs when she felt a stinging pain in her leg, then another in her back. She winced and glanced down, expecting to see blood spurting from a bullet wound, but instead there was a dart sticking out of her leg.

Tranquilizers.

She pulled them out and kept running, speeding up as she raced toward the atrium. "Landon!"

"Ivy!" Landon's voice was breathless in her ear. "Shit. I heard gunshots. Where the hell—?"

"Listen to me!" She didn't know how much time she had until she lost consciousness, and she needed to get as much information to Landon as she could. "Stutmeir's not making a bioweapon. He's making shifters. They've already hit me with tranquilizers. Get out of here while you can."

"I'm not going anywhere without you!"

"You have to. Someone has to warn the DCO." She'd made it to the first floor and began weaving her way through the maze of hallways. "I'll be right behind you."

She was almost to the atrium when the drugs she'd been hit with kicked in and she was suddenly light-headed. Ten feet later, it felt like her feet had turned to lead. Within ten more feet, she was on her knees, her muscles refusing to follow her orders anymore. As she collapsed, she caught a glimpse of tall windows with velvet drapes and realized she was in the atrium.

Somewhere above her, Landon swore.

She lifted her head. He was swinging his legs over the railing, preparing to jump down from the second floor so he could come to her rescue like he had so many times before. The thought of what those *things* in there would do to him made her eyes fill with tears.

"Landon, no!" she screamed at him. "Run. Get out of here. They're coming."

Gunfire came from the hallway behind her, drowning her words. Landon threw himself backward over the railing onto the second-floor walkway to immediately return fire. She thought she heard bodies hit the floor, but she wasn't sure. Those things were fast—faster than she was maybe—and they didn't go down easy. No one had ordered them to take Landon alive, either, so they were riddling the whole second floor with hundreds of rounds.

Her arms gave out and she felt her upper body hit the floor. She tried to lift her head again so she could see Landon one more time before the drugs took their full effect, but it was no good. Hands clawed at her, dragging her across the floor, and she knew it was too late. For her, at least. *Please God, don't let it be too late for Landon*.

"Run, babe," she begged. "Please."

Then even her voice stopped working as everything went black.

—◊◊◊—

Ivy's whispered plea tore at Landon's gut. He would do anything for her, except run. Unless it was toward her. And right now, that was looking more impossible by the second.

"Hold on, Ivy." He didn't know if she could hear him over the headset or not. It didn't matter. He needed her to know he was still there. "I'm coming to get you."

He ducked behind a support column to reload.

Why had she zoned out again on him and jumped over the freaking railing? He'd immediately raced for the stairs, but when he got to the fourth floor, he discovered the stupid staircase didn't go all the way down to the ground floor like it was supposed to. He'd had to run all the way along the concourse to the other end of the lodge to get to the stairs down to the third floor, then do the same thing to get to the second floor.

Slamming a magazine into place, he turned and emptied all thirty rounds into the swarm of shifters descending on Ivy. He might as well have been pelting them with spitballs for all the good it did. Some went down, but not many. The damn things were bulletproof.

He ducked behind the support column to reload, then stuck his head out for a quick look. In the atrium, one of the shifters picked Ivy up and slung her over his shoulder, then turned and ran back in the direction he'd come. They'd gone to great lengths to take Ivy alive, and that gave him hope. He still had time to rescue her. He just had to find a way to get through the pack of ravening beasts looking to put a hole in him.

He wasn't only taking fire from the shifters in the atrium. Two shifters were shooting at him from the stairwell leading down to the first floor, while two others pumped out rounds from the stairwell leading up to the third floor. He put half his magazine into one stairwell, then emptied what was left into the other.

He had to get to a place where he could both defend himself and put some of these creatures down for good. To do that, he'd have to abandon Ivy. At least for right now. He'd rather cut his right arm off than do that. But jumping over the railing into a pack of bloodthirsty shifters was only going to get him killed. Ivy needed him alive.

Landon grabbed his fourth—and last—magazine and

jammed it into his M4. There was no way that was going to be enough firepower to take down an entire lodge of shifters. He snatched the single grenade attached to his vest and pulled the pin. It was tempting to throw it into the atrium and blow the shifters down there to kingdom come so he could rescue Ivy, but without any backup ammo, he'd be toast. And Ivy would still be in trouble. He needed to clear his exit route, get to the packs he'd hidden in the forest and load up on extra ammo, then get back here as fast as he could. When he did, he was going to kill every single creature that stood between him and Ivy. First, though, he had to clear out the shifters in the stairwell. Trouble was they were too fast and could pick up the grenade and throw it back at him before it went off. He'd have to hold it for a few seconds before he threw it. Doing that was dangerous, but it was a risk he had to take.

He pulled the pin and counted to three, then tossed it along the concourse toward the stairwell. It went off two seconds later. The blast shook the floor, stunning the shifters in the atrium as well as the ones on the steps, and they stopped shooting momentarily.

Landon was up and running for the third-floor stairwell before anyone could start shooting. The grenade hadn't done as much damage to the two shifters blocking the steps as he'd hoped, and he paused just long enough to shoot both of them in the head before running for the stairs.

He made it up to the fifth floor and onto the wall before he heard someone behind him. That was fine. He didn't need a huge head start, just enough to get to the forest before they caught up with him. He knew where he was going—they didn't. That meant they'd have to waste time tracking him once they entered the woods.

When he reached the section of wall where he and Ivy had climbed up, he started thinking he may have underestimated the shifters' speed. Half a dozen of them were on the wall and headed his way, guns blazing. As if that weren't bad enough, he started taking fire from somewhere below the wall, too.

Swearing, he turned and put a few rounds into the shifters coming at him along the wall. Landon was sure he hit at least four of them, but only one went down.

Dropping to his stomach, he slid his feet over the edge of the wall. He climbed down the first few feet, then dropped the last ten. He hit the ground and rolled, making sure to take a second to put a few more bullets into the wall up near the edge before taking off into the forest. That might discourage the bastards from climbing down right away.

It didn't.

The shifters jumped down from the wall, hitting the ground so hard it vibrated under Landon's feet. And that theory about them having to waste time tracking him through the woods? He'd been wrong about that, too. They followed like hounds on a scent, which he supposed was an apt description.

Running through the woods while wearing NVGs was never a fun event—the lack of depth perception was difficult—but it was even worse when someone was shooting at you. Trying to focus on where his feet were landing at the same time he was worried about taking a bullet in the back didn't give him a lot of speed.

Luckily, the shifters were horrible shots. If he wasn't

in a heavily forested area, he might have been dead already. The trees around him were taking a lot of punishment, that was for sure. Sooner or later, the bastards would get lucky and hit him.

He returned fire as accurately as he could while on the run. He was pretty sure he hit a few of them, but not before they rerouted him away from where the backpacks of ammo were waiting. Then he felt a sickening sensation—the bolt on his M4 locked to the rear because there were no more cartridges in the magazine.

Knowing the shifters would figure out he was empty pretty quick, Landon turned and ran. He didn't want to think about it, but for the moment at least, his plans had changed. Now, he wasn't trying to get to his ammo and then to Ivy. Now, he was trying to stay alive for the next five minutes until he could think of a better plan.

Behind him, the pack of shifters howled. Landon threw a quick glance over his shoulder. They were gaining on him. He looked around for someplace—anyplace—he could use to set a trap. If he could take out the first shifter that caught up with him, he could grab the guy's weapon. It was a long shot, but it was all he had.

Landon was so focused on what he was looking for he didn't realize the forest had opened up in front of him until he was standing in a patch of moonlight. The ground around him erupted in a shower of dirt and rocks as the shifters immediately zeroed in on his location. A bullet ripped into his vest, grazing his shoulder, and he winced. He tried to run, twist, do something to find cover. But suddenly the ground disappeared from underneath him and he was falling.

A cliff.

Shit.

What the hell would happen to Ivy if he didn't make it?

———ᴍᴍ———

It felt like someone was driving a spike into her head. Either that, or a red-hot poker. Regardless, *ouch*.

Ivy opened her eyes and found herself staring up at fluorescent lights. The brightness only made her head hurt worse, and she squeezed her eyes shut as the room suddenly started spinning. She was going to throw up.

She tried to turn over so she wouldn't get sick all over herself, but something held her down at the wrists and ankles. Everything came rushing back—the red-eyed shifters, Stutmeir, the tranquilizer darts…Landon. She prayed more than anything he'd gotten away. She didn't care what happened to her as long as he was safe.

She opened her eyes again, more slowly this time. She squinted up at the light, waiting for another wave of dizziness to hit her. When it didn't come, she lifted her head slightly and saw that she was strapped down to the same bed as the red-eyed shifter she'd seen earlier. She was naked except for her bra and panties. Panic surged through her, making it hard to get enough air, and she forced herself to take a deep, calming breath. Freaking out wouldn't help her escape.

She lifted her head again to survey the room and was relieved to find she was alone. She wrinkled her nose at the scent of blood. It was old, as if it had been there for a while. It didn't smell like it came from a shifter. But it wasn't quite human, either.

More like a combination of the two. Like the

creatures Stutmeir had made. Suddenly, kidnapping genetic scientists and DNA experts made a lot more sense.
They'd thought the ex-Stasi was making a bioweapon,
but instead he'd been developing shifters. Why?

She'd have to worry about the answer to that question
after she got out of here.

She yanked at the leather straps around her wrists, but
they wouldn't budge. She jerked on the ones around her
ankles next. Same deal. The red-eyed shifter had made
it look so easy.

The sound of men's voices drifted in from outside the
room, and she froze.

"We can't leave now." A heavily accented man's
voice, German by the sound of it. Stutmeir, maybe?
"Not when we're on the verge of finally realizing our
goal. Last time we moved, it took weeks to get the lab
up and running again."

Lab? Ivy almost choked on a laugh. Of a mad scientist, maybe.

"Klaus is right," another man said, this time with
what Ivy thought was a French accent. "Now that we
have a naturally occurring genetic mutation to study,
there's so much we can learn. Her DNA likely holds the
secrets to allow us to overcome the rage and impulse
control issues the hybrids display."

"Which we'll study when we get to the new location,"
a second German said. Maybe this one was Stutmeir.
"Staying here is too risky."

"I don't understand why." The Frenchman again.
"The man who came with her is dead."

The second German said something about the organization that sent them having people combing the area

looking for them by tomorrow, but Ivy didn't pay attention to the rest of their conversation. She was too busy thinking about what the Frenchman said and desperately trying to convince herself she'd heard wrong.

Landon couldn't be dead. He was Special Forces. He'd been trained to survive every kind of dangerous situation that had ever been conceived and then some. He'd been to the most perilous places in the world, done things in his life that would have killed a normal man ten times over. The Frenchman wanted her to think Landon was dead so she would be more vulnerable.

Tears burned her eyes. What if the Frenchman was telling the truth? That would mean that Landon, the one man in the whole world who knew what she was and cared about her anyway, was gone.

Ivy wanted to scream and cry and tear whoever had taken Landon from her to shreds, but she didn't have the strength to move. She couldn't even seem to breathe. She was numb all over.

This was her fault. If she hadn't zoned out and jumped over that railing, none of this would have happened. Landon believed her little problem was something they could manage, something they could control, as long as they worked on it together. She'd thought so, too. But they were both wrong. And now the man she loved was dead because of her.

The light above her shimmered through her tears, and she closed her eyes. In the forest earlier, she hadn't been sure the things she'd felt for him were real, but she'd been wrong. If they hadn't been real, she wouldn't hurt so much. She loved Landon. Now, she would never get the chance to tell him.

Footsteps intruded on her misery. Part of her wanted to lie there and let them do whatever they wanted to her. Landon was gone and so was her desire to live. But then another emotion surfaced—one tied directly to her feline instincts. Yes, Landon was gone, and these were the bastards who had killed him. She owed it to Landon to get revenge on his behalf. She was going to kill Stutmeir if it was the last thing she did.

She opened her eyes to see the arms-dealer-turned-monster-maker leaning over her. His eyes were even colder and harder in person, but she refused to flinch. Even when he trailed a finger along her cheek, down her neck, and over the curve of her breast. She hissed, flashing her fangs and yanking at the restraints.

Stutmeir pulled his hand away, shock on his face. Then he grinned. "I heard stories, but you are even more remarkable than I realized."

Ivy growled. She'd enjoy ripping off his face.

Stutmeir shared a laugh with the other two men. One was the French scientist, Jean Renard. She didn't recognize the other man, but he must be the German they'd been talking to, Klaus.

"Well, she might be a natural-born shifter, but she acts just like all the rest of them." Stutmeir smirked as he turned to leave. "Feel free to conduct as much research as you want. You'll have at least five or six hours until we move."

Research? Her heart froze. What the hell were they planning to do with her?

She got the answer to that a few minutes later. Or maybe it was hours. Without any clock, she wasn't sure. She tried to ignore what they were doing, but the humiliation of being treated like a lab experiment made that difficult. Not to mention the incredible pain they inflicted on her as they took samples from every conceivable part of her anatomy. The agony was almost enough to momentarily make her forget that Landon was dead. Almost, but not quite. And the pain of losing him was worse than anything she physically endured.

"For the love of God, what…?"

The two men paused at the sound of the woman's voice. Tall and blond, she had her hair pulled back in a ponytail and wore a white lab coat. If that didn't give her away as the kidnapped doctor, Zarina Sokolov, her startlingly blue eyes would have.

"What are you doing to her?"

Renard barely glanced at the woman. "Taking samples. What does it look like?"

"Without anesthesia?" Zarina grabbed a syringe off a tray and filled it with something from a vial. "At least give her something for the pain."

"No." Klaus's voice was hard. "We want to test her pain threshold."

They wanted to watch her suffer.

The Russian doctor must have thought so, too. Muttering something under her breath, she shook her head and walked out.

Renard offered Ivy a small smile. "I'm going to take a bone marrow sample. This will hurt less if you remain as still as possible."

Ivy's eyes went wide at the sight of the long, needle-like probe in his hand. It looked like a gutter spike and had a blunt tip. There was no way that thing could puncture skin, much less bone.

Renard put the tip against her thigh and savagely pushed.

Ivy screamed. Right before she blacked out, she added Renard's and Klaus's names to the list of people she was going kill.

———

Landon smacked hard against the ground. Fortunately, it was steeply angled, so it was like hitting a ramp—one with sharp rocks. But he was still alive, and that was what counted.

He tumbled down it at breakneck speed, his NVGs going one way, his M4 going another, his head slamming into the avalanche of stone over and over before the ground disappeared out from under him again.

Double shit.

The fall was shorter this time, and instead of hitting rock, he hit water. Fast moving and icy cold, it knocked the air from his lungs and made his head spin.

Man, this just keeps getting better and better.

He gulped in air as he struggled to get himself turned sideways to the current. It was too dark to see much of anything, but from what he remembered of his map recon, none of the rivers in the area were more than twenty or thirty feet wide. If he was right, it shouldn't be too hard to get out of the rapids.

That didn't take into account the weight of his boots, uniform, and tactical vest. The rapids tried to drag him down the whole time, but he gritted his teeth and swam harder. Ivy needed him.

When he finally dragged himself out of the water, all he could do was lie on his back, gasping for air. Somewhere upstream, the shifters howled, like they were celebrating his demise. Bastards probably thought he was dead. He was shocked he wasn't.

How long had it been since he'd left the lodge? Fifteen minutes? Thirty? Long enough for Stutmeir to do whatever he had in mind for her. He had no idea why those animals had darted and dragged her off, but his mind went to a very dark place involving torture and experimentation—neither of which he was willing to contemplate.

So stop thinking and go get her.

A few hundred rounds of 5.56mm ammo and a handful of grenades weren't going to be enough to save Ivy. There were too many shifters and they were too hard to take down. As much as he hated to admit it, he needed help.

And where was he going to get it? Not the DCO, that was for sure. They'd given him orders to kill her if she got captured. If he told them what happened, they'd probably implement some kind of immediate scorched-earth policy and order every single living creature in that lodge killed, Ivy included.

Asking the DCO for help wasn't an option. But asking someone in the department he trusted was.

Using the satellite phone was not an option. He couldn't risk going back for it, not with the shifters prowling around. He'd have to use his cell phone. Which meant he'd have to go back to the Jeep—fifteen miles away.

Instead of sticking to the forests like he and Ivy had when they had approached the lodge, he navigated straight to the road, then ran from there to the Jeep. It was riskier, but time was the most important factor now. Luckily, he didn't run into any shifters on the way.

Back at the Jeep, he grabbed the first cell phone he came to—which happened to be Ivy's—and scrolled down until he found Kendra's number. It rang four times before she answered.

"Ivy? It's the middle of the night. What, you have so many roaming minutes you don't know what to do with them?"

"It's not Ivy. It's Landon." He rushed on before she could say anything. "The mission went to hell and Ivy got captured."

There was a sharp intake of breath on the other end of the line. "Oh God. Did you…?"

She couldn't seem to finish. Landon didn't need her to. He knew what she was asking. "No! I could never do that to Ivy." He ran his hand through his hair. "I'm calling because I need help getting her back. Stutmeir isn't making a bioweapon. He's making shifters. The lodge is crawling with them."

"Shifters? But how…?"

"I don't know. That's not important right now." He struggled to keep his voice even. "Have you gotten hold of Tate yet?"

"No. He still hasn't made contact, and we haven't been able to get through to him. He's probably still out of range."

"Shit. I need Tate's team to help me get in the lodge, and I need Declan to track Ivy once we're inside."

"Declan's nose isn't much better than yours or mine. He's better at super strength than a good sense of smell. You need Clayne for that."

Buchanan was the last person he wanted out here. Next to last if Landon counted Coleman.

Kendra must have interpreted his silence the proper way. "I know you two don't get along, but he's the only other person you can trust. He'd never do anything to jeopardize Ivy's life."

Landon squeezed the bridge of his nose between his thumb and forefinger. Kendra was right. "Okay. Tell him to meet me at the storage unit the DCO set up. And I need him there ASAP. Any way you can get him there"—he looked at his watch—"by 0800 in the morning my time?"

"0800? It'll be tight, but yeah, I'll get him there. If I have to tie him up, drag him on a plane, and fly it myself, I'll get him there. And Landon?"

"Yeah?" He already knew what she was going to say.

"Make it work with Clayne. For Ivy's sake."

He'd buddy up with Jeffrey Dahmer and Charlie Manson if it'd get Ivy out alive. "Just get him here."

Okay, it wasn't what he was hoping for, but it was a start. Problem was, Buchanan was only one part of the equation. He had a shifter who could track Ivy, but he still needed enough firepower to get in the front door. And he knew exactly where to get it.

He pulled out his cell phone and thumbed through his contacts until he found the number he was after. He hit the Call button and prayed. *Please don't be out on a training exercise.*

A sleepy voice answered. "What?"

"Angelo, it's Landon. I need a favor."

"Name it."

Someone else would have cursed and reminded him it was 0430 in the morning on the East Coast. But not Angelo. "Ivy and I ran into some trouble on a mission and I could use your help. As many of the other guys on the team as you can get, too."

"Where are you?"

"Washington State, three hours outside of Seattle."

Angelo sighed. "When do you want us there?"

"As soon as you can get here. Faster than that if possible."

Landon heard a woman's muffled voice in the background. "No baby, go back to sleep. It's work stuff." The bed creaked, like Angelo sat up. "Okay, I'm in. Where do you want to meet?"

Landon gave him the address of the storage unit.

"We going to need weapons?" Angelo asked.

"No. I've got that covered. Just get as many of the guys here as you can. And Angelo? I only want volunteers—this is going to be messy."

"When isn't it? Don't worry. I'll take care of it."

"Thanks, Angelo. I owe you one."

"Yeah, you do. And don't you forget it."

Landon would have laughed if he weren't so scared. If Angelo helped him get Ivy back, he'd repay him for the rest of his life.

Chapter 15

A NEEDLE PRICKED HER SKIN, PULLING HER OUT OF THE blackness for the second time since her capture. Ivy knew it was useless since she was strapped down to the bed, but she twisted away anyway. The needle jerked out of her arm. Someone swore.

Ivy opened her eyes and found herself staring at linoleum. She wasn't in bed anymore, but on the floor. Was she in the lodge, or had they moved her somewhere else? She pushed herself up. Her hands were bound together in front of her with a ton of duct tape. More of the stuff was wrapped around her ankles, immobilizing her feet. She gritted her teeth as pain shot through her thigh. It felt like she'd been beaten with a baseball bat.

Her long hair fell in front of her face and she reached up with her bound hands to push it back. That's when she saw Zarina Sokolov. The Russian doctor was kneeling on the floor a few feet away, a small syringe in her hand.

Ivy looked around. She was in a room with no windows, no furniture, and—thanks to the two shifters posted outside the open door—no escape.

She swung her gaze back to the blonde, eyeing her warily. The Frenchman Renard might have started out as a prisoner, but he'd clearly switched sides. Zarina Sokolov might have done the same. "What did you just stick me with?"

"I was trying to give you something for the pain, but you jerked away before I could."

Ivy pushed against the floor with her feet, scooting back against the wall. "I don't want any medication."

The woman moved closer. "What they did to you must still hurt very much."

It did, but she needed a clear head if she wanted to escape long enough to get her revenge on Stutmeir and the two doctors who'd thought she was a human pin cushion. That meant no pain meds. Besides, nothing could take away the agony of losing Landon. Compared to that, every other pain paled in comparison.

She glared at Zarina when the doctor reached for her arm. "I said I don't want it."

The woman looked as if she wanted to argue, but then she nodded. "I understand. I was only trying to help."

Maybe she hadn't turned traitor like Renard. "You're Zarina Sokolov, right?" Ivy kept her voice low so the guards at the door wouldn't hear.

Zarina's eyes went wide with confusion. She threw the guards a worried look over her shoulder. "How do you know my name?"

"My…" Ivy swallowed hard. "My partner and I were sent here to rescue you and the other doctors. But from what I saw earlier, Renard's already joined the dark side."

"Yes. He's completely on board with everything Stutmeir is doing." Zarina frowned. "But who sent you?"

"That's not important. What's important is whether you can help me get free."

Zarina darted another worried glance in the shifters' direction.

Ivy glanced at them, too. They were talking among

themselves, ignoring her and Zarina. "Please. I just need you to get me something I can use to cut the tape around my wrists. I'll do the rest."

She could have used her claws to free her ankles, but it would take forever, not to mention make a lot of noise. And then what would she do about her wrists, chew through the tape?

Zarina swallowed hard. "I helped someone else escape a while ago, so they don't trust me anymore. They search me every time I leave the lab."

Ivy wanted to know whom she'd helped, but there wasn't time to ask. "I need you to do this, Zarina. It's the only way I'll be able to get you out of here."

The blonde looked dubious. Why wouldn't she? Ivy was in her underwear, bound hand and foot. As helpless went, she was pretty much the poster girl here.

Zarina nodded. "I'll try." She got to her feet. At the door, she paused to talk to the guards. "I'll be back in a few minutes with something for her to eat and drink."

"What for?" one of the shifters demanded. "She's not going to live long enough to need it."

The other one laughed. "I heard Renard say he plans to take brain cell samples as soon as we get set up at the new facility. Can't imagine she's going to be hungry after that."

Zarina lifted her chin. "Actually, she'll be completely functional after the procedure."

The Russian doctor's voice was so cold it sent shivers down Ivy's back. She hoped the woman was faking it.

The first shifter shook his head as Zarina walked away. "Damn, that is one cold bitch."

The other made a sound of agreement, then turned his

attention to Ivy. "Sucks to be you. Bet you're wishing you died with that partner of yours."

A fresh stab of pain pierced Ivy's heart, and she added the two shifters to the growing list of people she was going to kill when she got free.

If she got free. When Zarina still hadn't come back after what seemed like forever, Ivy thought she wasn't going to. The Russian woman said she'd helped someone escape before. If Stutmeir figured out what Zarina was up to, he'd keep the doctor as far away from Ivy as possible.

She frowned at the duct tape around her ankles. It looked like she was going to have to claw and chew her way through it after all.

Ivy extended her nails just as Zarina walked in with a plastic cup of water and a granola bar. She kneeled down in front of Ivy, holding the cup to her mouth. Ivy didn't feel like drinking or eating, but she didn't have much of a choice, not unless she wanted to make a scene, and that would only make the two shifters by the door curious. She sipped the water. As she drank, Zarina pressed something rough and cold into her hands.

Ivy glanced down and saw a jagged piece of metal. She'd been hoping for a scalpel, but this might work. She darted a quick look at the shifters outside the door to see if they noticed, but they weren't paying attention.

As Zarina offered her the granola bar, Ivy caught a glimpse of the watch on the woman's wrist. Almost 0500 hours. She'd been out longer than she thought.

Using the doctor's body to shield her from the guards' view, she tried to saw at the tape around her wrists, but it was useless. She couldn't hold the piece of metal between her palms and get enough leverage. She considered asking Zarina to cut her bonds but quickly discarded the idea. Both the doctor's hands were full, and the woman was already taking a huge risk. So, Ivy did the next best thing—scraped at the thick tape around her ankles. If she could hold the piece of sharpened metal between her feet, she could saw her wrists up and down over it.

She took another bite of the granola bar as she worked. "Where's the other doctor, Sarah Beacon?"

Zarina held the cup while she drank. "I haven't seen her since we arrived. She played along at first, but once she realized what Stutmeir was trying to create, she refused to help anymore. I think he killed her."

Ivy figured as much. "Has Stutmeir said what he plans to do with the shifters? Maybe mentioned who he works for?"

Zarina shook her head. "I don't know who he works for. Only the German doctor, Klaus, is privy to that information. All I know is that he's not completely satisfied with our work. Stutmeir wants perfect soldiers with superhuman strength and animal attributes like yours but without all the violent impulses and control issues every hybrid we've created has."

She jerked around to look at the guards at the door, but they weren't paying attention. Could it be possible their hearing wasn't as well developed as a real shifter's?

"How many shifters—hybrids—are here?"

Zarina offered her another sip of water. "Thirty, maybe forty. When we started having success with the test subjects he'd kidnapped, Stutmeir turned his own soldiers into hybrids."

That was a lot to go up against. But she only had to fight off enough to kill Stutmeir and the doctors. And help Zarina get to safety. She owed the woman that much.

Ivy felt the bindings around her ankles begin to tear, and her heart leaped. Another minute or two and she'd be able to start on her wrists. "How did you create them?"

"Using animal DNA." She shook her head. "I didn't want to do it, but I was afraid they'd—"

"That's enough, doctor."

Ivy froze at the sound of the man's voice, almost dropping the piece of metal. She must be imagining it. She had to be.

Zarina stiffened. "I'm just giving her something to eat."

Booted feet crossed the floor. "You did your good deed for the day. Get out."

The woman gave her an apologetic look. "I'm sorry. Be careful. This man is cruel in ways you can't imagine."

Ivy didn't need to be told that. She was well aware just how sick and depraved her ex-partner could be. What she didn't know was what he was doing with Stutmeir.

She palmed the piece of metal and lifted her head to look up at Jeff. He stood in front of her, legs spread, arms crossed over his chest, an arrogant smirk on his scarred face. The memory of what he'd tried to do to her on that rooftop in Mexico came rushing back, and she had to fight to quell the rising panic. She forced herself to forget she was tied up and half naked as she glared at him.

"You're still as ugly as I remembered."

"And you're still as much of an animal as I remembered. I thought cats were supposed to land on their feet. Guess not." He grinned. "Of all the freaks the DCO could have sent, it had to be you. It's like Christmas and my birthday all rolled into one."

Ivy didn't ask what he meant by that, but she could guess. The bra and panties she was wearing suddenly seemed even more revealing. "You told Stutmeir about the EVAs, didn't you? That's what gave him the idea to make his own."

"I might have. I can't take all the credit, though. He heard rumors about a shadowy black ops unit that had operatives with amazing abilities for years. I merely filled in a few details and shared what I'd learned about your DNA."

"And helped him kidnap scientists and doctors who could make shifters out of humans."

"That too." Jeff shrugged. "We tried to track down natural shifters—start our own version of the DCO, you could say—but freaks like you are hard to find. Have to hand it to the DCO. They're damn good at spotting you in a crowd. And the ones we did find? Let's just say they weren't too interested in joining our ranks."

She strained at the tape around her ankles and felt it tear a little bit more. "So you killed them?"

"Guilty again."

Ivy bit back a growl. Trying to rape her had been bad enough, but using what he'd learned at the DCO and selling it to the highest bidder was beyond low. He was as much of a terrorist as the people he'd once sworn to fight.

"But enough about everyone else," he said. "You're

really the center of attention here. And from what I hear, you had quite the eventful night. Let's see. First, you get your partner killed—the second one, or so I'm told. Then you're poked and prodded like a lab rat. And to make things worse, you find yourself tied up and defenseless in a room with the one man who hates you more than any other woman in the world. I'd say things aren't going so well for you right now."

Ivy bared her teeth, hissing as she showed him her fangs. She might be tied up, but she refused to let him see how afraid she was. "I should have killed you when I had the chance instead of simply making you uglier than you already were."

His mouth twisted in a sneer. "But you didn't. And you're going to be real sorry about that."

She opened her mouth to tell him to go to hell, but Jeff drew back his foot and kicked her hard in the side. She fell over, gasping for breath, sure he'd broken a rib or two. She curled into a ball to protect herself from another kick, but it never came. Instead, Jeff dropped down beside her. He grabbed a handful of hair and yanked her head back.

"I'm going to finish what I started on the rooftop in Mexico, bitch. And this time, there isn't a damn thing you can do about it."

Wanna bet, asshole? Ivy lifted her bound hands to rake her claws across Jeff's face, but he caught her wrists, shoving them over her head and pinning them to the floor. He cupped her breast in his other hand, squeezing painfully.

Ivy growled. She'd die before she let this bastard touch her.

She strained her legs and almost cried with relief when she felt the last of the tape tear away. She twisted her body until she got one of her legs between their bodies. Letting the claws on her toes extend, she shoved him away, raking him from stomach to groin. He howled in pain and fell back. The second he did, she leaped to her feet and threw herself at him, clawing at his throat with her bound hands.

Jeff got his hands around her wrists before she could do any real damage. "Fucking bitch. Someone should have declawed you a long time ago. Guess I'll have to do it myself."

Letting loose a snarl, she bared her teeth and bit down on his shoulder. She felt her fangs crunch down onto bone. She'd rip out his throat if she had to.

Ivy lunged, going for the jugular, but hands gripped her, pulling her way before she could sink her teeth in. She fought, snarling and kicking out with her feet, but the hybrids were stronger than she was and subdued her within seconds.

"Sedate her!" Stutmeir ordered. "With a double dose this time. We'll be leaving in a few hours and I don't want her waking up before we get to the new facility."

Klaus hurried forward, syringe in hand. She couldn't let them drug her again. Ivy hissed and struggled against the men holding her, but she was like a doll in their grip. Klaus actually laughed as he jabbed the needle in her arm.

Ivy whimpered, not with pain but frustration. She felt the drug coursing through her body, pulling her back into unconsciousness. She tried to fight against it, but it was useless. Everything went black.

It had to be the longest night of Landon's life.

After talking to Angelo, he'd thought about going to the storage unit and picking up some weapons so he wouldn't feel so unarmed, but he didn't want to miss seeing Stutmeir if he left the ski lodge. The ex-Stasi had been one step ahead of the authorities the whole time, so it made sense he'd be leaving soon since his hideout had been compromised.

Instead of going to the storage unit, Landon was in an ambush position in some trees off the small, twisting road that connected the lodge with the main highway. Confronting Stutmeir and his pack of rabid science experiments would be suicide, but he'd do it in a heartbeat if that was the only option he had left. Anything to save Ivy.

If she was still alive.

The thought was like a punch to the gut, and for a minute, he couldn't breathe. If he thought like that, he'd go crazy. Then what good would he be to Ivy? She needed him to be on his game, not acting like a raving madman.

He tightened his grip on the knife. He never should have left her. He should have cleared out the atrium with that grenade, tracked down the animal who'd taken her, and killed the son of a bitch with his bare hands. Of course, if he had the foresight to go in with more fire-power in the first place, he wouldn't need to use his bare hands. He would have been a walking arsenal. He sure wouldn't have had to run and leave Ivy at the mercy of a man like Stutmeir, either. Then again, Ivy wouldn't be in that position if Landon had realized she'd zoned out and tackled her before she jumped over the railing.

If he got her back—*when* he got her back—he was going to make sure he never let anything like this happen ever again. He'd pay more attention to her moods and be more aware of when she was at risk from the very animal instincts that made her so valuable and dangerous to others.

He promised himself another thing, too. When he got her back, he was going to tell her how he felt about her. He hadn't told her before because he didn't know exactly what it was he felt. Or maybe he had and had just been too stupid to recognize it. Man, self-recrimination was a freaking bitch on PMS.

Landon glanced at his watch. 0615. He couldn't put off leaving any longer, not if he wanted to meet up with his reinforcements.

At least there hadn't been movement from the ski lodge. Maybe Stutmeir thought he was safe there. Maybe the German thought he and Ivy had attacked his hideout without backup or follow-on forces. From what Landon had read in the guy's file, Stutmeir wasn't that stupid.

Unless Ivy had tricked Stutmeir into believing that. The idea was comforting. It meant she was alive and well and controlling the situation.

He looked at his watch again. He really needed to go.

Landon had to drive like a maniac to get to the self-storage unit by 0800. The DCO had picked the last unit of the last building, so it was highly unlikely someone at another unit would be able to see what was inside it. Even so, he pulled the Jeep around to block the doorway just in case.

Landon was opening the first of the two security locks when a vehicle crunched to a hard stop beside the Jeep. He glanced at the car and saw Buchanan silhouetted behind the wheel. He could practically feel the big man glowering at him.

He started to turn back to the lock but stopped when movement in the passenger seat caught his eye.

Buchanan got out of the car and slammed the door, looking as pissed off as the last time Landon had seen him.

Landon dropped his hand down to the top of his knife and spread his legs, centering his weight as the shifter strode toward him.

He was so intent on Buchanan, he completely forgot about the second person in the car until a woman spoke.

"We talked about this, Clayne. Don't even think about it."

Buchanan growled low in his throat but grudgingly stopped at the sound of Kendra's voice.

Landon frowned as the blonde closed the car door and hurried over to them. "What the hell are you doing here, Kendra?"

"I'm here to make sure you two stay focused on the right enemy instead of trying to kill each other."

Buchanan took a threatening step toward Landon, his lip drawn back in a snarl. "If Ivy's dead, I will kill you."

If Ivy was dead, Landon wasn't sure he'd stop Buchanan from trying. He bent to open the second lock.

"What the hell happened?" Buchanan demanded.

Landon gave them a brief synopsis, starting with sneaking into the lodge and finishing with his header off the cliff. He left out the part about Ivy zoning out, saying they'd gotten separated and that he wasn't able to get to her before she'd gotten captured.

"So you just up and fucking left her without a fight?" Buchanan swore under his breath. "What are you, a fucking coward? The only thing that should have stopped you from going after her is a bullet through the spine—if you even have one."

Landon ground his jaw. The words hurt like hell, not because he cared what Buchanan thought of him, but because they were exactly the same things he'd been saying repeatedly to himself all night long.

"I tried!" An image flashed in his head of Ivy lying on the floor, half conscious, begging him to run. His gut twisted. "Fuck, don't you think I tried? I couldn't get to her, dammit."

The shifter growled, fangs glinting in the early morning sunlight.

Landon swore. He might need Buchanan's help, but he wasn't going to listen to his rantings to get it. If the shifter wasn't going to help get Ivy back, he'd do it without him. He didn't have time to waste trading insults. He needed to get back to the lodge. Problem was Buchanan didn't look like he was going to walk away until this thing between them was resolved.

"You want a fight, shifter?" Landon pulled his knife. "Let's fight."

He braced himself, waiting for Buchanan to take a swipe at him, but Kendra darted forward, putting herself between them.

"Stop it, both of you!" She held up her hands, her eyes narrowing as she looked from him to Buchanan and back again. "What the hell is wrong with the two of you? While you're wasting time yelling at each other, Stutmeir could be doing God only knows what to Ivy. Put your damn dicks back in your pants and think about her."

Buchanan flushed and retracted his claws, his yellow eyes going back to their normal color and clouding with pain. Turning on his heel, he walked away, then stopped and turned back. He pinned Landon with a glower. "Why didn't you follow DCO rules and kill Ivy as soon as it looked like she was going to be captured?"

What the fuck kind of question was that? "Seriously? I can't believe you'd ask me that when you know we slept together."

"You're banging her. So what?" Buchanan snorted. "That doesn't explain why you didn't pop her."

Landon stared at him, speechless. Why had he thought Buchanan might help? The man was too warped to give a shit about anything.

He shoved his knife into its sheath and turned back to the storage unit. "Forget it. If you have to ask, you wouldn't understand."

"What wouldn't I understand?"

Landon ignored him. He opened the second lock, then lifted the door.

Gravel crunched under Buchanan's boots as the shifter crossed the parking lot. "What. Wouldn't. I. Understand?"

Landon swore silently. He turned to face the other man. "That I'm in love with her, you fucking idiot."

The first time he said those words out loud, it should have been to Ivy, not this asshole.

Landon didn't wait to see what effect they had on Buchanan. He didn't care. Right now, he needed to rework his original plan—where the shifter used his keen sense of smell to track down Ivy so they would get her away from Stutmeir before the ex-Stasi knew they were onto him and decided to eliminate her—because that one was shot to hell. He walked over to the far side of the unit and picked up the M4 that was on the shelf.

"Do you even have a plan to get Ivy out?"

Landon looked over his shoulder to see Buchanan opening one of the crates on the floor. "What? You're in now?"

The shifter pulled an M203 rifle/grenade launcher combination out of the box. "That depends on the plan."

Outside, a vehicle pulled up to the unit and stopped.

"Who the hell is that?" Buchanan growled, looking around for the ammo that went with the weapon he was holding.

"Relax." Landon put the M4 back on the shelf. "It's only some reinforcements."

Landon ignored the frown Buchanan gave him and walked outside. He'd spent half the night praying Angelo would be able to round up one or two more guys from the team, so he was shocked to not only see Diaz, Mickens, and Griffen, but Marks, Deray, and Tredeau, too. He shouldn't have expected anything less, but it still brought tears to his eyes.

"As soon as Angelo said you and Ivy were in trouble, we were all in." Diaz's face turned apologetic. "Everyone else would have come too, but Johnson needed to keep a few of the guys with him to give us a legitimate cover story for coming out here on short notice."

Landon frowned. "What cover story is that?"

"We're supposedly doing survival training at Fort Lewis," Tredeau explained.

Landon looked at Angelo. "You told Johnson you needed to go out on a completely unauthorized training op, and he didn't flip out?"

"Nah. I knew he wouldn't." Angelo shrugged. "You're his commanding officer. Former commanding officer, anyway. He'd do anything for you. Besides, it was either talk him into coming out here with us or go AWOL—which we would have done if he'd said no, by the way. Top didn't even ask why you needed us. He just told me to get the team together and meet him at the airfield. By the time we got there, he was waiting on the ramp of a C-17 with that cigar shoved in his mouth. No idea how he did it, but he got the battalion to agree to a no-notice training exercise. He's got the rest of the A-team at Fort Lewis taking up space to make it look good."

Landon was speechless. He knew his team was incredible, but this was too much.

Buchanan grabbed his shoulder and spun him around. "Sorry to rain on the reunion, but who the hell are they?"

Leave it to the shifter to spoil the moment. "Guys from my old Special Forces team. We needed help; they came to help."

Buchanan swore. "Ivy's life is in danger, and you bring in a bunch of half-trained snake eaters to rescue her? Are you trying to get her killed?"

Landon shoved the shifter's hand away. "Dammit, Buchanan. This is more than we can handle by ourselves. When we go in that lodge, we're going to be facing twenty-five trained killers, maybe more."

"So? I can handle the first twenty. You just have to handle the other five."

Landon glanced at Kendra. She'd come out of the storage unit and was standing with her arms wrapped around her waist. She looked as terrified for Ivy as he was.

"You didn't tell him about the shifters, did you?" Landon asked. He didn't wait for an answer, but turned back to Buchanan. "The size of your balls might be impressive, but I don't think even you can take on twenty-five super-powered shifters."

Buchanan's brows drew together. "Stutmeir has shifters working for him? Where did he find that many?"

"He didn't. I don't know how he did it, but he found a way to make them. Test tube shifters, apparently—and vicious as hell. They fight like they're insane—sort of like you."

Buchanan grunted.

"When we go in there," Landon continued, "we're going to need a lot of firepower."

The shifter's gaze went to the other men and he shook his head. "There has to be another way."

"There isn't. It's these guys—whom I trust a hell of a lot more than I trust you—or the DCO. Do you honestly think they'll mount a rescue op when they find out Stutmeir took Ivy alive? My guess is it'd be more of a sanitizing mission, but what do I know?" He pulled out his cell phone. "So, you want to call the DCO, or should I?"

Buchanan ground his jaw, but that silenced him.

Angelo walked over. "What's going on? Who is this asshole, where's Ivy, and what the hell is a shifter?"

Landon shoved his phone back in his pocket. "This is Clayne Buchanan. He's a friend of Ivy's."

"Which is the only reason I'd ever get involved with you fucks," the shifter growled.

Angelo ignored the comment. "Okay, that answers one of the questions. What happened to Ivy?"

Landon swore under his breath as the rest of his former team crowded around them. While they were wasting time here, Stutmeir could be making his escape and taking Ivy with him.

"We came here to get some intel on an ex-Stasi-killer-turned-arms-dealer named Stutmeir, but there was a problem and Ivy got captured."

Angelo frowned. "And I take it these shifters you keep mentioning are the reason you couldn't get her out, and why you need our help?"

"What are these shifters?" Deray asked. "Super soldiers or something?"

"Something like that." Landon sighed. "Look, this is real black ops shit, and none of you are cleared to know a damn thing about it, so I'll keep it short and simple. Shifters are humans that are…well, part animal."

They stared at him like a pig with a Rolex.

"Part animal?" Mickens snorted. "You're shittin' us, right?"

"Do I look like I'm shittin' you?"

"Shifters." Angelo's voice was thoughtful. "You mean like skinwalkers?"

Landon wasn't surprised at the intuitive leap. Angelo's Native American heritage gave him a completely different set of beliefs than other people. "Not in the way you're thinking. They can't turn into animals. They only display certain attributes."

"I'm not sure if I'm following this." Mickens held up his hands. "No offense, sir, but it sounds a little batshit to me."

Landon knew it sounded crazy. He didn't believe it the first time, either, and he'd seen Ivy's claws with his own eyes. "I know this sounds like something from the SyFy channel, but shifters are real, and they're dangerous."

"So are we," Griffen said.

This was getting nowhere fast. "Maybe it'd be easier if I show you." Landon glanced at Buchanan. "Could you demonstrate?"

The shifter scowled. "I'm not a trained monkey, you know. I don't do tricks on command."

Kendra muttered something under her breath. "For heaven's sake, Clayne, just show them, dammit. The sooner we get out of here, the sooner we can get to Ivy. You do remember Ivy, don't you?"

Buchanan stopped glaring long enough to shift into the golden-eyed, clawed menace Landon knew and didn't love. Growling deep in his throat, the shifter whipped out his arm and raked his claws down the side of the building, leaving four long, jagged grooves in their wake. The whole show was probably only a second or two, but it was effective. Every one of his former teammates gasped and jumped back.

"What the...?" Marks said.

"Buchanan's a shifter. He was born with the DNA of a wolf," Landon explained. "The shifters with Stutmeir aren't natural born, though. He's figured out a way to turn humans into them."

"Damn," Deray muttered.

"It gets worse." Landon ground his jaw. "I'm only guessing here, but I think he might have taken Ivy to experiment on her."

Angelo's eyes narrowed. "You think he'll try to turn her into a shifter?"

"He won't have to," Kendra said.

"Why not?" Diaz asked.

"Because she's already a shifter," Landon said.

"Like me," Buchanan added.

No doubt that was for Landon's benefit. It was probably the shifter's way of pointing out how different she was from Landon, and that she'd be so much better off with him once they got her back.

"Ivy isn't anything like you," Landon told him.

"Is Ivy a wolf, too?" Mickens asked.

Diaz shook his head. "Man, did Ivy move like a dog to you? What are you, blind and dense? Gotta be a cat, with moves like hers. Am I right, Captain, or am I right?"

Landon knew Diaz was sharp. "He's right."

Diaz gave Mickens a smug look.

The medic's face flushed. "I knew that."

"Sure you did," Griffen said.

Landon looked from one man to the next. "Now that you know what you'll be facing, I'm going to ask you again—are you all okay with this? I don't want you to feel like there's any pressure here. I'm not your commander anymore. If you want to back out, I'll understand."

"Shifters or no shifters, I'm in," Angelo said.

"Me too," Diaz agreed.

Deray, Mickens, Griffen, and Marks echoed.

"Okay. Then we need to get moving." Landon jerked his head at the storage unit. "Weapons and everything else we're going to need are in here."

Tredeau let out an appreciative whistle as he and the others followed Landon into the unit. "Man, this stuff is top of the line. This organization of yours—what did I hear you call it, the DCO?—they don't mess around, do they?"

If they only knew. "No, they don't."

While Angelo and Tredeau grabbed weapons and loaded magazines, Diaz found the radios and ear pieces and started checking them out. Mickens was on the other side of the room, checking out the first-aid kit. Landon's mouth edged up. It was like old times. He wouldn't trade working with Ivy for anything, but he'd be lying if he said he didn't miss going to battle with these guys.

Landon was stuffing a butt pack with blocks of C-4 explosives when Angelo walked over. His friend leaned back against the shelf.

"So, I guess you and Ivy decided to go ahead and play with that fire, huh?"

All Landon could do was nod. "And it might just have gotten her killed."

"You know I'd be here having your back regardless, but I'm curious why no one but Buchanan and Kendra are here from this DCO organization of yours?"

Landon glanced over his shoulder to make sure no one else could overhear them talking. "Because I had orders to kill Ivy if there was even a remote chance she might get captured on a mission."

Angelo's eyes went wide. "What kind of fucked-up organization asks its operatives to murder their partners like that?"

"The kind that doesn't want anyone to know they have freaks of nature working for the U.S. government," Buchanan said.

Landon hadn't heard the shifter come over. That's

what Buchanan thought of himself, a freak of nature? No wonder he was so screwed up.

Angelo looked Buchanan up and down, as if evaluating how hard it would be to take the shifter in a fair fight. "Well, I don't know about you, but Ivy's no freak. So that tells me you two work for a bunch of assholes."

Landon couldn't deny that. Buchanan didn't either.

When they were all armed, Landon gathered them in front of the storage unit for a quick briefing before they left.

"I don't have time to give you a full operation order, so here are the essentials. Stutmeir and his men are located in an old ski lodge a little more than an hour from here. The place is made out of stone and built into the side of a mountain—think about that keep in the second *Lord of the Rings* movie and you get the idea." They nodded. "There are five floors and at least one basement level. My guess is that Ivy will be someplace on that basement level."

"What's the plan to get her out?" Buchanan asked.

"We break up into two teams. One causes a distraction and draws the bulk of the bad guys toward the front gate while the other one slips in and grabs Ivy. There may also be a couple doctors being held hostage, so if you see any nerdy types running, wait to see a weapon before you put them down. Other than that, it's your standard kill 'em all approach."

"Hell, yeah." Angelo grinned. "Mess with the best, die like the rest."

Landon ground his jaw. His friend had that right. If they hurt a single hair on Ivy's head, he'd track down every last one of them and kill them as slowly as he could—twice if he could figure out how.

Chapter 16

LANDON BREATHED A SIGH OF RELIEF AS HE SURVEYED the ski lodge from his position in the forest. Four large moving vans and a half dozen oversized SUVs were parked in the front of the lodge, doors open, boxes and lab equipment waiting and ready to be loaded.

They weren't too late. Now, he prayed whatever the reason Stutmeir had for taking Ivy alive had kept her that way the whole night.

He glanced over his shoulder and gave Griffen a nod. He'd picked the demolition expert to lead the team that'd take out the gate and—hopefully—draw the majority of Stutmeir's men in that direction.

Griffen returned the nod, then moved off without a word. Marks, Deray, Diaz, and Tredeau followed, equally silent. There'd be no radio communications until they initiated the attack just in case Stutmeir had a radio scanner.

Landon motioned his team around the far side of the lodge, to the same place he and Ivy had crossed over the wall last night. Had it only been that long? It felt longer. If luck was with them, Stutmeir's people would be so busy packing they wouldn't notice anything until Griffen's team started blowing up the place.

He glanced over his shoulder to make sure everyone was in position and saw he'd picked up a stray to go along with Buchanan, Angelo, and Mickens. Kendra was crouched down beside Buchanan with an M4 carbine in her hands like she knew how to use it.

"What the hell are you doing here?" His voice was a harsh whisper. "I told you to stay in the car where it's safe."

"I decided against it." She lifted her chin. "Ivy is my friend, Landon. I'm going to help get her out, whether you want me to or not."

"I don't have time to babysit you and find Ivy at the same time."

"Then don't babysit me. You find Ivy. I'll take care of myself." She held up the M4. "I don't just stand around and watch you guys all day, you know. I know what I'm doing. I've been trained by the best. And like you said, you don't have time for this. Griffen is already setting the charges, which means we have to get moving."

Landon growled loud enough for even Buchanan to look taken aback. He glared at the shifter. "She's your responsibility."

Jaw tight, he turned and took off toward the back wall. Kendra was right about Griffen setting the explosives. If they wanted to be ready to go over the wall the second the demo charge went off, they needed to move. He glanced at his watch. 0940. Shit, they were already five minutes behind. They needed to get up there now.

He scanned left and right, then motioned everyone up. He glanced at Kendra, half hoping she wouldn't be able to scale the wall and would have to go hide in the woods until this was over, but she got up the wall faster than he'd expected.

Landon just reached the top of the wall when it trembled under him. A split second later, he heard the distinctive crack of C-4 going off. He was over the wall and down the other side before the rumble of the blast faded away.

Once on the ground, he led his team across the grounds to the basement windows he'd remembered seeing during his reconnaissance with Ivy. He'd considered the idea of going in through the roof entrance again, but dropped that plan when he realized it'd take too long.

Gunfire erupted from the front of the lodge.

"Engaged," Griffen announced over the communication headset.

Landon dropped to his knees at the first window he came to and pushed last season's dead leaves out of the well. There were iron gratings over the windows. They were rusted, but looked stout. He could forget about the element of surprise.

He reached into his butt pack for a block of explosives when Buchanan reached down and grabbed the grating with both hands. The shifter wrenched the ironwork completely out of the stone, taking half the window casing with it.

Angelo grinned. "Damn. Maybe you're a freak, but you're a useful freak."

Landon silently agreed. "Let's go find Ivy."

Inside, Landon grudgingly let Buchanan take the lead. In theory, it was so he could pick up Ivy's scent faster, but Landon thought it had more to do with the fact that the shifter wanted to be the first one Ivy saw when they found her. Kendra and Mickens followed directly behind Landon, leaving Angelo to bring up the rear.

The basement was a maze with very little light and a

lot of doors, most of which were locked. On the upside, it was completely deserted. Based on the volume of gunfire, explosions, and shouts above them, Landon could understand why. Griffen and his team were obviously doing their job. Stutmeir and his men probably thought they were fighting World War III.

Buchanan didn't pick up Ivy's scent in any of the rooms, so Landon didn't waste time checking them out. As much as he hated admitting it, the guy was useful.

"I have her scent." Buchanan quickened his step. "I can smell her blood, too. Fuck!"

Landon picked up the pace to keep up with the shifter even as he braced himself for what they were going to find. Buchanan said he'd smelled blood, but would he know if she was dead just by the smell? Landon didn't want to think about it, so he focused on keeping up with the shifter instead.

Buchanan rounded the corner ahead of him only to duck back so fast Landon almost smacked into him. The shifter held up two fingers and mouthed, "Guards." Landon nodded, indicating he understood and was ready to take them down.

The men had their backs to them, but the moment he and Buchanan came around the corner, they turned. Landon knew it was too much to hope they were regular, everyday humans and not Stutmeir's homemade shifters. Their eyes went from normal to gleaming red.

The creatures snarled and sprang, one toward him, the other at Buchanan.

Landon put a three-round burst into the thing's chest, but all that did was piss it off. It stumbled once, then charged him again.

Landon squeezed the trigger. He'd empty the whole magazine into the creature if he had to.

Kendra, Mickens, and Angelo raced around the corner, all three of them shooting the monster as fast as their fingers would go. It finally went down, but not before getting hit at least twenty times. Un-freaking-believable.

Landon abruptly realized he'd never heard Buchanan get off a shot at the other creature. He spun around, expecting to find the wolf shifter in a pool of blood. But Buchanan was leaning over the second guard, his face a mask of rage. The creature was lying on the floor, his throat torn open. Amazingly, the thing was still alive.

As Landon watched, Buchanan grabbed the man's hair in one hand and chin in the other, then savagely wrenched his head, snapping his neck. The body convulsed, boots kicking the floor, then went still.

Buchanan stood up and wiped his bloody claws off on his jeans, then picked up his weapon and turned around. He frowned when he found all of them staring at him.

"What?" he demanded. "Is this guy any deader than that one?" He pointed at the creature they'd shot.

Landon didn't say anything. Buchanan had a point. Who cared how the monsters had been killed anyway? They were gone, and that left the door they'd been guarding free and clear.

He jerked his head at the room. "Is Ivy in there?"

He really wanted to know if she was alive, but he couldn't bring himself to ask. It didn't make sense for Stutmeir's men to guard a dead prisoner. If she was in there, he'd find out soon enough anyway.

Buchanan nodded in answer to his question. He

started for the door and probably would have kicked it in, but Landon beat him to it.

The room was a white square. No furniture, no windows, no wall hangings.

And in the middle of the floor, a half-naked Ivy was curled up in a ball, her hands and feet bound. She looked more fragile than Landon could ever imagine. But the thing that tore at him the most were the barely healed cuts, scratches, and bruises on her beautiful body. Stutmeir hadn't simply beaten her; the bastard had tortured her.

Landon hurried across the room and dropped to his knee beside her. He was almost afraid to touch her, terrified he'd discover his worst fear was real and she truly was dead. But he had to know.

Taking a deep, shuddering breath, he set down his weapon and tenderly brushed her long hair back from her face. She was so still and pale, there was no way she could be alive. He'd told himself he'd been ready for this, but he wasn't.

He leaned closer, praying for some sign of life, and saw a tiny pulse beating at the side of her neck. She was alive, but she was weak.

"Ivy?" His voice sounded hoarse, as if it was choked with tears. Maybe it was. "Oh God, what did they do to you?"

She moaned, her eyes fluttering open. "No more… please…"

Her pleading tore at his heart. He cupped her face. "Ivy, sweetheart. It's me. It's Landon."

She blinked up at him, as if trying to focus. Tears filled her eyes. "Landon? Are you alive, or am I dead?"

"You're alive, baby." Tears burned Landon's eyes. "I swear it."

"They told me you were dead. I thought you were gone."

"I'm not," he assured her. "I'm right here, and I'm going to get you out of this hellhole."

Mickens dropped down beside him. "Captain, let me check her before you move her too much."

Landon was afraid to let her go even for a minute, but Mickens was right. They didn't know how extensive Ivy's injuries were, and he didn't want to do more damage.

"She's pretty beat up." Mickens glanced his way. "It looks like she has a few cracked ribs and maybe a fractured arm, but the breaks must be old. They've already set."

"They're recent. She heals quicker than we do," Landon said quietly.

Mickens looked stunned at that but didn't comment. He pointed at the scar marring the perfect skin of her thigh. "I don't know what this puncture wound was, but it's like someone stuck her with a thin, dull knife."

Landon ground his jaw. He was going to not only kill Stutmeir slowly, but excruciatingly painfully, too.

The medic checked Ivy's eyes, and Landon saw her trying to focus on Mickens's face. "They drugged the crap out of her, too. But I think she'll be okay long enough for us to get her out of here. I'll check her out more when we get to safety."

As soon as Mickens picked up his bag and moved out of the way, Landon was beside her again. Ivy reached up with her bound hands to touch his face. He swore under his breath. Grabbing the knife from his belt, he sliced through the tape around her wrists, then pulled her into his arms.

Ivy laced her fingers in his hair, pulling his mouth down to hers. The touch of her lips on his did more to convince him that she was going to be okay than anything Mickens had said. He wanted nothing more than to sit on the floor and kiss her like this for the rest of their lives, but he knew their lives would be very short if he did.

He reluctantly pulled away to gaze at her. There was so much he needed to say to her, but the words just wouldn't come. Not now, not like this. He cleared his throat and turned his attention to the tape around her ankles, slicing through it with his knife. The skin was red and raw underneath it, just like on her wrists. She'd been fighting with all her strength to get free. He clenched his jaw so hard he felt his teeth crunch. Damn those bastards. They were going to pay for hurting her.

First, he had to get Ivy to safety. Landon shoved the knife back in its sheath, then shook off his tactical vest so he could take off the button-up shirt he had on over his tee. He'd worn it to blend in with the other hikers on the trail yesterday and had almost ditched it more than once. Now he was glad he'd kept it on.

He gently helped Ivy into it and buttoned it up, careful not to hurt her. It was way too big on her, hanging down to the middle of her thighs, but at least it covered her. He put his vest back on and slung his M4 over his back. Slipping one arm under Ivy's knees and the other around her back, he got to his feet and turned to the door.

Buchanan, Kendra, Mickens, and Angelo were waiting for him, their faces grim.

"We won't be able to get her through the window we came in," Landon said.

Buchanan let out a ragged breath and tore his gaze away from Ivy. "You just keep her safe. I'll find a way out of here."

They were halfway down the hallway when Landon's radio crackled.

"Captain, trouble is heading your way," Griffen reported. In the background, Landon heard the echo of automatic weapons firing and the thumping boom of grenades exploding. Griffen swore. "We're keeping the bad guys from getting out, but they're keeping us from getting in, too. Looks like some of them are starting to pull back inside. I don't know where they're going, but if you don't have company already, you soon will."

"Roger that, Griffen. We're heading up to the first floor with Ivy now. Try and make your way inside if you can. We'll need your help to get out of here."

"Wilco, Captain. We'll do our best, but these things are fast as lightning and damn near impossible to kill. They've almost gotten us a few times."

"Stop your whining," Angelo growled over the line, "and get your asses in here."

Ivy already felt better, and not all of it had to do with her super-fast ability to heal. It was because she was in the one place she wanted to be more than anywhere else, the one place she never thought she'd be again—Landon's arms. She closed her eyes and buried her nose in his neck, breathing in his scent. It warmed her right down to her very soul.

When she'd awakened from her drugged stupor, she was afraid it was someone coming to shove another needle full of tranquilizers into her arm. Then she'd heard Landon's voice through the fog and she'd seriously thought she was dead. She knew she wasn't the moment she'd felt his warm, gentle hands on her face.

She never should have doubted him. He'd told her he would come for her, and he had. She should have known nothing would stop him from keeping that promise. He was the most amazing man in the world. And she planned on telling him that as soon as they were out of this horrible place.

Ivy reluctantly lifted her head from his shoulder to look around. The first thing she saw was Mickens. So she hadn't imagined him. How had one of Landon's Special Forces buddies gotten here? Then she saw Angelo a little farther back and between them—Kendra?

The drugs must be making her see things. There was no way Kendra could be here. Ivy couldn't imagine why her friend would show up in her drug-induced hallucination, but there she was—and she was carrying a weapon.

Ivy shook her head and breathed deep to draw in more oxygen. That was when she saw Clayne running in front of them.

She wasn't hallucinating. Mickens, Kendra, Angelo, Clayne—they were all real. And they were there to rescue her.

Up ahead, Clayne growled. It was quickly followed by a woman's scream.

Ivy jerked her head around to see Zarina Sokolov standing in the middle of the hallway. She was holding a piece of angle iron in her hands like a baseball bat and doing her best to stand up to Clayne.

Clayne ripped the piece of metal out of her hands and flung it on the floor, then grabbed her by the arm.

"Clayne, no!" Ivy ordered. "She's one of the hostages."

He snarled, giving the doctor a glare. "She doesn't look like a hostage to me. She damn near brained me with that thing."

"Well, she tried to help me escape at the risk to her own life, so cut her a break."

Clayne grunted but released her. Zarina took a wary step back as she rubbed her arm.

"Doctor Zarina Sokolov, right?" Landon asked. "Don't be afraid. We're here to rescue you."

Zarina glanced at Ivy. "She told me that earlier, but I didn't believe anyone else would come." She wrapped her arms around her middle. "Stutmeir figured out I tried to help you escape and locked me in my room. When I heard shooting, I didn't know what to think. I took the bedframe apart so I'd have a weapon, then hit the guard on the head and ran."

"Stutmeir and his men are headed right for us," Landon said. "Do you know another way out of here?"

"Beside the main entrance?" She shook her head, then stopped. "Wait! I heard Klaus and Renard talking about a secret passage they found. It's somewhere off the main floor atrium."

Landon frowned. "Renard? The French doctor who was kidnapped?"

Ivy growled. "He's joined the dark side."

"Then he can die along with Stutmeir." Landon looked at Zarina. "How do we get to the atrium from here?"

Zarina gave them quick directions, then picked up the piece of metal Clayne had taken from her and fell into step behind Kendra.

If Stutmeir and his men were headed downstairs, it wasn't in their direction. They didn't run into anyone on their way to the main floor. Ivy told Landon to put her down several times, that she could be more use if he gave her one of the extra weapons they were carrying, but he ignored her.

As Landon carried her into the atrium, Ivy caught a glimpse of Stutmeir, Jeff, and several other men—including the two doctors who'd tortured her—rushing down a set of stairs on the other side of the lobby. Ivy's claws came out as she bit back a growl.

Landon's arms tightened around her briefly before he gently set her down on her feet. "Get Ivy somewhere safe. I'm going after Stutmeir."

Fear gripped her. "Landon, no. Not by yourself. He has hybrids with him."

"I'm taking Angelo with me." He cupped her cheek. "Those bastards are going to pay for what they did to you."

She covered his hand with hers, afraid if she let him go, she'd never see him again. But how could she talk him out of going when she'd vowed to get the same revenge a few hours ago? "Be careful."

His mouth curved. "Always."

Then he leaned in to kiss her—right there in front of everyone.

Ivy clung to him when he pulled away. "I love you," she whispered.

It wasn't the perfect time or place to say it. And she

certainly hadn't wanted to have an audience. But she didn't care. She wanted him to know.

"I love you, too." His voice was deep and husky, the words so heartfelt they made her want to cry. He kissed her again, then looked at Clayne. "Keep her safe."

Landon met her eyes for one long moment before he gave Angelo a nod. Ivy watched through tear-filled eyes as they ran across the atrium and disappeared down the steps after Stutmeir.

Ivy was feeling steady enough to walk on her own, but Clayne picked her up in his arms anyway. Mickens led the way this time, heading toward the front door. They were almost there when four hybrids burst into the lodge. The creatures looked shocked to see them, and it took a second for them to react, which gave Mickens and Kendra more than enough time to shoot them.

"Griffen," Mickens shouted into his headset. "We're coming out. Hold your fire."

The courtyard was littered with both hybrids and men alike. Thankfully, Ivy didn't see any of Landon's friends among them.

Griffen and the rest of the men were waiting for them outside the wall. Ivy was amazed to see how many of them there were. She was also horrified to see that two of them were injured. Diaz was sitting back against the stone, bleeding from a set of vicious claw marks across his chest. Tredeau was lying on the ground beside him with some serious bite wounds on his thigh and stomach.

Griffen frowned. "Where're the Captain and Angelo?"

"They went after Stutmeir," Clayne said.

Ivy held her breath as Griffen tried to contact them on

the headset. Her stomach clenched when neither Landon nor Angelo answered.

"They were headed underground," Kendra said. "They probably can't pick up the radio down there."

Ivy prayed she was right.

Griffen looked at Mickens. "Take care of Diaz and Tredeau. The rest of the team and I will go after the captain and Angelo."

As Griffen took off running toward the lodge with Deray and Marks, Clayne gently set Ivy down on the ground near the wall. He brushed her hair back from her face, his gaze unreadable, then cleared his throat and got to his feet, ostensibly to stand guard with Kendra while Mickens tended to Diaz and Tredeau.

Zarina came over, dropping to one knee beside her. "How are you feeling?"

"I'm fine." Ivy gave her a small smile. "You should help Mickens."

"I will, just as soon as I'm done with you."

Ivy sighed but sat still and let Zarina play doctor.

The woman's brows drew together. "You're a remarkably fast healer, Ivy. A normal person would have been incapacitated for days, maybe weeks if they endured what you did."

"Shifters heal fast."

"Klaus thought that might be the case, but until you arrived, he didn't have anyone to test his theories on." She gave Ivy a rueful smile. "I wish he'd never gotten to test them on you."

Taking Ivy's hand in hers, Zarina gave it a squeeze, then went to help Mickens with the injured Tredeau.

Ivy looked over at Clayne and Kendra. They were

talking too softly for her to hear unless she used her shifter abilities, and she was too tired for that.

"Clayne," she called.

He was at her side in a heartbeat. "What's wrong? Are you okay?"

"I'm fine," she assured him. "It's Landon I'm worried about."

His mouth tightened. "Donovan can take care of himself."

"I'd feel better if he had backup."

"He has backup."

Why couldn't Clayne ever make anything easy? "I meant shifter backup."

The muscle in his jaw flexed. "I'm not leaving you here unprotected."

"Kendra and Mickens are here. And even if they weren't, I can take care of myself. Besides, all the bad guys are gone. Please, Clayne."

His only answer was a low growl.

Tears welled in her eyes. "Fine. I'll go myself."

Ivy pushed herself to her feet—and swayed. She quickly put her hand on the wall to steady herself.

Clayne swore and caught her arm. "You're not going anywhere. Shit, Ivy. You can't even stand up." He gently but firmly pushed her back down. "I'll go rescue your boyfriend, okay? Just stay here."

She wanted to tell him Landon didn't need rescuing, just backup, but was afraid Clayne wouldn't go if she did. She caught his hand. "Thank you."

He grunted and was gone.

Ivy leaned back against the wall and flexed her legs, trying to pump the drugs out of her system. Regardless of what she'd said about the bad guys being gone, something told her this wasn't over yet. She needed to be ready.

———— ∿ ————

Stutmeir and his men had more of a head start than Landon thought. By the time he and Angelo got to the tunnel under the lodge, the ex-Stasi was nowhere in sight. He heard him, though. The bastard was running for his life up ahead. It wasn't going to do him any good. Landon would track him down to the ends of the earth and back.

Light filled the tunnel about a hundred yards in front of him, and Landon ripped off his NVGs. Outside, he found himself in the forest on the back side of the mountain ridge behind the lodge. Figuring Stutmeir and his crew had chosen the quickest path of escape, Landon ran down the only trail he saw as fast as he could, Angelo at his heels.

His gut told him he should slow down in case there was a trap waiting for him and Angelo, but if he did, he might never catch up to Stutmeir. He'd never wanted to kill someone so much in his life. Not the father who'd beat him, his sister, and his mother. Not the men who'd ambushed Jayson and left him for dead. Not every terrorist who wanted to destroy the United States.

No, this went way beyond any of that.

The sound of raised voices ahead made Landon stop in his tracks. He held his hand up, signaling for Angelo to do the same.

"Dissention in the ranks?" Angelo wondered.

"Sounds like it."

He couldn't make out everything the men were saying,

but they were definitely arguing. It sounded as if some of the men wanted to go back to the lodge and fight.

Landon looked around, then motioned to Angelo to leave the trail and swing through the forest. If Stutmeir and his men talked for another thirty seconds, he and Angelo would be able to flank them and take them by surprise.

He and Angelo worked their way through the thick fir trees until they were twenty yards from Stutmeir's group. Giving Angelo a nod, Landon stood up, aimed, and started shooting. Angelo did the same.

Landon wanted to take out Stutmeir with the first burst, but there were a half dozen men between them. Make that a half dozen shifters. The creatures didn't go down any easier now than they did before. After getting over their initial shock of Landon and Angelo's surprise attack, the hybrid shifters bounded through the trees like enraged beasts.

He didn't want to run, but he and Angelo had no choice but to retreat. They took turns covering each other as they fell back one tree at a time. Landon swore as the forest behind them disappeared and the sky opened up. They were headed straight toward a cliff. Hadn't he done this same thing last night? This time, he wasn't going over without one hell of a fight.

He and Angelo pumped round after round into the hybrids. They put down a few, but not enough to make a difference. Stutmeir was safely in the background standing next to a man with a scratched-up face.

Over the gunfire, Landon heard the pounding of footsteps behind him. He spun around, prepared to put down whoever it was, only to pull up when he recognized

Buchanan. The shifter slid across an open patch of ground like a runner sliding into home plate to cover the last few feet between him and Landon, gun blazing as he fired at the hybrids.

Landon glanced at him as he shoved another magazine into his M4. "Why the fuck did you leave Ivy?"

Buchanan drilled a hybrid that had gotten too close before glaring at him. "Because she begged me to come save your sorry ass. I told her it wasn't necessary, that you were this great Special Forces warrior and could handle yourself. Apparently I was wrong and she was right. Looks like I showed up just in time to keep you from jumping off a cliff. What the fuck is that about? You're ugly and all, but I didn't think you were the suicidal type."

"Not suicidal," Angelo said in between shooting at the hybrids who were jumping from tree to rock, getting closer with every second. "Just low on other options. Landon probably won't say it, but thanks for showing up."

Buchanan grunted. "Not only is he ugly, but he's an ungrateful bastard, too."

Even with Buchanan's added fire power, they were still outnumbered. It didn't help when Stutmeir and his men spread out and fired on the three of them from multiple directions.

"Jumping off the cliff is starting to sound better than I thought," Buchanan admitted.

Landon opened his mouth to agree when he heard Griffen's voice in his earpiece. "We're almost to your location, Captain. Sorry it took us so long. We got turned around in those passageways under the lodge. We're coming toward you from the trail. If you can move right some, further along that cliff line, we can get them in a crossfire."

"Copy that."

Landon moved to the right. So did Angelo and Buchanan. To Stutmeir and his men, it probably looked as if they were in panic mode and doing anything to avoid going over the edge of the cliff.

If Griffen and his other men didn't get into place soon, Stutmeir was going to get his wish.

That's when Griffen, Deray, and Marks opened fire on Stutmeir from the left. Stutmeir might have those hard-to-kill hybrids on his side, but Landon now had something he didn't—superior positioning. Stutmeir and his men were sitting at the two o'clock position and were taking fire from both the twelve o'clock and the four o'clock positions. They couldn't turn to face one threat without leaving their flank totally exposed. The loss of tactical advantage took them completely by surprise. Within seconds of the first few men going down, the others retreated.

Landon immediately closed the distance between him and the hybrids. Out of the corner of his eye, he saw Buchanan and Angelo doing the same. It was dangerous for all of them to move right into the line of fire that Griffen, Deray, and Marks were laying down, but his team had done this countless times before. He trusted his men to adjust their shot line as he moved closer.

Stutmeir shouted for his men to stand fast, regroup, and counterattack, but they weren't listening. One second they were standing strong, the next second they were running in every direction.

"Go after them," Landon ordered. "Stutmeir is mine,

but I don't want any of his hybrids making it out of here, either. Take them alive if they'll let you, but don't let them escape. And make sure those damn doctors don't get away, either. They did some things to Ivy that I plan to make them pay for."

Buchanan took off with a blood-chilling howl, and Landon knew the shifter wouldn't be bringing any hybrids back alive.

Landon looked for Stutmeir and saw him and the scar-faced man running for the tunnel leading back to the lodge. Evil bastards probably thought if they made it to the vehicles out front they could get away. They weren't going to get that far. Stutmeir was going to pay for what he'd done to Ivy—Landon was going to make sure of that.

Chapter 17

SOMEONE WAS COMING. IVY FELT IT. IN RETROSPECT, maybe sending Clayne after Landon had been foolish, but she cared more about Landon's safety than her own. Even drugged, she could handle whoever was headed this way.

She dragged herself to her feet, forcing her muscles to work even though they were doing their best to ignore her. She'd been drugged so many times in the last few hours it felt as if she was wrapped up in thick, wool blankets.

She looked over at Mickens and Zarina as she shook out her legs and swung her arms. The medic had given Diaz and Tredeau drugs for the pain and was now rigging IVs at the same time he was applying pressure dressings to the wounds. He moved with quick and efficient motions, a man completely tuned in to his task. Zarina was at his side, helping as much as she could.

Kendra was over by the gate, her back to them and her weapon at the ready, acting as if she was the lone protector for their makeshift MASH unit. Maybe she was. Zarina didn't know which end of a gun the bullets came out of while Mickens would be occupied with his injured charges. And Ivy was certainly still too wobbly to be much help.

But whoever was coming this way was getting closer. She opened her mouth to warn Kendra, Mickens, and

Zarina, but four hybrids hurtled around the wall before she could get the words out.

The creatures skidded to a halt, surprise on their faces. They recovered from their shock fast enough and lifted their weapons.

Kendra spun around and dropped to one knee, shooting the hybrid nearest to her. It caught the three men with him off guard, and they turned their weapons on her, forgetting about Mickens, Zarina, and Ivy.

Ivy gritted her teeth and forced herself to move. Her legs weren't as strong as they normally were, and the dull pain in her thigh slowed her down a bit, but she still managed a good leap.

She extended her claws as she flew through the air, raking them down one hybrid's face and chest, knocking him to the ground. He howled as her nails sunk to the bone, taking a large amount of flesh with them.

Ivy straddled his chest, swinging her clawed hands like sickles. Around her, she heard gunfire, but it seemed far away and unimportant. She was starting to zone out. Again. It would have been so easy to give in to her animal nature and let it take over, but she pulled herself back from the brink before it was too late.

She came back to herself to see that the hybrid underneath her was dead. Beside her on the ground was another hybrid, his body full of bullet holes.

Ivy sprang to her feet and spun around.

Zarina was shielding Diaz and Tredeau with her body while Mickens stood between a snarling hybrid and his wounded teammates. He might have been a medic, but he was Special Forces through and through, his face a mask of grit and determination as he pulled the trigger.

If the hybrid was going to get to his friends, they'd have to go through his dead body first. The shifter withstood a half dozen rounds of ammunition before he finally fell.

Off to the left, Kendra was putting the final shots through the last hybrid's chest. When the creature hit the ground, Kendra stepped forward and put one more round in its head.

Ivy gaped. Kendra had never done anything to make her think she was a cold and efficient killer. Clearly, the DCO was using her in the wrong capacity.

Mickens walked up to admire Kendra's handiwork. "Damn, girl. Are you an animal, too?"

She lowered her weapon and gave him a smile. "Only in bed."

Ivy almost laughed when Mickens's jaw dropped. She looked at Zarina and the two wounded soldiers to make sure they hadn't gotten hit in the barrage of gunfire when a scent on the breeze distracted her. It was faint but unmistakable.

Jeff.

He was close by, and he was running. He was…prey.

Her feet moved in his direction.

"Ivy?" Kendra called. "Where are you going?"

Ivy didn't answer. She couldn't. She felt herself slipping into the feline zone, felt that uncontrollable urge to let go and allow her animal to come out and play—and hunt. This time there was no way she could stop it.

"Ivy!"

She turned and ran toward Jeff's scent. Every other thought in her head disappeared, leaving only one—find the man who had tormented her and kill him.

Stutmeir was faster than he looked. Landon chased him for a solid fifteen minutes before getting a glimpse of the ex-Stasi again. It didn't help that the scar-faced man ran in a different direction, confusing the trail and making it tough to figure out which set of tracks belonged to Stutmeir. Luckily, Landon picked the right one.

Instead of going deeper into the forest, Stutmeir led him into a clearing. Strewn with small boulders, it made for dangerous footing, and Landon had to scramble to keep from falling as he ran across the slope. He raised his gun, aiming it at Stutmeir, but the German had already disappeared into the forest again.

Landon ran after him. He was halfway across the clearing when he heard the sound of rocks falling above him. He'd just fallen for the oldest trick in the book. Stutmeir had doubled back and gotten into position above Landon on the slope so he could ambush him.

He swore and threw himself behind the only cover he could find—a rock that wasn't much bigger than a coffee table. He'd barely hit the ground when the dirt exploded around him. He did his best impersonation of a groundhog and tried to bury himself to avoid getting shot, but the rock wasn't big enough to provide much cover. Landon wasn't sure exactly where Stutmeir was, either, so he had no idea what angle he had on him. He sure wasn't going to poke his head up to take a look. He prayed nothing important was hanging out.

What was Stutmeir carrying—an MP5? That meant a thirty-round magazine. But had the man started the ambush with a full clip?

A distinct clack of a bolt locking back as the weapon ran out of ammo answered his question. The sound was clear and unmistakable. Now was his chance to get to more substantial cover before Stutmeir could reload.

He had about two and a half seconds to cross the fifteen feet of rocky, uneven ground between him and the edge of the forest—unless Stutmeir was faster at reloading an MP5 than Landon thought. Not wanting to take the chance, Landon darted out from behind the rock and ran for the forest's edge. He threw himself the last few feet, hitting the ground in a roll and slamming hard into a tree.

Landon leaned against the tree, waiting for Stutmeir to open fire again. But all he heard was the sound of the ex-Stasi heading farther up the slope. Landon got up and ran after him.

Fighting gravity, the slippery rocks, and the thick undergrowth was hard, but all Landon had to do was think about how Ivy had looked when he'd first found her in the basement of the lodge. All the torture they'd inflicted upon her precious body. The drugs they'd given her. The countless ways they'd made her suffer. That gave him all the strength he needed, and by the time he crested the ridge, he could have killed Stutmeir with his bare hands.

Unfortunately, Stutmeir was nowhere in sight. He must have already gone down the slope and up the far side.

Landon's first instinct was to barrel down the slope after the man, but he stopped himself. Stutmeir had already proven himself adept at setting up hasty ambushes, and there was absolutely no way the other man could have made it all the way up the far slope in the time it had taken Landon to crest the ridge.

There was a blur of movement above him, then a stabbing pain as something sharp sliced down the outside of his right arm from shoulder to elbow. He swore, but barely got the curse out before Stutmeir hit him square in the chest. The impact knocked the air out of his lungs and sent both of them tumbling down the slope.

———~~~———

Tree limbs smacked against Ivy's legs. Rocks dug into her bare feet. She ignored them. She had Jeff's scent. Nothing was going to slow her down.

But then the breeze stilled in a heavily overgrown section of the forest and she suddenly lost his trail.

She froze in her tracks, the animal in her so frustrated she almost screamed out loud.

She turned in a slow circle, sniffing the air. She'd worked with Jeff, knew the way he thought. He'd stay on the course he'd been following. If she did the same, she'd catch him.

Letting out a growl, Ivy turned and ran. Within a few hundred yards, she broke out of the heavier old-growth forest, where she picked up his scent again. It was stronger now. He was close.

Movement caught her eye, and she saw him. He was running through the trees, toward the trail that would lead him to the main road. Ivy sped up, determined to cut him off before he got there. With a snarl, she launched herself through the air and pounced on him like the small, scurrying rat he was.

Jeff cried out and tried to twist away, but his own momentum worked against him and he fell to the ground.

She tumbled over him, digging her claws into his shoulders and the backs of his thighs as she rolled.

She landed on her feet a few yards away, hands on the ground as she prepared to pounce on him again. When she lifted her head, Jeff was already on his feet, flipping his submachine gun around. It was almost too easy to swipe it out of his grasp and send it spinning into the air.

Jeff swore, his eyes darting to the trees where it had landed, as if he wondered whether to go after it. He must have decided against it because he pulled a knife and dropped into a defensive stance.

Ivy approached him slowly, moving first one way and then the other, testing him. She'd injured him pretty good with her initial attack, not to mention when she'd almost gutted him back at the lodge when he'd tried to rape her again. He wouldn't have much mobility in his arm or be able to push off with his legs.

"What are you waiting on, bitch?" he demanded. "Attack if you're going to, so I can gut you like I should have done years ago."

Ivy stilled, then stared directly into his eyes, letting a slow, drawn-out hiss escape her lips.

Jeff flinched. But he quickly found his spine again and hissed back at her in his own crude way. "Maybe you're just thinking about letting me finish the game I started back in the lodge? Maybe you want to get on your hands and knees and take it like the animal you are?"

Ivy snarled. Jeff might get in one shot with his blade, but she was going to make him sorry he'd ever met her. By the time she was done, he was going to beg her to kill him.

"You sick bitch. I can see you want it." Jeff motioned her forward with his free hand. "Come and get it."

Ivy felt the last vestiges of her human side disappear. She could barely remember who Jeff was, much less what he'd done to her. All she knew was that she wanted to destroy him for it.

Only she didn't want it to be this way. She wanted to be there when it happened, wanted him to know it was Ivy and not some animal who finished him.

But she was too far gone to ever come back. She didn't even know how to begin regaining control. Being this deep, she wasn't sure if she would ever be in control again.

An image suddenly flashed into her mind of her and Landon sitting in a tent in South America. It was so vivid, she could smell him. So intense she could feel his fingers as he tenderly wiped away her tears.

Your animal nature is part of what makes you so good in the field, but it's not the only part. His voice was soft in the darkness. *Your human side plays a part, too. You can't let one part shove the other into the backseat. You have to be the one in control.*

Then he had kissed her, and in her memory, the feel of his mouth on hers was just as powerful as the real thing had been.

And just like that, a path appeared before her, showing her the way back to the Ivy she wanted to be. She grasped at the memory of the kiss as if it were a lifeline leading her out of a dark cave. She focused on Landon's face, on the touch of his lips, on the way his eyes had filled with tears when he'd rescued her.

"What're you doing, bitch?" Jeff smirked. "Daydreaming about what I'm going to do to your freak ass?"

Ivy smiled, showing him her canines. She was herself again. "I was just imagining how much better the world is going to be without you in it."

He snorted. "You don't have it in you to kill me. The only chance you had to finish me was while you were wrapped up in your inner beast."

Ivy didn't answer. Instead, she walked toward him, clawed hands down at her side.

Jeff lunged at her with his knife—just like she knew he would.

She knocked the knife aside with one hand and raked the claws of the other across his throat.

Jeff dropped the knife and clasped his hands around his neck, trying to stop the flow of blood.

Ivy watched as he slowly dropped to his knees, then crumpled to the ground. The anger she'd carried around for so long disappeared. She waited for the light in his eyes to go out completely, then turned and ran for the lodge. She was done here. She needed to find Landon and make sure he was okay.

———◊◊◊———

Landon lost his weapon somewhere on the headlong slide down the hill, which ended with him smacking against a jagged rock—hard. He ignored the pain and got to his feet as quickly as he could.

Stutmeir was already on his feet, a wicked looking survival knife in his hand. It was sharpened on one side and had a ragged set of saw teeth on the other. Stutmeir moved a little gingerly, as if he'd landed awkwardly. Or maybe the man was just faking it, trying to suck Landon into attacking him.

Landon took a quick look at his own arm, assessing the damage. The cut was deep and jagged at the top of his bicep, but it got shallower as it ran down his arm. It wasn't much more than a scratch near the elbow. It was bleeding a lot, but it wasn't life threatening.

Landon saw his M4 out of the corner of his eye. It was at the bottom of the slope, maybe fifty or sixty feet away. It might simply be how the weapon was lying in a crevice, but it looked like the collapsible stock had collapsed a whole lot more than it was supposed to. At least Stutmeir didn't have his gun, either.

Landon reached down for his knife, but the sheath was empty.

Stutmeir spread his legs as Landon approached, balancing his weight on his toes and keeping the knife low. The guy looked like he knew a thing or two about knife fighting. Landon hoped that Stutmeir's ankle really was gimpy. If not, this could get ugly.

Landon circled around to the right, trying to get on the same level with Stutmeir, but the man slipped sideways to stay in front of him—and keep him lower down on the slope. If his ankle was injured, he wasn't showing it now.

Landon was just about to move to the left when Stutmeir kicked out with one foot, showering him with dirt. The ex-Stasi immediately followed the move with a lunge.

Landon backpedaled to avoid the knife, then darted to the side and delivered a quick punch to Stutmeir's ribs. The blow wasn't hard enough to break anything, but it made Stutmeir grunt all the same. He'd felt it for sure.

Unfortunately, Landon wasn't able to capitalize on

the rib shot because Stutmeir quickly skipped back a few steps. Was he moving a little more gingerly on that ankle? Maybe, but it wasn't something Landon was ready to put any faith in.

So they played a game of cat and mouse, Landon moving in a feint and trying to draw Stutmeir into making a mistake, while the ex-Stasi did the same to him. Landon got in a few more body shots. Stutmeir got him with a backhanded slice across the chest. The wound was barely a scratch, but it demonstrated once again how fast the ex-Stasi was.

Landon clenched his jaw. This was taking too long. He considered running down the hill to get his rifle. Even if it was broken, he could use it as a club. But Landon still didn't know if Stutmeir was faking that bad ankle or not. Turning his back on the man would be suicide.

"Whatever the DCO is paying you, I can double it." Stutmeir's breathing was ragged. "I'll even throw in a few thousand extra if you bring that cat bitch with you. She could be a real asset to me."

Landon would have been more concerned with how Stutmeir knew about the DCO if he wasn't so pissed.

"Like hell I will."

Letting out a roar, he threw himself at Stutmeir.

They hit the ground hard, but because Landon was on top, Stutmeir took the brunt of the impact. That didn't keep him from trying to carve up Landon's face.

Landon caught Stutmeir's knife hand in one of his. Then he slowly forced the knife back toward the man's chest.

Stutmeir grimaced, straining to keep the blade away

with one hand while he used the other to punch Landon anywhere and everywhere he could reach.

Landon ignored the blows. He was focused on one thing and one thing only—exerting more and more pressure on the knife until he wore Stutmeir down.

"Name your price." Stutmeir's gaze locked on his, and for the first time, Landon saw real fear there. "Whatever you want, I'll pay it."

Landon shifted his body until he was directly over Stutmeir's chest, putting all his weight on the knife. Stutmeir gave up punching him and instead put both hands on the knife, doing everything to keep Landon from plunging it into his chest.

"Keep your money." Landon forced Stutmeir's hand back until the knife was positioned directly above the man's heart. "All I want is your blood."

Stutmeir whimpered as the tip of the knife touched his shirt. "Please."

Landon leaned down so his face was mere inches from Stutmeir's. "Is that what my partner said when you tortured her?"

"You're the cat bitch's partner? They told me they killed you."

"Guess your hybrids aren't as good as you think."

Tightening his hold on Stutmeir's hand, Landon shoved the blade into the man's chest.

Stutmeir gasped, his eyes going wide as he choked on blood.

Landon staggered to his feet. His radio headset had gone missing long ago, so he had no way of contacting the rest of his team or knowing where Buchanan had taken Ivy. The lodge was the most likely place.

Leaving Stutmeir lying there, he turned and headed in that direction.

He was just running down the hill on the far side of the lodge when he heard someone coming at him from the other direction. He hesitated, ready to duck behind a tree so he could jump whoever it was, but then he caught a glimpse of a plaid shirt and long, shapely legs.

Ivy.

Landon sprinted though the trees, desperate to close the distance between them. Ivy threw herself into his arms, holding on to him so tight he could barely breathe. He held her close, burying his face in her hair for one long moment before pulling back to look at her.

She blinked, her eyes going wide at the blood running down his arm. "Oh God, you're hurt."

"I'm fine. Stutmeir, not so much."

"You got him?"

"I got him." Landon frowned as he took a closer look at her. There was blood splattered across the shirt he'd given her to wear. And it was fresh. He didn't see any visible wounds, though. "Ivy, you've got blood all over you. What the hell happened?" He ground his jaw. "I'm going to kill Buchanan for leaving you alone."

"He left because I made him leave. And this"—she gestured to her shirt—"isn't mine. It's Jeff's."

"Jeff?" He frowned. "Your ex-partner? What was he doing here?"

Landon's blood went from a simmer to a rolling boil as she told him about Jeff working with Stutmeir, the DNA samples the two doctors had taken from her, and about Jeff trying to rape her again.

"That bastard." Landon clenched his fists. "I'll kill him."

"That's chivalrous, but unnecessary." She cupped his cheek. "I already killed him."

Landon shook his head. "You shouldn't have had to go through that again." He pulled her into his arms and pressed his lips to her hair. "If you're going to slay all your own dragons, what do you expect me to do?"

"Love me."

"I do love you. I love you so much it hurts." He gently tilted up her chin. "You'll never know how sorry I am for letting you get captured. I promise I'll spend the rest of my life making it up to you."

Ivy put her fingers to his lips, silencing him. "It wasn't your fault. I got captured because I zoned out again. We both know that. The important thing is that you came back for me. You risked everything to rescue me, and that means the world to me." She kissed him. "*You* mean the world to me."

Something clogged Landon's throat and he swallowed hard. He didn't deserve her.

He covered her mouth in a long, slow kiss, then reluctantly held her away from him. "We'd better get back and check on everyone else."

She nodded, entwining her fingers with his as he led her back toward the lodge. "I forgot to tell you. I figured out how to keep from zoning out."

"You did? How?"

She smiled. "I thought about you."

Everyone was already back at the lodge by the time she and Landon got there. Ivy was relieved to see no one else had gotten seriously hurt and the hybrids had all been killed. She only got a few minutes to talk to them, however, because Zarina appeared with her clothes and insisted she change out of her bloody shirt. When she came back a few minutes later, Angelo was telling Landon that none of the hybrids would let themselves be taken alive.

Ivy sighed. "I can't believe what you guys put yourselves through for me."

Angelo slipped his arm around her shoulders. "You and Landon are together, so that means you're family now. There isn't anything the guys and I wouldn't do for you."

"Even though you know what I am?"

"What you are is the brave, beautiful woman my best friend is in love with. Like I said before, that makes you family." Angelo grinned. "And it makes Landon the luckiest guy on earth."

She laughed despite the tears stinging her eyes. Going up on tiptoe, she kissed him on the cheek. "Thank you."

He hugged her tightly, then glanced at Landon. "I'll call you."

"Hey, Angelo," Clayne called as the sergeant headed for the door.

Angelo stopped, half turning to look at him.

"You and the rest of the snake eaters did good out there today."

Ivy looked at Clayne in astonishment.

Angelo grinned. "You didn't do too bad yourself, shifter."

Ivy gave Landon a curious look as he put his arm around her. "Snake eater?"

"Slang for a Special Forces operator." He eyed Clayne. "Tell me again how we wiped out a small army of hybrids and military-trained soldiers of fortune, and somehow end up letting the two doctors who tortured Ivy escape?"

Ivy held her breath, waiting for Clayne to blow up at Landon, but he only frowned. "I told you, I tracked them to the main road. They must have hitched a ride with a tourist or something because there was no sign of them when I got there. No scent, either."

Zarina worried her bottom lip. "Klaus and Renard have samples of Ivy's DNA. If they figure out how to manipulate it, they could make hybrid versions of Ivy. One that has the strength of the creatures you fought here today, but with Ivy's agility and control."

Landon swore.

"Zarina, there are people in the DCO who'd love to use this whole thing as an excuse to shut down the shifter program and boot Ivy and me out."

Kendra gave the Russian woman a pointed look. "Which means you can't tell anyone they have her DNA."

"I won't." Zarina looked at Ivy. "You saved my life. The least I can do in return is keep your secret."

Kendra visibly relaxed. "Okay. Now for our next problem. How are we going to explain all of this when you two"—she gestured to Ivy and Landon—"were only supposed to be out here doing recon?"

Landon exchanged glances with Ivy. "We'll say Stutmeir and his people were going to kill Zarina and that we had to move in."

"Then you'd better make damn sure you convince them you two did it on your own." Kendra folded her arms. "If you imply you had outside help or that Clayne and I backed you up, Dick will be all over it. He'll say it was a violation of every rule and regulation the DCO has, and talk the members of the Committee into shutting down the EVA program. Maybe even the entire DCO."

Clayne's mouth edged up. "The secret to making a lie believable is to limit the details and stick to the highlights. Don't give them any information they can use to catch you in an inconsistency. If they press you for details, pull out the old fog of war excuse."

Meaning she and Landon would be hazy about exactly how they had overcome such an obviously superior force all by themselves.

"You make it sound like you do this on a regular basis," Kendra said.

His grin broadened. "Practice makes perfect."

Ivy seriously doubted he lied as much as he claimed.

"The DCO's going to want you to secure the lodge until the cleanup team arrives," Clayne said. "I'm going to go pack up the weapons and whatever ammo is left so Kendra and I can drop it off at the storage unit. We have to make it look like most of that equipment was never used."

Ivy caught his arm. "Clayne, wait. Landon and I need to talk before you go."

"About what?"

Out of the corner of her eye, Ivy saw Kendra take the Russian doctor's arm. "Zarina, can I talk to you for a minute?"

Ivy could have kissed Kendra for being so perceptive. She waited until the two women were out of earshot before turning back to Clayne.

"Are you going to tell the DCO about us…Landon and me?"

She probably could have been a little more tactful, but with Clayne the direct approach was best.

Clayne regarded them for a moment. "No. If they find out about the two of you, it won't be from me."

"Why don't I believe that?"

His mouth quirked. "Because I just told you I make a habit of lying? Or maybe because I've been an asshole to the two of you?" He ran his hand through his hair, letting out a heavy sigh. "Look, Ivy, I did and said some things I'm not proud of. I've always just wanted you to be happy, and I can see Donovan makes you happy. I wish like hell he didn't, but he does. I know what it feels like when you can't be with the person you're supposed to be with. I won't do that to you."

Understanding from Clayne? He must have gotten hit in the head during the fight. Ivy wanted to ask what he meant, but now wasn't the time. She didn't have to worry about him telling the DCO about her and Landon—she could satisfy her curiosity later.

"Thank you."

"Sure. I, um, better go load up the car."

Giving them a nod, he walked out.

Landon pulled the satellite phone from the duffel bag on the floor. "I'm going to call John."

Ivy listened as Landon related what had happened—the fabricated version anyway. She didn't know if she should be impressed he could lie so convincingly, but she was.

Chapter 18

THE DEBRIEFING HAD BEEN HELL THANKS TO COLEMAN. If the assistant deputy director hadn't seen pictures of the hybrids' bodies, he probably wouldn't have believed anything she and Landon said. Ivy was just glad to be done with it.

Kendra was waiting for them outside the conference room. "Tate's team is back. They finally apprehended the shifter that ran them all over the mountains. They're taking him to an interrogation room."

They intercepted Tate's team on the way. The guys all looked like hell. It wasn't unusual for operatives to get beat up when they went after a rogue shifter, but Tate, Gavin, and Brent looked as if they'd been through a war—or at the very least, one heck of a nasty fight. Declan was the only one not sporting cuts, scrapes, and bruises. And that was probably only because they'd already healed.

Ivy tore her gaze away from Declan to focus on the shaggy-haired, bearded shifter shuffling between him and Tate. He had the look of a caged animal surveying his surroundings, waiting for a chance to bolt. As if sensing her gaze on him, the shifter lifted his head to fix her with a piercing look. She took an involuntary step back as she caught his scent.

Crap.

She leaned close to Landon. "He's a hybrid."

Landon stiffened and swore under his breath.

"Tanner? Oh my God!"

Ivy jerked her head up to see Zarina hurrying down the hallway. Shock flickered in the man's hazel eyes, and he probably would have met her halfway if Declan didn't hold him back. Tate stepped in front of Zarina, but the Russian woman brushed past him as if he wasn't there. Ignoring the restraints on the hybrid's wrists, she caught his hands in hers.

"I can't believe you got away," she said. "I was so afraid they'd catch you."

"They tried. I was more worried about you." He searched her face. "How did you get away?"

"They rescued me." Zarina threw Ivy and Landon a quick look over her shoulder. "This is the man I told you about—the one I helped escape."

"She could have mentioned he was one of Stutmeir's abominations," Landon muttered.

And that he was dangerous. But looking at the hybrid standing there with Zarina as if they were long-lost lovers, it was hard to picture him ripping poor innocent hikers to shreds. Ivy wanted to ask how Tate and his team had managed to apprehend him, but John showed up before she could.

"Take him to Interrogation One," John said to the two armed DCO operatives with him. "And keep the restraints on."

Zarina frowned at the cuffs on Tanner's wrists, then whirled around to face John, her blue eyes cold. "Why is he wearing those?"

"It's all right, Zari." Tanner's voice might have been soft, but his face was hard as he glowered at John.

"No, it isn't all right." She looked at John. "Why is he in handcuffs?"

John gave her a placating smile. "It's just a precaution, Doctor."

He nodded at the two armed guards. One of them walked over to take custody of their prisoner while the other took Zarina's arm to move her out of the way.

"Let go of me—"

Tanner roared. Fangs flashing, he lunged for the guard restraining Zarina, claws extended. Declan and Tate grabbed the hybrid at the same time the second guard drew his weapon and aimed it at Tanner's head.

Ivy shifted, letting out a soft growl along with her claws. Beside her, Landon tensed, preparing for a fight.

Zarina struggled against the man who held her. "No! Please don't hurt him."

"Then tell him to calm down and we won't have to," John said.

The Russian woman turned pleading eyes on the hybrid. "Do as they ask, Tanner. Please. For me."

The hybrid hesitated, as if torn between ripping apart everyone within reach and giving in to Zarina's request. After a moment, his claws retracted and he relaxed, the fight going out of him.

"Get him to the interrogation room," John ordered.

"I'll be right here when you come out," Zarina promised as the two guards dragged him down the hall and into the interrogation room. Her mouth tightened as she watched John follow and close the door behind them. "I don't understand why they're treating him like this. I know he's a hybrid, but he's not like the others."

"Zarina," Kendra said. "He butchered five hikers."

She shook her head. "He didn't kill those hikers. Stutmeir kidnapped them along with Tanner when we first got to the lodge. He tried the new serum we came up with on them. Tanner is the only one who survived. Stutmeir would have killed him if I hadn't helped him get away." She gave Ivy a pleading look. "Can't you help him?"

The pain in the woman's eyes tore at Ivy's heart. If Zarina wasn't in love with the hybrid yet, she was heading in that direction. "I'll try, but right now, Tanner is a murder suspect. Until that gets straightened out, that's how they'll treat him."

"For what it's worth, I'm inclined to believe her," Tate said.

Landon frowned. "You chased this guy for weeks, and now you decide he's innocent?"

"We chased him because he ran," Declan explained. "That damn guy ran us ragged. I don't know how, but he figured out we were on to him from the start. He doubled back dozens of time, took routes so dangerous we thought he might be insane, swam upstream through freezing rivers, covered his scent with deer guts, hid his trail by strapping the animal's hooves to his shoes. We're talking real survival skills here. The only reason we caught him was because he let us catch him." The bear shifter shook his head. "He stumbled on an old man who had a heart attack while he was camping with his two teenage grandkids. Tanner stopped and gave him CPR, then carried the man out of the forest—three hours back in our direction, with the two teens in tow."

"We caught up with him just as the EMTs put the old

man in an ambulance," Tate added. "He waited with the kids so they wouldn't be scared."

"He told us he used to be a Ranger," Declan said. "Just got out of the military after doing three tours in Iraq and two more in Afghanistan."

"Which explains why he was able to stay one step ahead of you," Landon said.

Declan opened his mouth to say more, but closed it again when John came out of the interrogation room. Ivy was hoping for a report, but instead her boss told Tate and his team he wanted them in the conference room for debriefing.

"What about Tanner?" Zarina asked.

John stopped. "Mr. Howe won't be going anywhere for a while."

"He didn't kill those hikers."

"Maybe not," John agreed. "But I think even you'll admit it's a little dangerous to let someone like him roam the streets. Until we evaluate how volatile he is, he's staying here."

Zarina folded her arms. "Then so am I."

John regarded her in silence. "I had a feeling you'd say that. We can always use a good doctor at the DCO."

Kendra watched John walk away. "When Dick finds out we have a hybrid here, he's going to have doctors poking and prodding him until they figure out how to create their own."

"Can they figure out how to make new hybrids by studying him?" Landon asked Zarina.

She shook her head. "Just because you can look at a Picasso doesn't mean you can paint one. Besides, I'll make sure I'm involved in whatever testing the doctors do. I'll know if they're getting close and I'll do whatever I have to do to sabotage it. Even with Tanner's DNA, the DCO could work for years and never get anywhere. Klaus and Renard are the much bigger threat. With Ivy's DNA, they could be well on their way to already creating the perfect hybrid."

Ivy's stomach knotted. "And if the DCO ever captures one of my clones, they're going to put two and two together and figure out what really happened at that lodge."

"Hey." Landon took her hand in his. Even that small public display of affection was dangerous in the DCO offices, but she didn't pull away. "We'll deal with that if—and when—it happens. When Klaus and Renard surface, the DCO will know about it. When they do, we'll make sure we're the ones John sends to bring them in."

How did Landon always know what to say? She gave his hand a grateful squeeze. "You're right. There's nothing we can do right now. For all we know, Klaus and Renard might not even get my DNA to work."

———◦◦◦———

He and Ivy hung around the DCO just long enough to hear the outcome of the interrogation with Tanner—where he backed up Zarina's story—then went to Ivy's apartment. Once inside, he set their Chinese takeout on the counter and pulled her into his arms for a long, thorough kiss that had him considering the idea of having dessert before dinner. But then he saw the worried frown creasing Ivy's brow. Clearly, dessert was going to have to wait.

"Hey." He smoothed her hair back from her face. "You okay?"

"Just worried about what those scientists are going to do with my DNA."

He kissed her again, then gently cradled her face in his hands. "I'm worried, too, but whatever it is, we'll deal with it together."

She smiled. "Together. I like the sound of that."

"Me, too. More than I ever imagined." He searched her face. "What do you think about making this together-thing a bit more official?"

"Official how?" Ivy's brow puckered in confusion, then her eyes went wide. "Oh! You mean...?"

"Yeah. I mean I think we should get married. We'll be able to stand up to anything the DCO throws at us if we know what we have between us is rock solid."

Ivy looked like he'd hit her with an axe handle.

He stepped back, ran his hand through his hair. "It isn't anything you have to answer right away. Just think about it."

"I don't have to think about it."

"You don't?"

She smiled. "The answer is yes."

He stared. "Really?"

"Yes. Really."

What had Angelo said, that he was the luckiest guy on earth? He was the luckiest guy in the whole universe. "I'm going to do this proposal thing right. Buy a ring, get down on one knee—"

She put a finger to his lips, shushing him. "Your proposal was perfect. Although, it might be a good idea to get a ring before we tell my parents. Dad'll shoot you if I show up without one on my finger."

He chuckled and kissed her again. "Deal."

Epilogue

Somewhere South of Khorugh, Tajikistan

MINKA PAJARI'S BREATH CAME FAST AND HARD AS SHE stared up at the ceiling above her head. She didn't know how long she'd been lying there strapped down to the cold, metal table, or what the two foreign men who'd kidnapped her wanted with her. It didn't matter that they hadn't raped and killed her yet. They would. It was the only reason men abducted women in her part of the world. But then why did they keep poking her with needles and taking blood?

She'd worked at the small U.S. military camp on the other side of the mountain for several years and had become good enough with the language that they occasionally paid her to be a translator. But the two men used strange English words she didn't know, and she couldn't make sense of the things they were saying.

Minka bit back a cry as one of the men suddenly loomed over her, another needle in his hand. Only this time, the vial wasn't empty. It was filled with a red liquid that looked suspiciously like blood.

She yanked desperately at the bindings around her wrists, but the leather straps held her fast no matter how hard she pulled, and she winced as the man jabbed the needle into her arm and injected her with the liquid.

"This might hurt a bit," he said in his guttural accent. "But it will make you better."

She opened her mouth to tell him she wasn't sick and that she didn't need to get better, but the words wouldn't come out. Her throat was locked tight.

Then the pain struck, and it felt worse than anything she'd ever felt in her life. She was on fire; she had to be on fire. When she looked, though, she didn't see any flames. But maybe that was because her vision went dim.

She squeezed her eyes shut, praying for relief from the unbelievable agony. But she only convulsed and quivered more violently on the table.

Then the pain receded. She ached all over, though. And there was something wrong with her eyes, too. She couldn't see right.

The man smoothed her long, dark hair back from her face. "There, there, girl. I told you we'd make you better, and we did. Look."

He held something over her face, and it took her a moment to realize it was a mirror. Minka tried to focus on the reflection, but it was hard in the darkened room, especially with her eyes not working right.

Then something appeared in the mirror. She stared at her reflection in confusion. It was her face, but it was different. Her eyes were not their usual cinnamon brown, but glowed green. And the small, white teeth at the corners of her mouth had been replaced with long, needle-sharp fangs.

She moved her mouth, sure she was wrong, but the image in the mirror moved, too. The man had injected her with something to make her look like this. Something that had turned her into a monster.

Minka screamed, and once she started, she couldn't stop.

Acknowledgments

My husband and I came up with the idea for the X-Ops series at the Lori Foster Get Together in 2012. I'd wanted to write a book I could make the jump from small press to New York with, and the idea for a romance pairing a shifter with a military guy had been dancing around in my head for a while. I wasn't quite sure what kind of adventure the hero and heroine were going to have, but I knew whatever it was, it was going to be exciting, action-packed, and sexy. So, we went to P. F. Chang's (our favorite restaurant!) and batted ideas back and forth over spicy chicken until we came up with our feline shifter heroine and Special Forces hero working for a super-secret government organization to keep the world safe.

I know I already thanked my hubby in the dedication, but I want to thank him again. I also want to also thank authors Kate Douglas, Monette Michaels, and Cynthia Eden for reading *Her Perfect Mate* and loving it; my agent, Bob Mecoy, for believing in me and encouraging me and being there when I need to talk; my editor Leah Hultenschmidt for loving this series as much as I do and bringing it to Sourcebooks; editorial assistant and my go-to person at Sourcebooks whenever I need something, Cat Clyne; and all the other amazing people at Sourcebooks, including Todd, Beth, Rachel, and their crazy-talented art department. I'm still drooling over this cover!